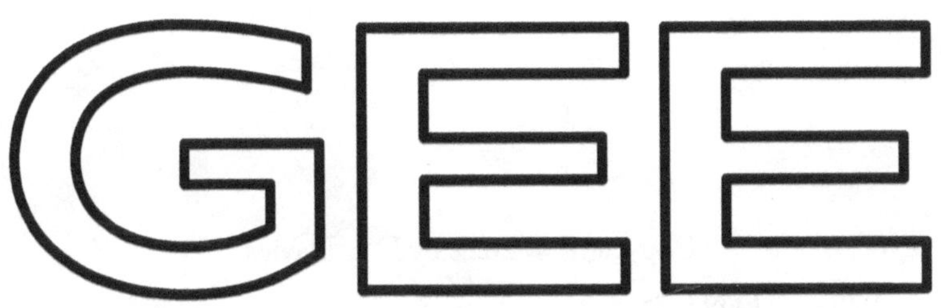

GEE

George Elandier Evansen

D L Davies

BookSide Press
877-741-8091
www.booksidepress.com
orders@booksidepress.com

CONTENTS

Prologue

There wasn't much about him that would stand out in a crowd. He was in his late twenties, of average height and build, black hair and dark eyes that were quick to glance about and laugh when the situation called for it. They could also express foaming rage when the need arose. At the moment, he was in a bazaar, looking for a very special thing. He stopped at one stall, checked out their wares but immediately turned them down. Not that they were of poor quality; it was just that he was very choosy when it came to certain things in life. He moved over to yet another stall and began to look their offerings over. What he was looking for was some hashish. What was being offered was nice, not at all objectionable, but not up to his specific standard as he was somewhat of a hashish snob and would accept only the very best. As he wandered from stall to stall, a young pair of eyes observed him, took note of what he was doing, and moved closer; he, too, had his own objective in mind. He was engrossed in the wares of yet another stall, when he became aware of a small form standing not far from him, eyeing him intently.

"Yes; you have a thought?" he asked the young boy politely.

"But of course;" the youth admitted. "I could not but help notice the care with which you examined the hashish;" the child stated. "You will not find what you seek in this area. I have an Uncle who deals in only the best. Perhaps you would like to come over and see what he has to offer?" The man who was running the specific stall glared at the boy but said nothing.

"Perhaps;" he admitted cautiously. Hashish was not illegal in the bazaar, but neither was it too openly displayed; and when someone did come seeking it, it was a high-profit item and therefore not something a stall owner wanted to easily lose. "Beat it; kid," the stall owner said, snapping at the youth. The child bowed politely to the man.

"This one's products are quite nice," the child allowed, "but my Uncle has a supplier from a distant farm and this one is known far and wide for the quality of his wares.

"I may have heard of this supplier. Tell me if you may; does his supplier live in the hills some distance to the southeast of here?" he asked. The boy flashed a brilliant smile and bowed politely; but said nothing.

"Please take me to this Uncle;" he said, glancing at the youth, and then back at the man who owned the stall. "I can easily come back here if his wares are not up to my standards."

The two walked off in a slightly different direction than he had been headed. They rounded a corner to their left, walked perhaps half a block down and then turned left again and went between two buildings. The man's dark eyes were alert, searching for potential problems. He was very good in martial arts but aware that even at his skill level he might be overcome. But the boy wasn't up to anything bad. He led him to a small building off to the right that was part of a much larger structure, bowed politely and waved him in. He entered, closely tailed by the boy. "Uncle; I have one here who is a true appreciator of your wares. See if you cannot take care of his refined tastes." The child bowed towards a man, who was just then stepping out from behind a wall, a broad smile on his face. "A connoisseur then, perhaps," he asked.

"I'm not sure what that word means; but I do seek something special in the way of hash; perhaps you have knowledge of such?"

But of course; I have a very good friend who grows only the very best, properly cared for, and only cut when the plants have reached optimum size." He reached under the counter that separated them and carefully unrolled a paper-clad bundle. The moment the scent reached his nostrils he knew his search was over. It was without question the best hashish he had ever come across; the color was a rich, dark green and the scent was exactly right. He haggled with the man as custom and mutual pleasure dictated and when the two reached a point at which both could agree; he bought the entire bundle.

He wrapped the bundle within the folds of his clothing; and before leaving, he ruffled the top of the child's head in a gentle, friendly manner and slipped him some money. It wasn't much, but from the grin that came into the boy's face, it was both unexpected and greatly appreciated.

He lived in perhaps the most beautiful city in the world; certainly thought so by those who lived there. It was also greatly loved; and considered by a vast many to be one of the most Holy Cities on Earth. It was also very much up to date and modern in the extreme and boasted a transportation system second to none. He found a place, waited until one of the rapid transit busses came along, and before too much time had passed he was home. It didn't take him long and he got his dinner inside him and he got cleaned up for the night. It was the weekend and he was off until Monday morning. This gave him more than forty-eight hours in which to enjoy his latest purchase. After dinner was over and the blare of distant vehicles and radios and voices began to die down, he dug out his trusty bong, got it ready and cut off a carefully chosen chunk and lit it. It was better than he had hoped or dreamed. He was one of the head men on a nuclear weapons facility some eighty miles south of where he lived. The money was great but the stress of being around nukes all the time sometimes got to him; but nothing a little time with his bong wouldn't cure.

He felt the influence of the drugs take effect and at first slowly and then with speed the pressures of the past week eased into oblivion and he was a peace with himself and the world. He spent much of the weekend eating, sleeping and enjoying his latest purchase. By the time Sunday evening came around he still had over half of his purchase left. This was a record for him; brought on by the potency of the herb he had bought. It just didn't take as much to relax him as a lesser batch would. By Monday morning he had his bong and hash carefully tucked away in a hidden corner of his room and by 6:30 am he was on a fast rail back to where he worked. The day passed peaceful enough. He was the top computer man on an extensive nuclear missile site. By the time 3PM arrived he had done all of his work, checked and double checked all of the soft and hardware within his group, and as was usual for him at this time of day; he engaged his computer into game mode and began to attack all of his country's enemies.

He was well known for his gaming. He was of superior intelligence; his memory near that of total recall and his speed and accuracy on a keyboard was second to none. He was also the man, who, in case of actual conflict, would push the buttons that launched the nukes and send them on their way. So, in the last hour or so of his shift, he attacked all of his county's enemies; starting with those closest and working outward. His mind was clear. Or at least, it felt clear to him. To himself and others, his hands and fingers flashed over the keyboard with lightning speed, clicking and clacking and setting up and arranging things until by the end of his shift and it was time for him to go home, he had entered from memory, all of the coordinates of all of the enemy cities within range and had his missiles up and ready to go. Or at least what he thought were the exact codes. In his befuddled state his mind substituted one set of numbers for yet another. He was bent over his keyboard, getting ready to launch yet another attack when one of his coworkers called his name. "Hey, man, it's time to close up;" he yelled. He waved a happy hand at the man, and in a blink, his smallest right finger lashed out and struck the 'delete' key and he was done.

"So, man, how many of the enemy did you kill today?" one of his friends called out to him.

"All of them;" he yelled back. In the next instant he picked up what needed picking up and headed for the door.

Actually; it wasn't his fault at all. Whoever designed the keyboard should have been more careful. Then again, in the infancy of computers, they weren't as fast and as powerful as the modern version; if they had been, perhaps someone would have paid attention and not put the 'enter' and 'delete' keys so very close together. His keyboard sat with a red light quietly blinking off and on and when the specified number of blinks had taken place and the particular number of seconds had elapsed, giant missile doors quietly slid to one side and somewhen in the midnight hours, one nuke after another left its silo; each tracking towards their programmed target and not much later than that; the beautiful city, the city wherein he slumbered peacefully, was suddenly lit up by a nuclear fireball that erased him as well as everyone else in the city from off the face of the Earth.

Bad news travels fast; even faster than a speeding missile. Before the next day was come, half of the population on the planet were tossing nukes at the other half, all in the hope of killing 'them' before 'they' killed 'us.' It, in time, reached such intensity that it seemed as if anyone possessing so much as a firecracker was looking for a match to light it with and someone to throw it at. Before sanity could once return; nearly half of the planet had been destroyed by the other half. All of the nukes had long since been used up; and most of the standard HE (high explosive) were also expended, and perhaps only for the lack of more bombs to drop and more missiles to launch, did the planet Earth finally return to a relative calm. Ever so slowly did the people left alive crawl out of their various holes and tried to yet again create a life for them and for their children.

Chapter 1

His name was Gee. Actually; it was George Elandier Evansen. His Mother just called him "Gee" because she was lazy of speech in the Southern way and tended to speak in short sentences. He was somewhat over four feet tall, had emerald green eyes, and a ragged mop of hair that missed being black by the narrowest of margins. He was also 10 years of age. Unless, of course, he was 9; he didn't actually know because he didn't know when he was born. What was fully established was, he had been taken out from within a home, totally destroyed by one of the bomblets dropped by the great rocket that had targeted their city some 8 years in the past. These bomblets were not the small, puny devises made up in years past, but were each very close in power to the infamous 'block buster bombs' that were dropped during WW II. Seen from the air, the pattern of destruction looked very much like what a shotgun might make on a large blank wall, with points of hits in places with other places having no damage at all. The people who were raising him had adopted him not long after he had been placed up for adoption and he knew no other home but this.

He was a 'finder' by trade. That is; he wandered around, snooping and prying and peering into all the corners and places he could find, looking for anything that was remotely edible. Or that could be sold or traded for food; for finding food was basically the full-time occupation of everyone who now lived in their land. At first, he thought of himself as a 'seeker,' but as time moved on and his skill increased; he changed his title to one he preferred. At the moment; he was snooping about in a blind alleyway. That is, it was an alley between two standing buildings, but instead of running all the way through; a tall wall stopped everything. He had searched this specific alley not much earlier and had found nothing of interest. But as his skill with finding things increased, he developed a sixth-sense about things and would at times get a sort of buzzing feeling up between his eyes, centered in his forehead and at the moment this buzzing was going full out. There was something in the alley and he intended to find it.

He was dressed in what could only be thought of as rags. Everything he had on to keep warm and covered had at one time been part of something else. Even his shoes, which had at one time been tennis shoes of sorts, were little more than some strips of rubber wrapped in cloth. His one claim to fame was a truly sad remnant of what had once been a sweat shirt that was several sizes too big for him; at best. What he liked most about the covering was that it had once sported a 'hand-warmer' pouch right under his stomach. Rather than something to keep his hands warm, he used it for an extra-large, spare pocket; most convenient for one who pursued his pastime. Among the odds and ends contained therein was the torn out corner of an ancient gunny sack. This was quite useful as it would cover his head and shoulders and much of his face and upper back when he had to crawl through one crack or another; seeking what he might find.

He had barely started looking when several voices sounded behind him. He turned around; scared. These were voices he knew well; the voices of the three Brandon brothers; boys who combined into their own little gang of bullies and thieves. What they would do to him, given the chance, did not bear thought. He looked about; frantic in his fear. Off in the left-hand corner of the alleyway there was a corner of sorts; habited by collections of every sort of junk one could think of. He immediately eased over, burrowed behind what he could, and then to improve his odds; took the scrap of gunny sack and pulled it over his head and back. From a distance, and if one didn't look too close, he now looked just like another bit of flotsam or jetsam on the ocean of life. He crouched down as far as he could, looked slightly in their direction, and froze.

"Now; this is what we gonna do;" Arvin, the oldest boy began. "Aw dang it Arvin," his brother Walt began to whine; "we been over this a dozen times." And we gunna doos it another dozen ef yous don't pay 'tention;" the bigger boy bellowed. The second boy ducked, nodded his head and at least tried to pretend he was listening. As Gee listened, with growing horror, he heard the three plan out a raid on Forrester's Grocery store; just listening to the three boys made his blood run cold. The three were not noted for their intelligence; just the opposite: virtually every plan they had ever made was flawed and doomed to failure even before they were begun. But this time was different. As Gee listened; he could see in his mind's eye what the boys were plotting. Even with the vagaries of outraged fortune against them; the plan was fool proof. And Mr. Forrester was one of his favorite people.

He crouched; listening with every pore in his body. It didn't take long. For one thing; the key part of the plan centered on hitting the owner of the shop just as quitting time came around. It was Friday; and Mr. Forrester always took his week's earnings over to the nearby Bank where he would make his deposits and replace the change he often needed. Gee knew that his only chance in stopping the three was to find some of the policemen that patrolled the neighborhood and fill them in on the plan. The moment the three slipped out of the alley and turned left and headed eastward toward the grocery store as well as the general area that police were often found; Gee found his own feet and began his assault.

He scurried on; frantic in his need. It didn't take long. There were two officers standing on what was left of a badly demolished street; several street punks were eyeing the cops, who were in turn, watching them. He couldn't just walk up and start telling the officers what he'd seen. The kids watching didn't like the cops; and they liked considerably less, anyone who would rat on other kids. There had to be another way of getting the job done and even as he walked up a plan began to unfold. He faced the two cops.

"Hey; you gots anythin' to eats? I'm hungry!" He stared the two in the eyes and his lips moved almost soundlessly; "Tells me no; says 'git;'" he said. The two looked at him; puzzled. "What?" they said quietly.

'I'm hungry; you gots anything to eat?" he demanded. Again, he whispered, "Tells me no; say's git."

"Gowan; beat it," one of the men growled loudly. His eyes told a different story and he gave the smallest nod his head was capable of. He was starting to understand.

Gee softly said "chases me;" stuck his tongue out between his lips and blew a noisy, juicy raspberry, turned and started to run. "Come back here you little snot!" one of the two cops yelled, and in the next instant, they began to chase after him. The men didn't run nearly as fast as they could, for they understood that whatever Gee was up to, he didn't actually want to be caught; but to be chased.

He led them off towards Forrester's grocery, his right hand wind-milling beside him, beckoning them onwards. There were a large number of empty fifty-gallon oil drums stacked up and lined up around this side of Forester's market and he led them that way. There was a narrow trail that led between the barrels and off towards what could be thought of as open land; or at least as open as one would ever get in a city. He led them that way and once in the trail, he crouched down and beckoned for the men to do the same. "Hats," he said. This; the men understood instantly. The hats that the police wore had octagonal tops: these would be recognized instantly by any punk who had ever tried to evade the police. He led them along a narrow, unused trail to a place where a number of barrels had been removed or had never been put, this offered a minimum of cover for their needs.

He crouched down and the men did as well. With a few well-chosen words he explained everything he had overheard; including the speakers names and what they had said. Even as he spoke; he was rummaging around in the pouch on the front of his shirt. Several days earlier, he had found a fairly long length of heavy wrapping twine, perhaps fifteen feet long. The twine looked potentially useful and he had picked it up. He brought it out and even as he unwound it; he explained what his plan was. The two men listened, thought it through, and nodded their heads: it could work. Off in the distance the three heard a male voice bellow; "Come back here you little punks!" Wild laughter followed as did the thudding of feet; coming closer with every heartbeat.

He got one cop into each recess and drew out the heavy twine and tossed it across between them. The two, trained professionals in any such thing, instantly understood; they wrapped the twine around their night sticks and laid them out of sight. Gee quickly flipped some loose soil over the twine so that only small parts showed. "Watches me," he hissed at the two men, then added; "does they askes, tells 'em 'lectric ears." In a blink he pivoted and was gone in direction they had just come from. "Electric ears?" one asked the other; confused. An instant later, Gee's head popped up from behind yet other drums. He pulled out the gunny sack corner, flipped it over his head, the longer part down his back and crouched. In an instant he changed from being a recognizable human head to an odd-looking blob among the barrels. "Now that is just plain sweet;" one officer said to the other. Gee's right hand came up where they could see it.

They were crouched down between drums and couldn't see what was coming; but Gee could. His right arm came up, formed a small fist, and began to bob, as if a head was nodding. Like the beating of a heart his fist bobbed up and down and the sound of feet and excited voices closed in. The small fist bobbed and bobbed again and then formed a thumb with two fingers exposed. The next bob and it was only a thumb and one finger and then just a thumb. Then his fist formed again and pulled backwards and in the same instant both officers pulled away and the heavy twine came up to shin level and the first pair of flying feet hit the twine, tripping the boy, who went screaming; face first onto the ground; promptly followed by the second and then the third.

The officers were well trained professionals and knew exactly what to do next. Rather than trying to unwind the twine from their nightsticks, they simply slipped the string off the ends and in the next instant they were in the middle of the three, whacking heads and arms and legs impartially while yelling at the tops of their voices to the three to stop fighting and to surrender. The boys were naturally stupid, but even they figured out they had lost the cause and curling up into human balls, stopped fighting. Other feet were coming fast; these belonged to the grocer and his long-time employee. They stood and gaped in astonishment at what they saw. "What? How? How did you know?" Mr. Forrester demanded of the police men. The two officers stared into each other's eyes and understanding came to both.

"Electric ears," one of the men said; confidently. The second nodded confirmation and then cracked one of the three on the head because he was trying to get back up. "This is something new that the department is trying out. Not many know about it so keep it to your selves." Even as he spoke he eyed the three boys and then quickly shook his head at the two men when he knew the boys weren't watching. The two stared at the cops; interest clear in their eyes.

"Awhile back, the department began to put Electronic Listening Devices out; what we call 'electric ears.' Mostly; what the listeners get is just random noise. Wind, dogs barking, that sort of thing. Sometimes it's just people talking; gossip; the weather; who is thought to be sleeping with whom else; and so on. Just a short while ago; we got a heads-up that these three morons were going to rob your store. Thing is; evidently the three of them decided to talk about it right under one of these ELDs and HQ got an ear- full and called us." "And, as they say, the rest is history;" the second officer injected.

"Electric ears?" Mr. Forrester asked; confused. The officer speaking glanced at the three boys, nodded at them and then shook his head to the grocer when he could see that the boys weren't watching. "Gee; how else would we know?" he asked softly. Mr. Forrester and his helper looked confused; the office pointed at the boys and then tapped his own ear with his right hand; the side of his head away from the three. The two men stared, glanced at the boys, and then nodded.

"How else," Mr. Forrester admitted with a growing understanding coming into his eyes and face.

"How else indeed;" the officers agreed.

The two men got the perps cuffed. With only two handcuffs between them they linked the three together, then just to make sure the three didn't get any ideas, they put the boys on the ground; sitting upright and tied their ankles together with the twine. The three weren't going anywhere. One of the officers called headquarters to have the three perps hauled off to jail; the second man pointed at the cash bag lying off to one side; he pantomimed picking it up and holding it close to his chest. Mr. Forrester immediately obeyed.

"We are supposed to tell you that we have to take that cash to headquarters so it can be properly counted," the officer stated. At the same moment he shook his head and pantomimed holding the bag even closer to his own chest. The grocer got the idea and did exactly that. "No doubt you have to pay taxes with at least some of that money," the officer continued in a conversational tone of voice. "Taxes that help pay the police for their service to you." Mr. Forrester nodded his head; a thoughtful expression on his face. In the distance a siren wailed; growing closer and louder with every passing moment.

Soon, a paddy wagon pulled up, and two more officers stepped out of the vehicle. They came over to where everyone was, glanced down at the three on the ground and then at the two patrolmen. "Good work!" one of the men commented.

"Sorry sir;" the second man said, looking at Mr. Forrester and the bag that he still held. "We are required by law to take that bag of money down to the station so it can be officially counted."

Tom Forrester held the bag closer yet to his chest and shook his head. "No; I have to take this to the bank and deposit it. There are tax dollars in there; money that helps pay both the police and fire departments; among others."

"But Sir;" the officer started to protest.

"No," Mr. Forrester insisted, "I have to take it to the bank. I know exactly how much money is in this bag; I can give you a signed certificate stating the amount, but in no way will I give the money to you. If anyone in your department doesn't like it; have them call me. Or come down in person and I'll explain it to them; but under no circumstances will I surrender it; and I'm convinced that you do not have the authority to take it out of my hands."

That ended the conversation. The officer in the van put the three in the back, cuffed them both hand and ankle and returned both the cuffs as well as the twine to the two arresting officers. "Great work guys;" he admitted. "I especially like how you used two cuffs and some twine to contain three perps; great job all around. I'll be sure to mention it to the Chief," he added.

"Thanks, Greg," they replied. "And we're more than pleased with the quick response and for taking the perps off our hands."

Gee was long since on the other end of their block away from them. The Brandon brothers were well known for taking their displeasure out on the younger kids that lived nearby, and the failure of their pet plan was sure to put them into a most foul frame of mind. This would include beating up any young boy who happened to cross their path once they were released, which was inevitable, considering how overcrowded the jail cells were. Only the most desperate criminals were held there for any length of time. It wasn't more than a few days before the three were out on a bond of sorts and looking for someone to blame their failure on.

Gee had his own problems; his father disappeared some weeks earlier; leaving the family in dire straits. This was quickly compounded when his mother, who actually lived in a fairly decent home, all things considered, took up with another man who had a 15 year old boy named Clarence. Gee had nothing against the man nor did he blame his mother. She was a weak woman, both in mind and morals, and the loss of a man in her life was more than she could stand. Unfortunately for everyone involved on his end of the equation; Clarence was a major pain even before he got himself moved in.

Gee's father had been a Professor at the nearby college. When the war and bombs erased both the college and the need for such, his father fell back on his earlier trade; being a carpenter. He had put himself through college during his younger days doing this; and with the college gone, it seemed logical to him that with so many buildings having been destroyed, there would be a great need for such. Unfortunately; the bombs also erased much of the building materials and the family fell into dire straits. His dad vanished one day without the slightest clue he was leaving; it didn't take his mother long before she found another man. Not only was she still considered a good looking woman for her age, she also had inherited a fairly nice home, one that had managed not to be destroyed by any bomblets. Not long after the new man and kid moved in; all of his father's carpentry tools vanished without a trace. And while Clarence denied any knowledge of such; there was no one else who could have taken them. Gee despised the boy almost before he came to know him, and once that hurdle was past, he hated him even more.

The boy was the most arrogant, selfish, egotistical being he had ever met; he would actually take food out of Gee's sister's mouth and eat it himself; and she was a very young girl who had very little defense other than Gee. Who would attack Clarence in a heartbeat when he caught him abusing her; the mere fact that the boy was half again bigger than him gave him no pause, and he would attack without hesitation when Clarence began to pick on Susie, his little sister.

The Brandon boys had been released the previous week. The evidence against the three was overwhelming. In another time and place they would have undoubtedly gone to jail or prison, but the nearby prison had been taken out by a direct hit by one of the more potent bomblets, perhaps the only good thing to have come out of the attack. And the local jails were full of people who were considered a greater risk to the public than the Brandon's. Now they were once again prowling around; looking for someone to blame their lack of success on. Several young boys got beaten up by the three; who somehow always had an alibi to keep them out of trouble. That; and many of their little victims were too scared to actually admit who had done what.

Gee was on the more southeastern end of the street he lived on. One of the bomblets had struck very near the intersection of that specific block, strewing wreckage near and far. One of the buildings that had been, perhaps not actually destroyed but nearly so, was just ahead of him and somewhat to his left: sort of northeast as it were. He moved between two buildings. The one behind him was basically totaled; the one directly ahead had taken a near direct hit on the southeastern part of the building with northwestern intact, and impossible to enter. He was wandering in what at one time had been a parking lot that sat between two buildings that were, perhaps, large apartments; or a business building of some kind. The area between the two was strewn with rubble; bricks, pieces of roof tops, and cars that had either been parked therein when the bombs had fallen or were somehow tossed that way by the blasts. But one entire wall just to the east of him was intact. This was both good and bad. Good; in that it offered a place that he had never searched. Bad; in that it was impossible to get into. Perhaps three floors up from the rubble on the ground a single piece of rusted railing, and steps leading downward, projecting out from around a doorway that could clearly be seen.

He was wandering about amid the rubble, trying vainly to figure out exactly how he was supposed to jump three stories up into the air, when he heard the all-too-familiar sound of Arvin Brandon's voice. "There; he just went into the alleyway; they's no way out. We got's him cornered now. By the time we get's done with him he'll know bette'n to rat us out." The other two boys voices called out eagerly and he heard the crunch of feet coming towards him. He glanced about; truly frightened. He *had* informed on the boys; would do it again in a heartbeat, but that did not mean he wanted to get beat up for it. He squatted down in a corner and gazed up at the partial stairwell that jutted out from the wall and had once been used for emergency exits. He bowed his head and squinched his eyes closed; he thought that if only, just only he could be up on that exit ramp, he would be safe because not only could the boys not reach him up there; they wouldn't even think to look up there to see him. He wanted with his entire mind to be up there; there was no room for any other thought. For just a blink, he felt as if something had somehow shifted within him, and in that same moment a small gust of wind blew up against him; a gust that somehow smelled ever-so-much cooler and sweeter. His eyes popped open and he found his nose no more than a very few inches from a brick wall. He stared around; astonished.

The boys yelled again, threatening him, but now the sounds came from below. He looked down. He had done it. He had no idea of how it could be, but in the blink of an eye he had gone from the ground to the stairwell that projected out from around the door in the wall and the three punks who hunted him and wished him harm were now far below. He squatted there, staring through the bars that still remained, and watched the boys as they waded through wreckage and garbage; trying to find him; to no avail.

It actually didn't take the three all that long to decided they couldn't find him; and then finally thought that maybe they had seen him duck into a different alleyway as it was obvious to even the dullest of them that there was no other way out of here other than the way they'd come in. Disgruntled, disappointed, the three turned about and wandered off, muttering imprecations against him and anyone else they could think of and never once thinking that this was yet another of their plans that failed.

He watched from above. It was not until the three were entirely out of sight that it occurred to him that he was now in more trouble - if that were possible - than he'd been in before. It was a good 25 feet to the ground, and if that wasn't bad enough, the ground was littered with busted bricks and broken glass and smashed up cars and no matter where he hit, he wouldn't survive a jump. Moving as carefully as he could, he stood up. There was a door next to him to his left, leading inward, but this door had no knob on the outside. It was not designed as a door to enter a building, but one to be used as an emergency exit and all such things as knobs and levers were, logically, inside.

The exit was made up of steel rod; metal that was now badly corroded in places by rains and time, and thus, none too strong. He moved carefully until he could see through the glass window. Almost! A great deal of dust and other debris covered the glass; both on the inside as well as out and he couldn't see any way out of his predicament. He peered, trying to look through the grime in the faint hope that he could figure out exactly how he was supposed to do this. He tried opening his eyes as wide as he could and he tried squinting; all to no avail. He tried looking at it from an angle; from as much above as his slight stature permitted, and close up and as far away as possible. It was somewhere in the middle of one of these exercises when he somehow looked at it differently. Not like he was on the outside looking in; but the other way around.

In that blink of time, his perspective changed and he could see it clearly. Totally covered with a grimy layer of dust; it is true, but clearly. He could see the release mechanism just on the other side of the door where he couldn't reach it. He reached out, not with his physical fingers but with his mental ones and felt a resistance. He pushed; but nothing happened. He pushed harder and still nothing. He looked again. Aha! He could see it; the locking mechanism was to the left. Even with all the grime in the way he knew that it had to be in the opposite direction: he pushed. The small devise resisted for just an instant and then, it slid out of the way. He tried the lever again. This time, with only a little reluctance, it slid out of the way; there was a muted click and the door swung a few fractions of an inch outwards. He grabbed the edge of the door with his fingertips and with only a small amount of resentment, the door swung open and he gratefully slipped through.

He found himself inside the building. Before his wandering gaze he could see clear blue sky ahead and to his right; what might be the southeast as best he could figure it. He was on the third floor. To his left, a walkway continued north inside of the building for perhaps ten feet and then made an abrupt turn to the east; the direction he now faced. On the northern walls were three rectangles that were without question; doors. Below him, under the floor beneath, another three doorways were, and then out of his sight were presumably three more doors. A nine-unit apartment building! And, as memory served, not just any building; but where some very wealthy people had once lived. His finder's sense should be buzzing like crazy, but for reasons he couldn't guess at, his other sense was silent. Most strange! Perhaps it was just overwhelmed by all that surrounded him. Or maybe it was just taking a nap.

He moved forward, enough to look over the railing. Below, where there undoubtedly was once a lobby of sorts, was a humongous pile of fallen bricks and roofing tiles. To his right the remains of the front of the building lay crumpled and torn; as it had been ever since the bombs had hit some eight years in his past. His eyes swung in a great arc; checking out all that he could see. In the end, he looked at the doorway that was nearest him, no more than eight or ten steps; at most. He eased himself that way. He found the doorknob, as logic dictated, totally covered with dust. He turned it carefully and then tried harder: it didn't budge. Nor had he expected it to. He turned his head slightly and stared at the doorway he had recently entered. He had managed that door; he should be able to do this one as well. He bent slightly over and eyed the door. He tried to look into it as he had the outer door. In a blink, he was looking at a number of tiny little springs and rods that pushed upward with a corresponding number of other small things pointing down with yet other cylinders and such that make up door locks; none of which were familiar to him nor did they make any sense. Then, on the other side, he saw a small protrusion that did make sense. Turned one way; the door was locked. Turned the other way; it was not. He tried to turn the door; with no success. He mentally reached in and turned the small protrusion perhaps ninety degrees and tried the door again; it opened. He walked in.

He was now in the hallway of a large apartment. As was plausible, everything around him was covered with a thin layer of dust, actually quite thin; all things considered. There was a light switch on the wall just to his right. He gave it a light flick of his fingers and the hall lights came on. So; there was still at least some electricity to this building? Interesting! He flicked the lights off because they were unneeded right then and headed on into what was unquestionably the living room. As reason suggested; everything he saw was of excellent workmanship. Off to his far right was a giant screen. His limited experiences with such suggested that it was a TV of sorts, but the few of them he had ever seen, were no more than a tenth this size.

He moved on. Just to his right was a door; he opened it. It was a closet; of sorts. Instead of clothing, there were shelves loaded with many boxes, none of which made sense to him just yet. He started to move on; but his eyes were now constantly flicking between his normal vision and whatever it was that had enabled him to look through the dust and grime of the door. As he looked at the back of the closet; he first saw just a blank wall. In the next instant there was a large metal box with a knob in the middle. Then it was back to being just a blank wall.

He paused. He moved forward; trying to stabilize his vision as it bounced between one and the other. Somewhere along the way he noticed what looked to be a release of some sort. He reached out and pulled it. It slid out slightly and then before he was actually ready, it started sliding downward into a recess made for this very thing. Then he was looking at a fairly large wall safe with the knob in the middle and a handle. He had seen safes before, knew what they were, but had never actually tried to open one. He knew that he had to turn the knob one way a bit, then the other way, and then back again. What he didn't know was how far to turn it nor how many times. He did know that the knob represented numbers of some sort and that only the proper numbers, and in the right sequence, would allow the handle to come down. Or was that up? Move, anyway, and therefore permit the door to be opened.

Gee loved a mystery almost more than he loved to breathe. He reached out and tried to turn the handle, in the off chance it had been left openable, but it was not to be. He turned the knob one direction and then the other, but other than the faintest clicking, he got nowhere. He stopped and thought. He had looked through a cruddy window; and more recently, through a regular door. He thought; "What if?" He tried focusing his eyes as he had on the door; and at first slowly and then with increasing confidence he started looking in. He did not actually understand what he was looking at. There seemed to be a number of circular discs that had a notch missing in one place. The next disc had a notch somewhere else. As he rotated the knob he noticed that some sort of catch would move one of the discs in one way; another twist in the opposite direction would turn yet a different disc in another direction. He fiddled and fooled with the safe and at first slowly and then with increasing speed and confidence he figured it out. All he had to do was to align all of the disc notches in the same direction, at the same time, and do it in such a way that when he pulled the lever down, a rod of sorts would slip into the gaps and the door would be openable. He did so, and with a minimum of adjustments and a shallow learning curve, he cracked his very first safe.

The first thing that met his gaze was the handle of some kind of gun. He understood such because his father had one and had showed him how to load and unload it and had taught him how to handle one safely. It was one of the first things that disappeared when Clarence and his Father moved in. He picked the pistol up by its grip, and with a reasonable amount of confidence, he pressed the release on the side of the weapon and the cylinder swung open. There were six small metallic circles facing him; he pulled one out and examined it closely. On the back, it said that it was a .32 long Colt; whatever that was. He could read, but only after a fashion, and only after a certain amount of head-scratching. Script; he couldn't read at all. He put it back where he found it and started poking around some more. He found a number of boxes inside, each were full of coins of one denomination or other. These, he knew were highly sought after because the people who had enough sense to stash cash money away tended to hoard the paper monies; especially the larger bills. Smaller bills and change were therefore a valuable find. And the safe held many rolls of such. These, alone, were very desirable and sought-after items. His next interesting item was a box that held, among other things, several straight razors; the kind once used for shaving, as well as a number of both folding and solid spine knives in various sizes. This was also a great find. He moved further back into the safe, but other than more of what he'd already found, there wasn't much. He closed everything back up, slid the cover back up to where it had been before, then turned around and started searching the boxes.

All of the boxes he had noticed when he first walked in were made up of seamless plastic, with a lid that snapped over the top. Many of the boxes were translucent; yet others were not. Now, more than just curious, he began to lift them down from off the shelves; and one by one he opened them up and looked inside.

Some of the boxes seemed to hold clothing and towels and other things made up of cloth. One box held only soap; some in bar form, some in plastic bottles that was liquid; yet others were powdered; what might well be used for laundry. One fairly large box held only first aid things; this box had some red tape stuck to the front in a large plus sign. The next box he pulled from off a lower shelf was quite heavy. As he pulled the lid from it, he found it full of canned meat of one type or another. He had personally never eaten anything like this and his own stomach immediately approved. He pulled out several cans to investigate later and put this box back where he'd found it. There were many more boxes that he'd not yet tried.

His own time sense was nudging him; suggesting that he should go back home. There was yet one more box he wanted to try before leaving for the day. By now, he had picked up enough things to more than compensate for any delays he might have, but the feather-weight of the box, when compared to the other's he had examined, aroused his curiosity. He lifted the lid and peered inside.

For a brief moment he didn't understand what he was looking at. In the next instant; it all came to focus. The entire box, which wasn't that small, was stuffed to the top with individually wrapped packages of cookies and crackers of every type. He grabbed a hand-full. "Sis gunna flip when she sees this;" he chortled in glee. He stuffed some of the cookies and crackers into his pouch and once he'd put the boxes back where they belonged and closed the room's door he turned to leave. He immediately faced an insurmountable problem. He was three stories up, and as far as he'd been able to see, there was no way down to the ground other than the front; which was filled with debris.

He thought for a moment. He had gotten up here because he was in a panic and needed to get away from the boys who wanted to hurt him. Maybe it wasn't just fear that had done it; maybe it was the wanting. He stood for a moment; his front pouch bulged slightly from the crackers and cookies stuffed therein. There weren't many, but a few of each, enough to make his little sister grin; and yes, even a few for the others. Whether he intended to give Clarence any was still up for grabs. He paused and thought. He focused his mind; outside, just inside the alley way there was a small area basically devoid of trash; for whatever reason. He focused his mind and tried to once again touch upon the driving need that had put him up on the exit in the first place, and almost before he began, he found himself standing exactly where he wanted to be. "Nice;" he muttered to himself; turning around in the proper direction he started home.

Chapter 2

He had not gone far when he passed Forrester's vegetables. Mr. Forrester also had a small café off to one side where he could also serve people meals as well as drinks. Just to his side of the building as he approached there was a large trash can. This was obviously used to throw away things that were worthless. As Gee looked, he saw that once again the can was upside down with the contents strewn far and wide. He shook his head sadly. Mr. Forrester did not use that specific can for anything except things that had no further use; there never was any food in them, but people – mostly kids – would turn the can upside down and empty it out, all in a very vain hope of finding something of value, or to eat. The perps, obviously, never bothered to put any of the junk back in, leaving a mess for Mr. Forrester or his hired man to clean up. As was usual for him, he promptly headed that way.

Gee bent over and began to scoop up the garbage and other things and tossing them back into the can. As he got the last bit of trash back in where it belonged, his eyes swept the area to see if he had missed anything. He was about to put the lid back on the can when his wandering eye spotted an unlikely-looking object up against the wall, laying on a largish grey stone. It looked suspiciously like . . . a wallet. As he leaned down and picked it up, he knew that was exactly what it was. Not only a wallet, but one bound with twine; a wallet he had reason to know quite well. He took it and headed for the door.

He walked into the grocery store. As he entered, Mr. Forrester and his helper were rushing about, picking things up and setting them down; sliding things out of the way and each of them yelling at the other. "It's here, I only had it a short while ago;" Mr. Forrester was yelling at the top of his voice. Both men saw him enter; the owner gave him a quick glance. I'm sorry Gee, but I can't stop to help you this time. I've lost . . . and he looked again at Gee . . . or more specifically; at his left hand.

"I was passin' by, Mr. Forrester," he began. "I looked over and seed you garbage can was flipped over again. I went over to pick it up. I wuz about t'put the lid back on't and I seed this over agin'st the wall, layin' on a grey rock. Ah thinks it might be youse, so I bringed it inside right smart so's t'sees if it's youse. He held the wallet out. Mr. Forrester came over and with tears in his eyes, hugged Gee, ignoring the wallet he had just been tearing his store apart; looking for.

"It is indeed, Gee, that's the exact thing we were looking for. Now I remember. I went outside and saw the can lying on its side. I put my wallet on the rock where I could see it clearly and not forget it. Then Tom Parks came by and started helping me. Then we went inside so I could help him get what he needed. Now I remember; that's where I put it down." He looked at his employee. "I knew I had it not long ago; I just couldn't remember putting it down. I must be getting old; more forgetful in my old age."

Gee gave Mr. Forrester hug for hug, then told him; "You's not getting' ol', Mr. Forrest' yous's just bein' 'uman. You din't forgets puttin' the wallet down 'cause you never thought o' putting th' wallet down. You thought of pickin' the mess up, and in orders to picks up the mess, you gots to empty you's hands. But folks don' think "ahm emptin' my han'"; they thinks ahm pickin' this up. And you's can't remember thinkin' what you never thunk."

The two men looked at each other, then Mr. Forrester slapped his forehead with his hand; "Out of the mouths of babes and children comes forth wise sayings;" he quoted.

"Amen; brother;" his helper added.

The two men looked at Gee. "Son; it's getting so I can't turn around but what you're doing something good for me. And, yes, just between the three of us; I know that you were responsible for stopping the Brandon brothers last week."

"They's already out and lookin' for trubbles." He admitted. "They's spotted me earlier today and was gunna give me what fer 'cuz ah rat' em out. I dunt thinks they actual know who did what as they's also been beat up some other younger kids; jest sum'thin to pass the time ah suppose. Anyhows, I managed to gives 'em the slip and stumble onter some very interest things; sumpin' you's might be interest in." He reached into the pouch at his waist, but what he actually wanted wasn't there; it was locked up in a safe about two blocks away. But he remembered exactly what it was that he wanted, and he reached, not so much as into his pouch, but to the safe where the coins were stacked up. He grabbed a roll of dimes and of quarters and pulled them out and handed them to Mr. Forrester, who stood and gazed at the coins and gaped. In a hushed voice he asked; "my God! Gee; where . . . oh; never mind, I shouldn't be asking such questions . . . especially of you. Will you sell me these? I'll get the cash right out of my till; I'll pay top dollar; I swear I will." He was going to add more but Gee held up his hand.

"I'll sells 'em to you, Mr. Forester, but I sells 'em for eats. Good eats, fresh eats, 'zactly like the monied folks buy. And don' charges me a cent less'n you'd charge 'em; an', yes, I no's where more monies is; how much; I dusn't no; but more. An' I promises to brings 'em to yous and no one else. Just makes sure you doesn't mention my name; 'bout this nor that I was the one who ratted the Brandon's out; they'll kills me if they knows for sure. They's already beating up some of the smaller kids who had nothin' to do with anythin;' just 'cos they's mean; and mad 'cos they dint gets away with stealin' you's money."

"You've got yourself a deal; Gee. And it's both an honor and a privilege to know you and to serve you. And I promise you full value, the best I've got. And if you insist; for the same price I charge all the others. And I didn't know about the Brandon's. First chance I get; I'll get one of the Patrolmen to one side and give him an ear-full."

"They is one other thin' you might's be interest in;" Gee said, and once again stuck his hand into his pouch. This time, he was reaching for something he actually had with him. "This be sumpin' else I comes across whilst runnin' from the Brandon's" he admitted; and pulled out one of the small packages of cookies he intended to take home for his family.

The two men stared at his hand; wordlessly. Hesitantly, almost fearfully, Mr. Forrester reached out and took the package out of Gee's hand. "Oh . . . my . . . God!" He said softly. He was holding a package of Oreo cookies; still in the original wrapper. "They; they look like they're brand new! Where. . . wh . . .never mind. You're not about to tell me and I shouldn't be asking, but you wouldn't believe how much you can sell one of these for. May I presume this isn't the only one you have?"

"Nope! I also gots some of these;" and he handed the man yet another package.

Tom Forrester gazed at his hand, his expression almost deadpan. "Ritz crackers. Of course you have Ritz crackers! You have Oreo's; why wouldn't you have Ritz as well? Anything else you might have in that handy little pouch?"

"Wull; maybe yet one more;" he admitted. He remembered some chocolate bars he had seen back in that closet. He focused his memory, stuck his hand back into the pouch at his waist; his hand appeared within the plastic box, seized one of the bars and pulled it out and handed it to Mr. Forester. He stared at the object in his hand. And stared some more. He handed it back to Gee.

"Where ever you got that from; put it back;" he ordered. "You never had that, it doesn't exist anywhere on the planet and if anyone ever asks you about it you will deny that you even know what they're talking about. Is that clear?" he said, staring directly into Gee's eyes. "My wife is a hard-core chocoholic. She is addicted to chocolate. Before the war started and certainly before the time the bombs fell here, she was well over two hundred pounds. Exactly how much over; I have no idea because she wouldn't tell me. But that woman could eat more chocolate that any six humans I ever saw, and if she had a hint that there was so much as a Hershey's Kiss somewhere, she would kill everyone in sight, including me, just so she could stuff it into her mouth and eat it. Put it back; put it back right now and should the subject ever come up, you don't even know what chocolate is. Is that understood?" Gee stared into the man's eyes, saw only truth in them, and promptly nodded his head. He took the bar from the man's hand and in the next moment, it was back where it had been for more than eight years.

The three got up from where they were sitting, and with the help of the two men, Gee selected some of the most beautiful apples; both in ripe red as well as others which were also ripe, but green. He picked out some carrots, radishes, cucumbers and even celery; all of which were in season at the time. By the time he was done, he had a very large bag filled with fruit and veggies and had still not used up all the money. It was getting late and the two men were ready to close down for the night. Gee helped them the best that he could, and then when all was done, they put his produce in a back pack of sorts so that people wouldn't be able to tell just by looking that it was food that he was carrying. All things considered; having that much food on one's self was even worse than walking around with conspicuous amounts of money.

The three parted company and Gee headed home. He felt for his little sister, but as it had been most of the day, he couldn't sense her; what he thought of as "'melling" her. Not smelling, which was of the nose, but 'mell, which in him seemed to be in his forebrain, directly above his nose; in the exact same area where he would get his "buzz" when he was about to find something new; or sometimes; in case of trouble. But at the moment; there was an absence of anything.

He walked into his home; before he was well within the door, his 'meller started acting up, warning him that something was not right. And this was not good. He walked in, turned left and entered the living room. His Mom stood off to his right, her back up against the wall. The man she was currently with was on the opposite side of the room, but well away from the wall and Clarence was in the middle of the room. He had something in his hand, what looked to be some rolled up paper and he was bragging incessantly. "Yeah; I sold the worthless little bitch; got top money for her. She's goin' to the sex slavers; she'll get plenty to eat. And plenty else; you bet."

"You sold who?" Gee demanded of the older boy.

"That worthless little bitch;" the bigger boy bragged. "And you're a sawed-off little punk and there's not a damned thing you can do about it." The boy strutted about, proud as he could be, while Gee's brain tried to make sense of it. He had been bragging about selling someone to the sex slavers; and there was no one in the house he could have . . . and then Gee snapped the final piece of the puzzle in.

"You sold my sister?" he screamed in rage. It all fit. He couldn't sense her because she was no longer in the house. But he could always sense her no matter where she was; there was a rapport between them that verged well into the eerie. It came to him in a blink. He could always sense her, always knew when she was scared, or sad or mad or happy or hungry or anything else. Even when she was asleep, he always knew if she was dreaming and whether the dream was happy for her or not. And he didn't have to be close. Sometimes; he knew her moods when he was blocks away. And he hadn't sensed her most of that day. It all came together for him in a rush. The only way possible that he couldn't sense her would be because she was no longer alive. There was no other alternative.

Gee screamed in rage. He tossed his backpack on the nearest table and attacked Clarence with mindless fury. The older and bigger boy immediately began to laugh. Gee wasn't much more than half his size and definitely not half his weight; he would teach the young punk something soon enough. Unfortunately for him; he was quite dumb. He had never heard the phrase 'catatonic frenzy' nor of any other frenzies that can come upon people; but he was watching one develop right before his eyes. And the frenzied one was exceedingly angry with *him*.

At first, he tried to fight back. He was, after all, older and taller and should have the edge in such a situation but whatever edge he thought he had; went promptly out the door . . . along with everyone else in the room. Even if Clarence was too dim to realize just how much trouble he was now in; everyone else in the house figured it out for themselves in the first few seconds and the room was promptly vacated except for the two fighters. For a few frantic seconds the larger of the two tried his best, to first, fight and defeat the younger and smaller. Lacking that; at least break even. When it became obvious even to his limited mind that he wouldn't be able to do either; he tried to bribe Gee. "Look man; there's plenty of money. "I'll even give you some." That made Gee even angrier. "OK; OK; you can have it all; look, there's a whole roll of money; I'll give you the whole wad!" In the next instant he got a fist in his mouth that took out two of his upper incisors.

"Look, Gee, I'm sorry. I'll go and get your little sis back for you; I dint know she meant that much to you." He was lying; but he would say anything to get Gee off his back. By now, Gee had stopped his screaming, now he had only one thought in mind: to kill Clarence and avenge his little sister's death. Nothing else mattered. Nothing else could.

He tied into Clarence. The older and larger boy was now in full retreat; wanting nothing more than to abandon the money, abandon the house, and abandon the city he lived in: he would willingly move anywhere; anywhere there wasn't a Gee: that is. But it was not to be.

All of the screaming and shouting and people abandoning a house were more than enough to attract other people's attention; especially if the people involved were patrol officers, walking a beat, specifically to keep peace in their little corner of the world. News travels fast, especially in circumstances like these, and it didn't take long for two of the local officers to show up at the house. The pair poked their noses in, took a single look at what was happening within, correctly analyzed what was taking place and while Clarence wouldn't know a frenzy if he stepped in it; both officers did. They promptly backed out of the house.

"My God! I've no idea what set Gee off," one officer said to the other, "but I sure don't want any part of him."

"Not in his present mood;" the second amended. "What do you think? Better call in for backup?"

"Better yet; call for an ambulance or a meat wagon;" the first admitted. Both agreed on this plan of action and promptly did so.

All things must come to an end and that even includes frenzies. Gee stood and stared around the room; he was the only one within; disregarding the broken and bleeding form that lay either unconscious or dead on the floor not far away. He walked over and picked up his pack from the floor. He wasn't sure he was able to carry it back to where he now lived. He *was* sure that he wasn't going to leave it anywhere the people inside this house could eat it; and that included his Mother. She was a weak woman and of limited mind but even she should have known what was taking place and should have moved to stop it. He held the bag in his left hand, thought of it for a moment, and in the next blink it was lying on the counter in his new home.

He turned. He bend down, picked up the roll of money, and headed out the door. There were a great many people outside; all of whom stared directly at him. He walked over to where the two officers stood. "I'm sorry for the ruckus;" he admitted to the pair. "Does you wants to arrest me? I'll go quiet. But that bastich in there sold my little sister to the sex slavers. Onlyest: there don't be any sex slavers in this city; it be against the law. But there do be cannibals. And my little sis is dead 'cos I can't feels her no more, and I thinks maybe-so himself in there also be dead. And neither way doos I care if he be. Is you gonna lock me up? I'll goes quietly does you wants to."

He handed the roll of money to the officer on his right. "This be what he gots from the people who takes my lil' sister off. I dunt knows how much is there but I wants to gives it to the police department; use it to help keep peoples like him inside lock up. . .or better yet; hung."

"I like that thought, 'hung,'" the second officer admitted. "And, no, you're not under arrest. If some bastard did that to my sister I'd have done the same. And I don't even like my sister all that much.

"What about you? Is there anything the police department can do for you? You look like forty miles of bad road, Gee, tell us what we can do and we'll see it is done;" the first officer said.

"No; I'm gunna be alright. I gots me my own place now; it's actual kinda nice; good view of some of the trash heaps in the area; that sorta thing. I'll be out and about soon enough. Does you wants me for ennythin, y'just gots to says so." He nodded to the two officers and then turning, walked quietly away. He got a few paces, stopped, his head down in thought and then turned around and came back; "one other thin' you guys might wanna know 'bout. A few hours ago the Brandon's tuk atter me, yellin' I'd ratted 'em out and they wuz gunna beat me up for it. I managed to give's 'em the slip, but I gots t' thinkin' 'bout it later. They's been a number of young boys limpin' 'bout, sayin' they tripped and fell. Personal; I thinks the Brandon's been beatin' kids up just cos they's mean and they's got to blame someone for they's mistakes. It can't be that they's at fault atter all. Maybe-so, iffn some of you boys got together and introduce they to you nightsticks, they might sees the light and leaves the littler kids alone. They's don' mind handin' out pain t'others but they's don' want any of they's own. Just a thought; y'might wanna thinks on it." He nodded politely to the officers, turned about and walked off, his head dropped in thought.

"Ya know,' the first officer said, "that's one hell of a kid there. Just imagine what he's going to be like once he's grown."

"I'm kinda looking forward to that myself; seein' what he'll be like when he's grown," the other admitted quietly. In the distance a siren wailed and wavered and grew louder with every beat of the heart.

Gee continued on and as he reached the next corner he started to turn left and promptly blinked out of sight. He timed the jump to just as he turned the corner because he didn't want anyone notice that he'd just winked out. This way, if those behind him were watching, they might think that he had somehow just ducked around the corner very quickly. And if someone saw him coming around the corner and then vanish, they would suppose he had started to turn that way and then for reasons of his own, had simply just backed up. In the next instant he was in his living room.

He was tired beyond his ability to understand or say. He shed his clothes, dropping them in the middle of the floor. He was unbelievably dirty and covered with blood; none of which was his. He walked the short distance, nude, turned the shower on and let it run. Once it was at the temperature he liked, he stepped in, grabbed a bar of soap and proceeded to clean up; from the top of his head to the soles of his feet. He had a lot of grime all over him, not all of which was physical in nature, and he needed - more than wanted - to both physically and symbolically cleanse himself of the day's events. In earlier investigations of the apartment he had found a very nice terry cloth bathrobe; a thing he liked and instantly adopted. He took it and put it on, tying the waist strap around him. Next he wandered out to the kitchen area. The backpack he'd carried earlier was exactly where he wanted it to be. He opened pockets and flaps and pulled out some vegetables and fruits and then sitting at the table, proceeded to eat until his stomach could hold no more.

He was now tired beyond belief. He went into the master bedroom, threw back the blankets and sheets, crawled in and covered himself up.

Much later, he couldn't be sure if he fell asleep the moment his head hit the pillow or immediately before. He slept.

If he dreamed, he didn't remember any. When he awoke he went through a few moments of extreme confusion; nothing looked right to his eyes, and the sister whom he usually slept with was nowhere to be seen. Then, in bits and pieces, memories floated through his mind and he remembered everything. Sadness filled his soul; he would never see her again and a bitter hatred welled up inside him against Clarence. That set him wondering if the boy was still alive. Part of him intensely wanted him dead. Not only had he stolen everything he could lay his hands on, he had murdered his little sister. Then his mind corrected him. Clarence hadn't murdered anyone. And it was a very possible fact that he was unaware that he was selling the little girl to be killed; he might well have believed the sex slave lie. Which, when looked at with a non-critical eye, was scarcely better. He did his best to think of else.

He got up, slipped on the robe and walked out into the living room. His clothes lay exactly where he shed them. They, too, were spattered and dirty and in dire need of cleaning. That, at least, was something constructive he could do. He went over to where the washing machine sat, dropped in what he had and could find, set the dials to the lowest setting as his entire load wasn't much, put in the appropriate amount of soap and turned the machine on. This, at least, was something that was familiar to him as his family had a washing machine that still worked. He then went into the kitchen to find something to eat.

His earlier forays into the kitchen had uncovered some very interesting items; things he only knew from what he had been told. One of these was some cans labeled SPAM. This was unknown to him other than hearsay. He pried the small key off the end of the can and tore the lid off. The most enchanting smell reached his waiting nose. He used a knife to slice a small piece off and with a certain amount of anticipation; he stuffed it into his mouth. It was the best tasting thing he had ever eaten.

He poked around the kitchen; in one of the upper cupboards he found a box. He opened the box and found four long squared off rows of what turned out to be crackers. In the refrigerator he discovered two bricks of cheese. One brick was covered in mold and was inedible from his viewpoint. The other brick had been better sealed, perhaps, and still looked as good as the day it had been purchased. Or he imagined it to be so. He remembered his Father talking about small sandwiches made from these things and with a minimum of fuss and bother; he made up some and ate them.

By now; he was full; as full as he could ever recall. He got up, put everything back into the fridge much as he had found them; took his clothing out of the dryer, redressed and began to look around. The night before, he had looked into all of the main rooms but had not made a careful examination. Neither had he gone outdoors. The living room had a large sliding glass door. This he slid aside with only a minimum of pondering and stepped outside; to his right, east of him, the cement floor stretched out and two more doors beckoned. He walked that way.

The middle door had a drape pulled across it from the inside. He couldn't see in but he could look down at the floor just inside. He pushed carefully on the protrusion on the door but it wouldn't move. He glanced down again. He could see the mechanism that kept the door locked; it was identical to the one on his own door. He thought for a moment, then in a way that was rapidly becoming a habit with him, he mentally moved the inside latch out of the way and slid the door open. He moved the closed drape to one side and walked in.

It was very much like the place he had just left. The furniture was different and arraigned differently and other things were not the same; but the floor plan was identical. He walked over to where the closet was on his own place and opened it. This was different inside; instead of shelves there were just boxes and chests piled up and there was no safe imbedded into the far wall.

He prowled around. Again, there were two bedrooms, each with its own share of clothing and other belongings. From what he saw, two adults and perhaps two young boys had lived here. This; most definitely caught his eyes. The 'shoes' he wore on his feet were little more than rags, wrapped around rubber soles. He started making a more careful investigation. One of the boys had definitely been older and larger than he; the shoes he found around his bed were far too large for his own feet. But the second boy must have been very close to his own size. Not only did the shoes he found fit; so did his clothes. This was a very nice find indeed, as his own clothing was little more than rags. He sat down, removed the clothing he had on and began to dress anew.

He stared in the mirror and did not recognize himself. There was a distinct downside to this; no one on the street would recognize him either. Worse yet; they would see him as someone to attack and rob, that they might have better things. He took almost everything off, put most of his original clothing on, keeping only a shirt and the oldest-looking tennis shoes there for his feet. The sweat shirt covered the shirt and the tennis shoes fit very well. He could, and would, over many weeks add first one thing and then the other. There would still be the inevitable envy and greed, but spread out over time, it should work out better for him.

He looked for a safe, and found one in the master-bedroom, tucked into the corner of the closet. By now, he understood how to open one as well as most experts in such and it only took him a few moments to crack this one. The first thing to meet his eyes was the butt of a handgun. This was logical; for if one were being forced to open the safe they would reasonably want something ready to fight back with. He pulled the weapon out, pushed the small lever on the side and flipped the cylinder open. These bullet cases had .357 Mag. on them, were silvery instead of coppery as the other gun and the bullets instead of solid lead, were jacketed, with a hole in the front of each bullet. He pulled one bullet out and examined it, then put the bullet back where it belonged, closed the cylinder and set it off to one side. The next thing his eyes found was a great many boxes that unquestionably held money. Most were imprinted with \$250. This looked interesting. Mr. Forrester just last night had said that there wasn't enough metal money and that too many people who had saved up money for a crisis had not only saved paper money, but paper in larger bills; \$50s and \$100 for the most part, and the smaller bills and coins were hard to come by in many cases. He took two boxes out of the safe, thought of the counter in his kitchen and placed the boxes there. He replaced the revolver in the safe, closed it up and arose. He had yet one more apartment to examine on this level with yet two more levels below him.

He turned his head and looked at the sky. There were clouds scudding by, looking ominous, and the sun was heeling over towards the west. It wasn't actually late yet, but he had several other things he wanted to do. He decided to put this off until tomorrow. He closed everything back up, relocked the door and went back to his own home.

It didn't take long as he knew exactly what he wanted to do. He hadn't been back to Forrester's since yesterday and the find of the golden dollars was something Mr. Forrester would surely be interested in; as well as the local banker. Perhaps he would open an account. Over a discreet period of time he could add to his balance and thereby increase his own security. He went into the bathroom, examined himself in the mirror. There was a definite improvement in his appearance, but not blatantly so; not enough to attract the attention of every goon on every street corner. He most definitely needed a haircut. His Mother had been the one who took care of that chore, but ever since his Father vanished, Mom had let a great many things go around the house. Perhaps he could find a barber and get that done. He pulled out two of the golden dollar rolls, stuffed them into his pouch and thinking of the place he wanted to be; promptly winked out.

He was there. He walked around the corner, went a short distance and started to turn into a path that would in time lead him to the grocers. Standing in his way were the Brandon boys and they were looking at him with evil intent.

"So; we got you at last," Arvin snarled at him. "When we get done with you, you gonna look like sumpin' the dog drug in." He didn't think; he reached into his pouch; not for the coins that were in there but for the revolver in his safe.

"Oh Momma; help me!" Arvin wailed. "He's gonna frow a stone at me. Momma!" His two brothers laughed sycophantly; sounding more like mules than anything human. In the next instant he pulled the gun out and aimed it directly at Arvin. Laughter left the three faces in a blink.

"A gun; he's got a gun, one of the three screeched in terror.

Arvin stared at him, a calculating look on his face. "Tell you what, Gee; I'm gunna over look all that you done to us. You just give me that gun and we'll call it even." He started to move forward, evidently confident that his ruse would work. Gee cocked the gun.

"You takes one more step and I shoots you," he announced. Arvin snarled and took one more step. The gun in Gee's hand came up and cracked loudly and the next instant Arvin was holding the side of his face. "The next one goes into you head," he warned the boy. Arvin was the largest of the three boys and was on the fleshy side. His nose was oversized, as were his lips and chin, but the most prominent features of his face were the lobes of his ears; which were enormous. Well; one of them was. He had his hand over the other one, or what was left of it, because Gee had just shot it off. Arvin thought of what Gee had just said and put a tentative hand to his forehead.

"Wrong head, stupid; he said. He cocked the revolver and aimed it between the boy's legs. Understanding came to him and a hoarse cry sprung from his lips and his face went white.

"What's going on here?" a baritone voice demanded off to one side; two police men that Gee knew well; stood, watching the four, their own guns drawn and aimed; but not at Gee.

"Well, officers," Gee began, "evident these three did sumpin' they wasn't 'posed to. Then, when thins went wrong, 'sted of understandin' they's stupid and they's plans is stupid, they starts beatin' up all the littler boys around, tryin' to makes themselves feel adequate. Only; they isn't. Then just now, they comes ater me, to beats me up. Onlyest thin is; they didn't no I has a gun; found it just t' other day. Nice little gun; too. Anyways; Arvin, bein' the biggest stupid of the lot, tries throwin' him chest out ats me and I just shoots his earlobe off. Was just now threaten' to shoot 'im in the head; onlyst thin is, he guesses wrong and thinks I'm talkin' 'bout the head on him neck when I'm talking 'bout the one 'twix him legs." Gee delivered his monologue in a calm, serious manner, nodding at each of the boys in turn as he spoke of them.

The two officers looked at each other and both broke into grins; "You're going to shoot him in the head?" one of the officers demanded. "Man; this I gotta see!"

"Ditto;" the other one chortled in glee. The three boys just looked sick. Once again their plans had gone into the toilet; just when they thought they had the upper hand.

"K!" Gee said; wanting to be agreeable on it. "Just steps a bit to your left Arvin; so's we can get this done up proper." And he once again aimed his gun at Arvin's crotch. Arvin's face went white and he made an incoherent sound in his throat and chest and he began to wail; "M-o-m-m-a."

"Well; maybe not;" the other officer offered. Gee; willing to go along with whatever the two adults said, nodded his head and stepped back two steps and lowered the gun to his side.

"What do you want done with them; Gee?" one of the officers asked politely.

"Not sure;" he admitted. He stared at the three; then looked at the two younger, smaller brothers. "Why doos you listen to him ennyways?" he demanded of the two.

"We gotta;" one of the two replied. When Momma died; she said we have to obey him 'cause he's the oldest."

"You Momma tol' you that?" he demanded of them. "To you face she say that?"

"Wull, no, not exactly; that's what she told Arvin; that we had to obey him because he's the biggest and oldest."

She never tol' you that to you faces?" he demanded again. Again; the boy shook his head.

"Tha's not what my Momma wooda tol' me. What she wooda said to me, was I oldest, is to takes care of you two 'cause you littler. To protects you two 'cause youse too small to takes care of youselfs." The money's you gets; do him splits it with you two equal?" The two boys stared at their brother and glared. "What I thought. Now then; I wasn't 'round when you Momma died but I do knows that Mommas love they's kids and wants the best for 'em. And I'm right sure no Momma would tell an older boy that the younger two had to obey him and do whatever he said; 'special if it was crooked or bad. I thinks that Arvin, bein' the liar he be, is lying to you all along. If you Momma tol' him anythin'; it would be to watch over you two 'cause you is smaller and weaker. I thinks he's been lyin' to you's all along, just like he's been lyin' to everyone elses." The two younger boys glared at their older brother and the glare that they sent him did not bode him well.

"Rights now; none of you three has a future; all you gots is a past . . . an' it aint a good past. All littered with bad thin's you's done, times you's been lock up, the little kids you kicked 'round. And most of it be Arvin's fault. He's' the one who's made you the bad folk you is. And for as long as you listens to him; nothin's gonna change. Now then; maybe you otta trys sumpin' different."

"Does you know what they pays workers?" he asked one of the cops, who were watching.

"Right now; the going rate for grunt workers; that is, unskilled, is $1.25 an hour; or $10 a day;" one of the two officers volunteered.

$1.25 an hour; $10 a day; $50 a week an' 'bout $200 a month; Gee declared. Did you ever have $200?" he asked the brother nearest him. From the resentful expression on his face, the answer was no. "Wull; I gots no rights to tells either of you's what to do's, but was it me in you place, I'd kick Arvin in the butt and shows up at the work center first thin' on the morrow and ast fer a job. And does they say 'no' tells 'em you understands and that you's will be back t'morrow. And then shows up. And keeps showin' up 'til they gives you a job. Then does that job to the best you can, gives it all you gots, and when in times they offers you a better job at higher monies; takes that one. Then maybe one days you'll be the man at the desk handin' out jobs to others . . . and makin' more than just $1.25 an hour." Or you kin keep on doin' what you's been doin' all along 'til somebodies gets 'enuff out of you and they takes a gun an' blows you brains out. The choice be you's; makes sure you chooses well."

Gee turned to the two officers. "I gots no more words for 'em;" he admitted. Do got some other thin's I needs to do. Mind ef ah slopes off f'now? The officer shook his head and waved Gee off. He nodded to the officer and making the gun secure; stowed it back in the safe where he'd got it and headed towards Forrester's Groceries.

He walked through the door. Mr. Forrester was bent over, his back to him, helping one of his customers. His assistant was off to the left, rearranging some lettuce heads; he looked up and spotted Gee. "He's here; Mr. Forrester" he chortled in joy.

Mr. Forrester immediately raised his head, waved at him and bellowed; "Be right with you; Gee: just as soon as we're done over here." Gee waved back and began to look through some of the produce that had come only that day. Mr. Forrester's helper came over to him; a broad grin on his face.

"Gee," he said softly, "you wouldn't believe the fuss those coins of yours made when Mr. Forrester showed them off at the Bank; I thought the teller was going to have a coronary."

"Wull; you best have a Doctor handy when you shows him what I found t'day;'" he whispered back. The man looked impressed but didn't ask for a preview of what was to come.

Mr. Forrest finished with his customer, and then since there were no others in his place, he came over to Gee, the biggest smile he was capable of pasted on his face. "Gee; I am so pleased to see you again. No doubt, as William already told you, I took those coins in to the bank today and nearly caused a riot. Coins that old and never been in circulation. Banker Robbins all but lost his mind."

"Wull; you best have a doctor standin' by t'morrow," Gee admitted, "'cos I finded a bunch of others that's gunna put his shorts in bunches. I couldn't begins to brings 'em all; but I brung a few so's you kin looks 'em over and says whats you thinks. They was some boxes sayin' dollar sign two five oh and they was mebby ten boxes there. Here; you's can see f'yself and says what you thinks." The two men stared at him, looking very interested, and then gasped when he brought out the two rolls of Sacajawea coins and held them out for them to see.

"Dollar sign two five . . . O . . . My . . . God; golden dollars!" Mr. Forrester erupted. For a few minutes Mr. Forrester was not completely sane. "My dear Lord; how many boxes of these did you say? I won't insult you and ask where you got them; but . . . where did you ever find these?"

"I finded 'em," he said. "I'm not gunna tells you or anyone else's where. I thinks that makes sense if you thinks about it. And I reminds you; don't be tell ennybody wheres you gets them. Does anybody thinks I knows where they's more, I'll never be able to shakes 'em and I'll never gets back for enny more. Not never. An' they's mor'n of 'em than o' me. Peoples; that is."

Both Mr. Forrester and William crossed their hearts with their fingertips and then held their hands up as swearing an oath. Mr. Forrester gave the coins back to Gee and then went to his own safe and pulled out two twenties and two fives and brought the bills back to Gee and gave them to him. "I dislike being in debt to anyone, Gee, so if you don't mind too much, please let me pay you cash for these two rolls. He willingly agreed and handed Mr. Forrester the rolls of coins and the deal was done.

"I hate to have to say this, but I'm not sure any of these coins are going to get into the public's hands," Mr. Forrester admitted. Our banker is a fine man, but he's a banker, and as long as these coins are this rare, he's likely to just keep them."

"In that case; doesn't gives him all of them; gives some of them out in change to folks who comes in to buys you groceries. That way; some of the peoples gets some of the coins and maybe some of 'em will keeps 'em too; you spreads 'em around; so t'speak."

"Y' know Gee; that's a brilliant idea; give them out in change. That way not only do the coins get out into circulation, people will notice and talk about them."

"And that can only be good advertise for you," Gee replied.

Chapter 3

Gee and the two men shook hands, sealing the deal and Gee got up and left. He hadn't seen any of the officer's since getting the Brandon's heads in a sling and he wanted to ask about that as well as some other things that had popped up in his mind. He set out, moving in a circuitous route so he didn't always seem like he was coming from Foresters; that could potentially cause future problems and he had more than enough on his plate for now. It didn't take long and he caught up with two of his favorite people.

"Gee!" the first officer exclaimed with a smile; "we were just looking for you. I don't know if you've heard the latest, but someone just shot Arvin Brandon's right ear off."

"Left," he corrected, "it were his left ear. And it were his lobe; not entire ear. Y'see; he, uh, I means . . . . someone shoots Arvin Brandon? Tells me 'bout it!" As he spoke the words "someone shoots," he came up on his toes and made a massive flinch in his shoulders. The two officers laughed at his theatrics and nodded their heads.

"Why don't you tell us instead?" the second of the two men asked. He nodded his head and with an economy of words, filled them in on what happened. At no time did he mention his visit with the grocer and his worker, nor anything else that was not part of the specific event. By the time he was done, the pair understood as clearly as if they had seen the entire affair in person.

"So; this gun you have. Would you mind showing it to us?" one of the two asked. He nodded, reached into the pouch at his waist and the safe and withdrew it.

"Gee; you're wearing something different," one of the officers said very quietly.

"Yup. I be a finder. And this times I finded the jackpot. Or whatever it's call. Notices; I gots a new shirt . . . new to me ennyways; and looks at my feets!"

"Gee; those shoes haven't been available for the better part of eight years. Where did you ever . . ? and his eyes locked on the revolver Gee pulled out of his pouch. Gee understood the way of things; his father had trained him well; he pressed the release and the cylinder popped out. He turned the gun slightly and handed it to the man on his right; the one who had just been speaking. He, also well trained, took the firearm and further conversation about shirts and shoes promptly stopped.

"Oh nice," the officer he'd handed the gun to said. "An old Colt in . . . .32 long." That caliber is not much in the way of a man-stopper, but it's taken its share of perps out. As well as ear lobes," he added with a soft chuckle. The second officer laughed softly along with his partner, then as it often is among those whose interest lie along such lines, the two men began to talk about Gee's gun in particular and other guns in general, including those they carried every working day of their lives. In time, the two men gently pushed the cylinder back in, carefully aligning the bullets inside to come up with a fresh round should the need arise. Gee took the gun and tucked it back into the safe where it was.

"I gotta tell ya, Gee; you're not supposed to be packin' a gun. That's partially because of your age and partially because civilians aren't supposed to have guns. Not on their persons when they go out; anyway. Thing is; from what I've seen of you, we cops are better off if you are armed. If you wish; I'll warn my fellow officers that you're packing and that it's OK."

"Thanks;" he replied. "Truth be, I won't be carry it much ennyways, I dusn't likes 'em all that much but knows that many times they's the lesser of evils. Not only that; but I has a way of carryin' that can't be found."

"Now that I'd like to see," one of the two officers said.

"Arright; you's seen me put it in my pouch; sees if you can finds it." Rising to the challenge, the two frisked him. Thoroughly. He was unarmed. They both patted him down. First; with the thought that they would find it immediately. Next; more carefully, and finally, as professionally as possible. The one fact remained; Gee was unarmed.

"Alright; we give up; where'd you put it?" one of the two demanded.

"I can't tells ya. Not 'cos it be a deep dark secret but 'cos I dusn't know the words. My Mamma is a good woman; she loved her husband and kids and couldn't do ennuf for us all; but she not very bright. She talk in small sentences and only knows a few words. At least, I never herd her use many different words. And bein' 'round Mamma most of the time, that's where I learn to talk. They's lots o words I dusn't know. Know to says; and unnerstand when others says 'em. I just makes my best guess and chugs on. Onlyest thin I can say is: I puts it somewhere else; but not on me."

"I'd like you to explain that;" one of the men began, "but from what you just said, you probably can't tell us because you don't know how. Is that right?" Gee nodded his head. "At least that's something I can understand."

Gee filled the two on everything that had happened with the Brandon boys with a condensed version of what he had told the younger two. "I dunt no ef th' boys will takes me up on it, but does the two show up for the work center t'marra, it be a good thing for them what needs thin' done and good for them two boys. I dunt think they's all that bad; it just be that Arvin be a back-sides hole and was usin' 'em to does his dirty work. Does they settle down an starts doin' what's right, they be a lot less crime 'round here and a lot less little kids getting' theyselfs beat up. And that be good for the kids, the grownups and the police all at once."

"Good job; Gee," one of the officers said. "You take the Brandon's out of the equation and that's going to make our jobs a lot easier."

"Not sure what a 'quation be; but if it calms things down roun' here, it can't be bad," he admitted.

"We're not sure if you want to talk about this;" one of the officers started off a bit hesitantly, "but we've got some news about your home. That is; the place where you were raised. Not long after Clarence was hauled off, your Mother walked out of the house and hasn't been seen since. Because the house was unofficially empty, a number of folks had a squabble and one group took over and they've moved in. As far as we police are concerned, the house is now yours. Just say the word and we'll kick them out."

"Nope; let's 'em have it; I gots a lotta memories there; manys of them awful good. But the last while, ever since Da vanish, things went downhill. And a'ter Clarence and his ol' man move in; things went in the trash. The final straw was what Clarence do to my baby sis. They be no excuse for that. I doesn't know do he live and doesn't actual care. And does I sees him on the street, walkin' 'round free, I mights just starts in on 'im again; just f' somthin' to pass the time."

"Well; that's one thing you don't have to worry about;" one of the two began. "After they hauled him away, the doctors had their hands full, just getting him stabilized. To the best of my knowledge, he'll live, but he's so torn up that he'll never be normal again. I didn't see him, but from what I heard, you flat opened a can of 'whup ass' on him. And from what I've heard of things; it was well deserved. And I want to tell you how sorry all of us are that it happened. You're one of the nicest kids we've ever known and no one deserved that less than you. And if there's every anything we can do to help you in any way; just ask."

"Thanks; I 'preciate the kind words; I doesn't wants the house; the folk who move in can have it; I even signs a release if it be needed. I be a finder, and the older I gets, the better I gets at it. The gun and clothes and shoes only be a bit of the whole. I won't tell you more, but don't feels sorry f'me 'cause I gots me a nice enough place and I finded somewheres I can picks up a lot of things that be real hard to get right now. It won't last f'ever, but does I be careful, it'll get me through 'til I'm older and more able to do better."

He gave the two men a hug each and then turned and headed off towards the east. In the distance, dark clouds were beginning to gather. In the area they lived in, major storms often came from the southeast and from the looks of things; this might just be one of them . . . or maybe it would just be a flash in the pan. With storms; no one knows for sure until they've arrived. A moment later, when no one was looking and he was surrounded by debris of every type and description; he winked out.

In the next moment he was standing in his living room. He reached into his right hand front pants pocket and pulled out the bills Mr. Forrester had given him and put them on a shelf, directly behind a picture of a middle-aged couple dressed in clothes that had been out of style for at least thirty years. Someone's parents; no doubt.

He was getting hungry. He went over to the fridge, pulled the door open and pulled out one of the lower bins. There were still some of the apples and veggies from the previous days; he poked around, found what he wanted and began to eat. By the time his belly was full, the day was starting to close down. Thus far, the impending storm had not landed, nor did it look like it intended to. He went outside. He had started to look into the final apartment east of him and had done other things instead. He started that way, took only a few steps, when a small ball of grey fur shot around the corner ahead of him; closely followed by an orange ball and then another grey. He stopped and stared; he had no idea of what they were.

At first slowly, and then with increasing speed, he began to recall. His mother had told him about cats and how much she loved them. She had described them in great detail, including what she referred to as 'kittens'. From everything his mother had said and from what he'd heard from others; that's what the little animals had to be: kittens. His mind, for the moment, forgot about investigating anything else; he now thought only of cats. As he tried to recall all that he had heard, he remembered that within the place he now called his home, there had been some boxes and bags that had pictures of cats on them; clearly cat food. And the small animals would obviously be hungry; this, especially, if the mother cat wasn't around. He thought for a moment, concentrated and in the next instant he was holding one of the boxes in his left hand. He had no idea how he could do this, was reasonably sure that most people could not, but the usefulness of the act was so obvious that he didn't give it a second thought.

He pressed in the front of the box where there was an obvious flap for such and in a matter of moments, poured out a palm-full of small kitty kibbles. He moved over to where the nearby wall was and sat down and leaned up against the wall. The three animals, alerted by his movements, started to scamper off. But his motions were not towards them; if anything, it was further away. He took a few of the small kibbles and tossed them in the general direction of the three small animals. He didn't throw them hard enough and they fell well short of the goal. He focused on the small bits of cat food with his mind and began moving them across the floor in small twitches. This; the animals liked. Three small pairs of eyes tracked the progress, then when at least one of them decided they were within their striking range; it attacked; closely followed by the other two. They pounced on the kibbles in true feline form and once they had sniffed their "prey" they proceeded to gobble the bits of food down, growling at each other, and anything else that might be in sight.

He repeated his actions for the better part of fifteen minutes and the small balls of fluff were more than willing to play this game. Especially since they were getting fed at the same time they were being entertained.

In time; they slowed down. Either they were getting tired of it, or more likely, getting full. From his own experience, once he started filling up, he got thirsty. This should be true of kittens as well as kids. He got up slowly and eased towards the door. The three animals were starting to get used to him; they stared at him, moved slightly further away but did not run for cover. He went in, found a bowl that looked kitten-sized and filled it mostly to the top with water. He carried it carefully outside. The three watched him warily, moved away in case his motives were not to their greater health and stared as he put the bowl down and eased away.

There may not be another creature on the Earth as curious as a cat. They are most intelligent, within their limitations, and the bowl was both new to them as well as something that needed to be investigated. First one, and then the following two eased over, sniffed the bowl daintily, then understanding; began to lap at the water thirstily. He backed off and watched them.

Off in the southeast; thunder rumbled. The storm, if that was what it was, seemed to be dying out. To the west, the sun hung low and lower, just now starting to touch the far horizon. He got up slowly, trying not to alarm his little neighbors, and eased towards the door. Instead of closing it all the way; he left it ajar. At first cautiously, and then with increasing trust, one little hairball followed by another slipped into his new home. "At last, a family," he thought. He took one of the smaller plastic trays he had found in his closet, got a small shovel to dig with and went down to the ground floor and scraped up a generous amount of 'kitty diggings' and brought it back up to his place. He found a convenient corner and put it there. The animals would smell the dirt and use it for the intended purpose. He laid out yet another bowl full of cat food, as well as water, then went over and sat in one of the stuffed chairs and relaxed. He thought of the day and all of its unexpected events. Even by his standards he had accomplished a great deal. Fatigue caught at him. He got up, took off all his clothes, climbed into the shower for a quick rinse and a dry off and then climbed into bed and went promptly to sleep.

If he dreamed, he had no memory of it. He did wake up once in the night to the sensation of a small creature crawling up the side of his bed, and then curling up in one corner. Before he fell back asleep he became aware of a second little body, followed by a third. What happened next he had no idea; because he slipped back into slumber before he was fully aware he had wakened.

There was a small ball of fur on the next pillow, just inches from his left ear when he finally did wake. There were no windows in either bedroom but the doors faced south where the living room drapes were and he had pulled them wide open before he had gone to sleep. The increasing light of impending dawn had brought him awake: that; and a second small ball which was at that moment walking across his midriff. He woke, stretched briefly, scattering kittens to the winds. He got up, did what everybody does upon waking, and then moved out into the living room to see exactly how early it was.

Dawn was upon them and it was still quite early. He still didn't know exactly what the correct time was. There were electric clocks all over his place as well as battery-driven clocks that had quit working some years back. In one of the safes he had poked through, he had found one of the older style, wind-up wrist watches that almost everyone once wore, but had yet to set it to the correct time; or had he wound it. It, like a great many other things, was new to him and he preferred to have someone who understood such things show him how; rather than stumbling along on his own and risk breaking something valuable.

He checked the cat's food and water bowls; both had been used and both needed refilling; he did so next. Then he checked the kitty diggings. That, too, had been used. He used a small scraper and got the solid parts out and flushed them; the rest he left as is. In time, that too, would need attention.

He went to the refrigerator and dug out the remains of what food he had picked up at Forrester's the day his little sis was taken away. In time; perhaps the pain would leave his mind. He would never forget; that he knew. But perhaps in time the memory wouldn't be so raw. He ate, then got busy and got dressed. He still had no idea exactly how early . . . or late . . . it was. On further thought, he went over, found the wrist watch and placed it upon his wrist. His body, and therefore his arms and wrist, were still quite small so he only barely found a hole that would keep the watch safely on him. He double checked his shoes. He hadn't been tying shoes very long and he wasn't all that good at it. Perhaps he could ask one of the police men who patrolled the area; or some other adult. He knew better than to ask one of the bigger kids; one of them might decide that the shoes would fit him and then there would be a fight. He double checked everything he could think of, and then in the last moment, went over to where he had put the money Mr. Forrest had given him, plucked out a five dollar bill; glanced at it and stuffed it into one of his pants pockets. He might need it for something. He looked around, made sure that the door was cracked open in case one or more of the kittens decided to go outside. He focused his mind, could not detect anything living in the immediate surroundings that might see him arrive and popped out of the room.

He turned to his right and walked out of the alleyway as if he had been there all along. He headed towards the more central part; at least it was more central for his section of the city. He hadn't gone far when one of the patrol men; one he didn't know, yelled at him and beckoned him over. "What's this I hear about you packin' a gun; he bellowed at Gee.

"I has no gun," he said truthfully.

"Well; I'll just see about that!" the patrolman snapped. He spun Gee around and began to frisk him. He found no weapon; not even a pocket knife; but he did find the five dollar bill. "Ya been stealin'" the man accused him; "We'll just take care of that!" and stuck the money in his own wallet. Gee looked over the man's shoulder. It was time for the change of shift and the two officers coming towards him were well known to him.

"Exactly what is going on here; Wallace?" his own coworker demanded.

"None of your business," he told the man; then turning, shook his finger in Gee's face. "An' you keep your mouth shut;" he snapped.

Gee stared the officer in the eyes and then calmly turned to the two who were just now walking up on them. "First; he accused me of havin; a gun. Thens he frisks me. Then he finds money in my pockets; takes it and sticks it in his own wallet;" Gee said calmly.

"The little bastard's lyin'" the officer snapped.

"Then how comes I knows you has a five dollar bill in you wallet and how does I knows the last four digits of its serial number?" The two men who had just approached him promptly produced their guns and shoved them in the other mans' face. "Pull the wallet out; Wallace" the first officer said. "If you've a five dollar bill in there and if this kid knows the last four digits; you're under arrest. We've had entirely too many complaints about you and your light-fingered ways; but this time you've gone too far."

Wallace glared at Gee. When he didn't comply, one of the officers spun Wallace around and plucked out his wallet. He opened the wallet, looked and found several bills therein as well as a five dollar bill. "Well; Gee?" the officer holding the wallet asked.

"Three, three, three, nine, C" he said calmly. The first officer looked at the bill closely and then showed it to his friend. He, in turn glanced at the bill, and then looked back at the one in his clutches.

"Congratulations; Wallace," he said. "Not only have you just lost a job, you're getting a free ride back to the station. Then you get to face Captain Taylor and explain to him just exactly why Gee knows the last four digits of a bill that's in *your* wallet. Captain Taylor's gonna be very interested in this; very interested. You're not gonna like it one little bit, because he for sure isn't gonna like it. The two put the patrolman's own cuffs on him, took his gun and badge and picking up the small radio that all such officers carry; called Headquarters. That Captain Taylor was going to be interested in this was, perhaps, the understatement of the year. Mount Vesuvius was just a small firecracker going off by comparison.

The squad car arrived and two officers got out. Information was exchanged; the look the first officers had given Wallace was echoed by those in the squad car. They shoved Wallace in the back seat and closed the door. The insides of the door had no way of either opening the door or rolling the windows down and the section between front and back seats had a screen that permitted no exchange of anything much larger than a paper clip. One of the two officers turned and looked Gee in the eyes. "Thing is, Gee, Captain Taylor got wind of this and he's dog-bitin' mad. Not only that; he knows who you are. Fact is; you've been building up quite a reputation among those who cover this section of town and he's more than interested in you. If you don't mind, and can spare the time, the Captain would like to meet you. But I gotta warn you; we might not be able to bring you back."

"That be alright," he admitted. "I be kinda interest too. I heered lots a' things 'bout him, and I'd actual like to see the insides of you place. As a guest and not a perp; that is." The men laughed at the comment, then sandwiching Gee between them and with their latest guest locked up in the back, they pulled out and drove away.

It wasn't that far. They pulled up to the precinct and got out. Several other officers, aware of what was going on, met them at the door. They transferred custody of Wallace to the others, and then with a courteous gesture, waved him inside the building. Captain Taylor was aware of what was happening, and specifically, who was coming in. He left his office, and came into the room where the other were, a broad smile on his face. "So; I get to meet you at last;" he said. "Please come on in. I've heard so much about you over the last few months and I'm delighted to meet you.

"I've heered lots 'bout yous too; he admitted. When the Captain extended his hand he immediately stuck out his own. There weren't many people whose hands he had ever shaken but he knew what to do and what was expected and did a respectable job of it. Captain Taylor waved him in and as he entered, followed him.

"So then, Gee," he said; please explain to me exactly what happened. I've already heard it from others and have even read the latest report; but I'd like to hear what you have to say.

"From the horse's mouth," he said with a smile. The Captain laughed and nodded his head. "Wull; backin' ups a bit . . . I be a finder; that's how I keeps myself fed. Afore everything went in the toilet, I'd goes out and looks for things. Mostly suthin' to eats. Lackin' that, anything as can be sold for food or otherwise use. M' Momma took care of much of that; she and my Da. At first, being small and new to it, wasn't often I'd find much of use. But as I growed, I learnt, and after awhiles I got better at it; comes back with useful stuff: that sort of thin'. Then my Da vanishes. He be there one day; the next he wasn't. Folks jest sed he'd sloped; tuk off; left fer greener pastures and that sort of thang. Onlyest; I knowed 'im; 'im and Momma. They loves each other; dint want t'be away from each other enny longer than they had to. I knows my Da would never leave; I knows him and I knows the onlyest reason he woudn't comes back is he couldn't; or he was dead.

"By then, I wuz getting' better; findin' more thins. Mostly by takin' bigger risks; goin' in places most folk won't go. Bein' small has it's 'vantage. Don't weigh a much; being smaller, I kin slip thru littler places, that sort o' thin. An' I started findin' more thins. Lookits the shoes on my feets;" and he stuck his feet out where the Captain could see them. He, in turn, looked and nodded his head. Everything about him; the expression on his face, the way he was sitting, all showed that he was very interested in everything this boy had to say. "Puttin' a point on it; I started findin' more thins; better thins. Some's o' the thins I sells. That's where I got that money I had in my pocket; I sells suthin. I doesn't wants to say to whos or what. But I finded suthin' o' value and sells it to someones. Again, I doesn't wants t' says who. It be legal and all, and him din't does wrong, but its not important who so I not gonna says who. But he gives me the moneys for value received and we both be sa-tis-fied. I goes to wheres I now lives. I looks at the money and notice the numbers on the bill. They ends in 3339C. That means that 'three threes makes a nine' . . . see? It kinda stuck in my mind and when that man frisks me for a gun and I don't gots one, he finds the money and sticks it in his wallet. Then the other two men comes up and things kinda fell apart for Officer Wallace an' they hasn't got better f' him since an' 'spects they won't."

"You have that right;" Captain Taylor said emphatically. "That man has been pushing the edge all along, but here of late, he's gotten so that nobody actually likes him anymore. What's worse; no one trusts him. What he pulled on you is the last straw. He's going to face a Judge over this one, and knowing the Judge in question as I do, things will not go well for Wallace; not even a little. But just a few minutes ago you said something that caught my attention; you mentioned a gun. I presume you mean a handgun; a pistol; a revolver. Is that correct?"

"Not sure what them words means; but if you means a gun youse can hol' in one hand, yes, that's whats I means."

"Something like this?" the Captain asked. He leaned back in his chair, reached down to his waist and pulled out a small, short barreled revolver. He opened the cylinder, emptied the cartridges onto the table and extended the gun to Gee. He looked at the gun and then instead of taking the gun in hand, which was obviously what the Captain had in mind, he reached out and picked up one of the cartridges and eyed it carefully.

"I seed sumpin' like this not long ago; he admitted. He turned it around, looking at it from its side, the front and then the back; "much the same; onlyest different. Th' one I looks at was silvery, like this one, but it looked longer. And the bullet part was longer toos and the back side said .357 Mag; not .38 + P like this one doos."

"Son; for the first time in ages; you give me hope. The cartridge you hold is called 125 grain hollow point and the case is in .38 plus p. That means that the bullet, while being a bit lighter than regular 38s, is much faster and more powerful. My thinking is this: if I actually have to shoot a perp, I do not want him getting back up. Not ever! If it gets to the place where I have to fire a round, then it's already gone past the point of no return, and I do not want that one to live. It's sad that it has to be that way, but from where I stand, it's either him or me. If I have to shoot him; he's already gone beyond the point of no return. Do you think you can find any more bullets like this? I'll pay you top dollar. I've got to admit; I've contacted all of the Districts that I can and nobody has any. Or if they do; they won't admit it; which, under the circumstances, is both logical and understandable . . . but not very helpful.

"I doesn't know of such right now, but doos I sees such, I'll see what I can doos for you. Since we be here, talkin', I gots a couple of questions I'd like to ast. F'one; these shoos I finded. I never had such, and whiles I nos a bit 'bout 'em, I still doesn't know how to ties 'em. Ef y'could shows me how; I'd be grateful."

"This is a glad thing I can do for you, Gee," Captain Taylor promptly replied. He was a man in his very early forties; slim of build and broad shouldered and brown eyes with a dark mass of black hair on his head that was gradually going gray. The shoe strings were nowhere near properly tied. Instead of normal bows; they were wrapped around each other in a random manner; enough so that for the most part they stayed at least relatively together. He undid the mess on Gee's right foot, and then moving carefully, slowly and methodically tied them properly. He talked Gee through the motions, and then on the next shoe, he had Gee do the tying; correcting him when he started down a wrong path and urging him on with compliments when he was doing it right. Before long; Gee had both shoes properly tied and knew how to do it the next time he needed to do so.

"Thanks you; Sir," he said, once the chore was done. "I knowed it weren't hard; I seen my Da doos it mor'n once but never did think to ast him how it were did. Seems like there were somethin' else I wan . . . oh yeah; now's I 'member. He exposed his left wrist; a watch was strapped there with at least reasonable correctness. "I finded this in a safe I comes across. I knows it be a watch, and that it 'posed to tells time, but I'm not sure I knows how to tells time and I'm right sure I doesn't know how to wind nor set it. Anythin' y'kin do will be 'preciated."

"Another glad thing I can do for you; Gee," he said. Gee extended his wrist and the Captain took the watch off. A moment later he whistled appreciatively.

"Nice watch; an Omega; and a very nice one at that!" he exclaimed." Once it was off Gee's wrist and with a few words and a short learning curve, Gee learned about not only the proper way to wind a watch, but also how to read one; for this specific watch did not have numerals all the way around and Gee had virtually no idea of how time was told.

"So where did you find that; on some shelf somewhere?" the Captain asked politely.

"Nope; I finds it locked up in a safe. And dun't ast me what safe nor where 'cos they be other thins there and I plans on either using 'em or maybe sells some of 'em. Depends on."

"It was locked up in a safe?" Captain Taylor demanded sharply.

"Yup! Tucked inter a corner. That; an' else that were in it.'"

"You cracked a safe?" Captain Taylor demanded again.

"I dunt know what's you means by 'cracked' but I opened it up. There was a gun in there; kinda likes the one you gots, but bigger and 'stead of blue, the metal was white or silvery or whatever it were.

The Captain got up, went over to his desk, pulled a key out of his pocket and unlocked a drawer. He pulled a revolver out and showed it to Gee. "Did it look anything like this?" he demanded.

"Yup! Thas' the same gun alrite; how'd you gets it here?" He asked the officer.

"I didn't. I don't suppose you would know this, but this gun is made by Smith and Wesson, model 686 and is one of the most sought after guns on the market. And I suppose there were two or three there?"

"Nope; prolly ten or fifteen of 'em; I dint has time to count 'em."

The captain went over to his chair and collapsed into it. "You're lying; right?" he demanded.

Gee grinned at him and nodded his head. "Yup!" he replied. "They were only the one. I din't spend much time searching as I was looking for else, but they was some boxes of what I suppose is bullets as well as a bunch of papers and stuff. Alsos too; what looks to be a lot of monies. But they was also in boxes and I dint goes through them neither. I was lookin' f' else and was busy doin' else and the guns 'n' stuff dint' interest me then."

Captain Taylor sat in his chair and stared at Gee. For a moment; stare was all that he did. Then at first slowly and softly he started to chuckle. That turned into giggles; which was closely followed by laughter. In the end he was all but helpless in his hysteria. Those who were outside, opened the door and poked cautious noses in, trying to learn what was going on; this seemed to strike the Captain as even more hysterical and he roared.

In time, he was laughed out. He blotted his eyes on his sleeve and found a piece of cloth that might have been a handkerchief and blew his nose. Then he wiped his eyes on his sleeve once again.

"I gotta tell you, Gee, that's the best laugh I've had in many years. And your delivery was perfect. I can now see why some of my men are so fond of you; you have a wicked sense of humor, and like I already said, you delivery couldn't be faulted. But if I got anything out of this, I understand that you said that you can crack a safe; that is, open a safe that is otherwise closed and the numbers are unknown. Is that right?"

"Yup" he admitted. "Actual; it be purdy easy. I jus' listens to the clicks an' clucks an' ticks an' tucks and works accordingly. It really isn't all that hard . . . but I gots to listen . . . and watch. Not sure I can 'splain it better than that.

"I'll put a point on this, Gee. I have a safe down in storage. We've had it some time now; we've had some very good people try and crack this fool thing; all to no avail. I can't get it up here right now, but maybe in a week or so when some of this latest mess is cleared up, I'd like you to take a shot at it. As I've already said; some of our best folks have worked on it, but for whatever reason the tumblers are exceptionally quiet, what you were describing as 'clicks and clucks'. You are much younger than we; maybe your hearing will be better and we can get it popped open. The fool safe has been around for several years; it was found not long after the bombs fell, and for whatever reason, we've been saddled with it ever since."

"I'd be pleased to gives it a try," he admitted.

It seemed like all of the needed business was taken care of. He gave everyone there a parting hug, and once that was done, he walked out of the front door, turned to his left and began to walk. He was aware that many watched him. As he cleared the corner and turned left, he triggered his inner transport and in the next instant he was walking in his living room. Several kittens, startled by his sudden appearance, hissed in fright and headed towards which ever corner or shadow that made them feel safe. He was home.

Chapter 4

He had yet to do any serious cleaning to his own home. There was a vacuum cleaner in a closet; this, he knew how to use as they had one in his old home. He dug it out, plugged it in, and started cleaning. This; the kittens definitely did not like. En masse they headed towards the gap in the outside door and in the next instant turned to their right and headed back to more familiar territory. He knew that being animals, they were easily frightened or startled, and once their fear was overcome they would return.

He vacuumed, dusted and cleaned all the chairs, shelves and other things he could see and reach. In time, that little chore was done. Next he headed for the fridge. Most of what he had brought home earlier was long since eaten. He went into his closet and selected some cans of soup; this was something he had yet to try and was most interested in it.

In due time, everything was little more than a contented belch within, and the kittens, having overcome their anxiety, returned one at a time. He checked their food and water bowls – which pleased them very much – took care of his immediate needs and was done with his normal routine.

It was getting late. The sun had long since set. Since he didn't have much else to do, he slipped out of his clothes and into bed and shortly thereafter was joined by first one little animal after another. The kittens had not learned about being petted yet. He spent the next while trying to gain their further trust, and ever so gradually, they started to become tamer. Somewhere along the way his eyes drooped and he had no awareness of exactly when he dropped off into slumber.

He awoke. For some reason he felt tense, like there was something that needed to be done. But the inner sense that prodded him did not suggest exactly what. He got up, dressed, checked both the food and water bowls and once again cleaned out the cat box. But that was not it. He looked out the door. From the amount of light outside the sun was long since up; he had slept through the night and most of the early morning. And still; something was prodding him. His 'meller, that part of his brain that warned him of danger and helped him find things, was buzzing non-stop. There was something that he needed to do . . . but what?

He looked around his apartment; it wasn't here. He thought of his gun, of getting it, but even as the thought entered his head he knew that wasn't what he needed. He mentally scanned his favorite site, detected no one near, and popped over there. His sense was buzzing madly now. He started looking around; hoping that he would find something that would give him a clue. Off to his right and slightly ahead; was a broken brick. For some reason the brick seemed to beckon to him; he walked over and picked it up. It was an ordinary baked red brick such as many of the surrounding buildings were made of; but this one had become broken: perhaps due to the explosions that had destroyed so very much in the area. He stared at it. It was perhaps two-thirds of a brick and the broken off part, instead of being directly across as was logical, was a double bevel. As he held it, the upper break formed a steep angle descending forward from the base, perhaps one third of its depth. There was a very rounded fracture point and then the break formed a much shallower bevel and moved back towards to where he now held it. An odd sort of break to his way of thinking; he personally had never seen such. Somehow; the brick seemed to call to him. He stuck it into his pouch and moved on. No more than a very few steps and he saw yet another piece of brick. This one had broken so that it was very nearly perfectly square with rounded corners. No more than another step further was an identical brick. He stuffed both of them in with the first.

He raised his head and looked around. Something was calling him and he couldn't figure out what or why. But not only was most insistent; it was getting obnoxious. He started off in one direction, took two steps and the buzz in his brain assured him that was not the way to go. He veered, first to his right and then to his left. Only after he'd taken a few steps in that direction did he feel he was headed where he needed to go. He put his legs to work and began to walk. He walked the entire block and then turned to his right. Well ahead he saw a group of young boys. This was definitely off his own turf; if he went that way the three would unquestionably stop him and rob him of anything he had. And beat him up if he didn't have anything for them. He didn't hesitate. The moment the boys saw him and started to react, he stepped backwards and immediately teleported to the corner well behind them. He glanced behind him; the three were staring where he had been an instant before; staring and pointing and talking excitedly between them. He continued on.

He reached the end of that block. The buzzing in his head had reached crescendo. He looked more to his right. There, a group of men stood with yet others standing back away, just watching; and in the midst of the men stood a young golden-haired girl. He knew that he had arrived; he walked up.

"Arright;" the man to his right said; "that'll do. But you better have all the money here. Last time; it was mostly 'funny money' and that can get a man thrown in prison."

"Yeah, yeah, mistakes can happen. And don't worry; this little gal will be very popular amongst the other young girls;" and he smiled. But he did not show his teeth. And it all came together for Gee.

"You be a liar;" Gee announced; "you not a sex-slaver; you a cannibal. And you the same bastich as kill and eat my little sis." His eyes flashed green fire and his face held both fury and hate in equal measure.

"An' you Pa, an' your Ma, and now we got you too." The man grabbed his left arm with his right hand and grinned widely; exposing front teeth that had all been filed to chisel points.

Gee didn't think; he just reacted. His left arm was being held in a grip of iron but his right was free. He reached into his pouch and in a blink he was holding the larger brick. Like a cobra's strike; his hand shot out and buried the broken-off piece of the brick into the man's face. In much less than the blink of an eye; from his eyebrows to the roots of his upper teeth and from outer eye corner to outer corner was instantly a giant, gaping, bloody hole. The man dropped to the ground; dead before he hit; lifeless before he knew he was about to die. Gee swiveled on his feet and faced the next man behind the one.

This one stared at Gee with growing horror. The act had happened so fast that his sluggish thinking couldn't possibly keep up with it, but the one thing he did know, was that he didn't want to be here any longer. Shrieking insanely, he spun, his right foot reaching out to take the first step. Again; Gee's hand shot out like a serpent's strike and the rounded edge of the brick caught the second man right at the base of his skull. In that instant the brain stem was smashed beyond recognition and he, too, dropped to the ground; dead before he even started to fall. Gee turned to the other two men who were further out; standing guard and watching. They, seeing the fate of their two comrades, instantly spun on the balls of their feet and took flight.

Gee didn't want this brick further; instead of putting back into his pouch, he placed it on the shelf, right next to the picture of the older couple with outdated clothing. He plucked the last two brick pieces out of his pouch; one in each hand. He advanced; leading with his right side. He took three quick, small steps, wound up his left hand and pitched the brick piece at the fleeing felon; it spun through the air, hit the man at the base of the skull and that one went down, skidding across the ground on his face. That left only one other.

By this time the fourth man, now more than just alarmed, was in full flight. It wasn't that far and the block ended, going left and right as well as straight ahead. Just to the left, up next to what remained of a curb, was the twisted wreck of a car; one that clearly had been destroyed both by falling bombs and rubble as well as the explosion of its own gas tank. The fourth felon, legs and arms windmill churning, headed that direction. Gee took two quick steps and drawing back with his right hand, threw the third and final brick. That rose quickly, seemingly moving to the fleeing one's left, sure to miss. But as the brick descended, the running man swerved to his left, obviously intending to duck down that street. Descending brick met up with his left temple and energy from the brick combined with the momentum he had from running and he as much flew as stumbled into the car's rusted remains; twitched briefly and was no more.

Gee stood where he was and did a relatively quick three sixty; staring at everything and everyone, but all were quiet, peace-loving citizens who wanted no trouble . . . especially with him.

He walked the short distance and faced the golden haired girl. "You all right?" he asked politely.

"Yes;" she replied. She looked to be perhaps seven or eight and was without question the most beautiful girl he had ever met. Her hair was the exact color of gold and her eyes were the bluest he had ever seen. She was petite of build and the smile she gave him surely had diamonds in it for it seemed to him to glisten and gleam in the sun's light. Then again; maybe it was because he was still high from all the action.

"What be your name; girl? My name be Gee. Wull, actual, it be George Elandier Evansen but Momma was kinda lazy o' speech and she just call me 'Gee' and I jus' kinda sticks with it."

"My name is Maria Cole," she said, with a shy smile.

"Maria; that be a beautiful name; a beautiful name for a beautiful girl; tells me, Maria, what doos you wants? Doos you wants to go back to where you was or do you wants to go somewhere elses?"

"I want to go with you;" she said quite bluntly.

'NO!" the man said and started to reach out and grab Maria by the arm. With a lightning-like flick of his left hand he batted the man's arm away.

"The moments you put this chile ups for sale, you gots no say in it. You still gots the money you gets for her; she not yous enny more. An' she do have a right to decide what she wants for the rest o' her lifes; it be her's; ater all. An' doos you wants to argufry 'bout it, I can gets another brick quick enough, and you can join them other four." He stared up at the older and taller man before him and his green eyes held no room for arguments or debates. The man, showing uncommonly good sense for him, immediately backed off.

Among the slowly gathering crowd were two patrolmen; both eased their way between one citizen and another and stood almost directly in front of him. "Excuse me, citizen, but did I hear you right? Is your name Gee? He nodded his head in agreement. That one, without further discussion, pulled his two-way radio from off his belt and raised it up to his head. "Patrolman Frommeling; this is Patrolman Dickenson; do you have your ears on right now? Over."

A moment later a familiar-to-him voice sounded over the man's speaker: "This is Patrolman Frommeling answering; what's up besides the sky? Over."

"One of your little lambs got out of his cote and has wandered over here and the dust he's kicked up since he arrived has yet to settle. I've been in actual combat and never seen this kind of destruction. And for whatever its worth to you; from now on, I'm gonna believe anything you say about this young man: and everything! Over."

A moment later the radio again began to crackle. "This is Captain Taylor; did I understand you right? Is there any chance that's Gee over there on your patch?"

"Ten-four, Captain; in person and breathing fire. I stood here with my mouth hanging open and watched him wipe out four cannibals like they were nothing; meanwhile rescuing the most beautiful little gal I've ever seen. I'm telling you; this child is a one-kid demolition team and I don't *ever* want to get on the wrong side of him. Over"

"Gee; get yourself over and on this phone right now; that's an order; over."

In years past and two-way radios were first invented, one had to hold a button down when they were talking and release when they wanted to hear. Those days were long past but people still used the 'over' to help those on the other side know when they were finished talking. It could save some confusion and it was still useful.

"This be Gee;" he admitted into the radio. "I gots t' tell ya; it be a right mess 'round here 'bout now. I thinks maybe-so somebodies needs to send a meat-wagon or two out here 'coz we be up to our ears in stiffs. And these cats goes bad on ya atter awhiles. Over."

Soft laughter came from the speaker; followed by the Captain's voice. "That sure sounds like you Gee. For whatever its worth to you, I was able to get that safe up to my office. It's out of my way; whenever you have the time; you can take a look at it. As for me . . . do try to not kill anyone else until I get out there and see for myself exactly why you've been kicking up so much dust. Please! Captain Taylor: out."

Gee handed the phone back to the officer he had taken it from.

It actually took a surprisingly short time before a police car pulled up and Captain Taylor stepped out. He stood briefly and stared about. The two closest corpses he located immediately; the third he found not long afterwards. The furthest, the one still stuck in the destroyed car, was beyond where he was looking and he couldn't find it until one of the officers pointed the body out to him. He walked the distance, counting paces as he did so. He turned and went over to where Gee stood; watching. He held out his arms and Gee willingly went to him and gave him a hug. "Son; I don't know what I'd do without you;" he admitted gladly. "It seems like every time I turn around; you've done something else for me and for the Precinct. Now then; fill me in on your end of things."

Gee started out, not with the actual event, but the odd feeling that he had that morning and the things that had happened on the way. He made a clear and specific report, without mentioning the other things that he could see and do. The Captain understood as clearly as if he had followed the child and had seen things with his own eyes.

"I gotta admit, Gee, that's one of the more interesting stories I've ever heard. It is clear to me that you can do things with ease that most people find hard; or can't do at all. You truly are an exceptional child. Whatever your needs may be; be sure to tell me or some of my people and we'll do all we can to help you; because it's becoming increasingly clear to us that most of what you do is helping our community at large and that specifically helps us."

In the distance the wail of an approaching ambulance sounded, followed by a second. The men in the vehicles were already aware that they were picking up the dead; and they didn't waste any time in doing what they had come for. Over the past ten minutes or more, people had begun to gather, and by now there were at least 20 gathered around in a loose group. The man who had sold the girl, vanished the moment he heard the conversation between Gee and the Captain, closely followed by several bystanders who potentially had guilty conscience's. In time; things were as picked up as anything got picked up in the day and age and people moved off to go about their own concerns. Gee hugged the patrolmen and Captain, goodbye, then he and Maria moved off, headed towards the northeast and where he lived.

He approached the corner that he had teleported to. He sent his mind out; detected the same group of boys in the same general place. They were just a single step from making their left turn around the buildings. "Be readies for a right turn;" he told her. The turn was obviously a left turn; she was about to tell him that for it is in the female mind to do such things. In that instant; the buildings which had been to his left were now to her right; and they turned right. They complete the turn. "I tries to 'splain later," he whispered. "It takes a while and I dun't wants to takes the time now. She promptly nodded her head and made a mental note to hold him to it.

Patrolman Frommeling had finished his shift and had already left. Instead he saw Patrolman Trent and the woman he presumed to be his wife. At least, they acted like a married couple and were almost always on the same shift together. They both walked up; observed by the two who knew they were coming.

"Just had to go out and kick up some dust; did you? the man asked. Gee grinned and nodded his head.

"An' this be Maria; this be who the dust was all 'bout;" he admitted. The two females eyed each other, and then of a common mind, both closed in and hugged one another. He looked upwards; towards the sky. The sun hung overhead; looking very much to him like midday. Then he remembered that he now had a watch. He looked down at his wrist and recalled that he still couldn't read it properly.

"Gee; you've got a watch!" the man exclaimed. Both females stopped hugging and turned to see what the males were up to now.

"Yup;" he admitted. "But I still can't reads it very well. Mebby some days I'll understand better, but f'now, I keeps just lookin' up ats the

Sun. I don't knows 'bout enny one else; but I'm getting hungry. What abouts you? he asked; and looked Maria in the eyes. She immediately nodded her head and got excited for she was very hungry. He turned to the two adults that were watching them with great interest. "An' what about's you?" he asked them. "I gots some monies and I knows that Mr. Forrester has a small café where he serves some food. Does either of you's gots the hungries too?" They did.

They were allowed to take such breaks from their duties and it wasn't long before they stood at the Café's door. He pulled the door open, and let first Maria in, followed by the two adults. He entered afterwards and carefully closed the door behind them. There were an even ten tables with four chairs each. Two tables were taken; one by a man well known to all of them; known and not liked. For a moment, Gee thought of going elsewhere, but Mr. Forrester spotted him and immediately waved him over to where one of the tables was. He smiled, waved, and continued in. The unliked man and his two personal guards glanced at them and then promptly went back to their meal.

The menu was quite limited. There were some meats for those who liked steaks and such; and the specialty of the place was a stew that was made fresh every day. This was the one many chose and what Gee and the others also went for.

It wasn't long and their meals were brought before them, along with some freshly baked bread, glasses filled with water and two cups of coffee that was ordered by the adults. Gee sampled his stew and found it bland. Without thinking of where he was nor who he was with; he reached into his pouch. Back at his own apartment was a small, compact container that held something that he had only recently found: found, tasted, and immediately adopted as a necessity when he ate. A moment later he brought the small cylinder out, snapped the plastic cap back, and began to sprinkle it over his food freely. For reasons he could not understand, in that blink of time, all movement ceased and every eye was upon him.

"What, may I ask, is that?" Patrolman Trent asked curiously.

"I doesn't actual know;" he admitted. "As everybody knows, I be a finder. I creeps and snoops and checks out all the cracks and crevices I can finds and then I looks 'em over. Was this one place in a kitchen. It had been looked over a'fore, but in a corner I finded this and some other things. But I doesn't know what it be; I only know I really likes the taste. He turned to Maria and offered her some. "Want any?" he asked politely. She nodded her head. He sprinkled her food freely and then she stirred her stew and took a cautious taste.

"Salt!" she squealed enthusiastically. An eye blink later and Gee would have given almost anything if she had just kept quiet. Every eye in the place turned upon him and those with him, and several started to get up out of their chairs. Mr. Forrester and his assistant immediately came over.

"What did you say; Missy?" Mr. Forrester demanded.

"That's what Gee has; salt!' she enthused.

"Thief; thief; you stole that; you stole that from me;" the unliked citizen began to shriek. The two men did their best to quiet him down but he was overcome by his own innate greed; and the word "salt" had triggered his insatiable desire to own and possess any and all that was remotely of value; whatever the reason for that value. The man was in his mid-late forties, blue of eyes and brown hair; hair that was going silver, and slender of build. He was also immaculately dressed and obviously very wealthy. His two men had their hands full, just trying to calm him down, but they more they labored the more he screamed.

Maria, now understanding what she had caused, hunched down in her chair and looked ashamed; he reached over and gave her a gentle hug. As he touched her mid-back, she flinched and pulled away. She had done that earlier; he remembered. Perhaps she wasn't used to being hugged. From what he'd seen of the man who was trying to sell her; it seemed a logical conclusion. He patted her on her shoulder; that, she seemed to take better and she gave him a wan, half-smile back as an apology.

Things got calmed back down; at least as calm as they were going to get for now. Officer Taylor looked Gee in the eyes. "Gee; you very likely don't know this, but at least here in our area, salt is almost impossible to find. And if anyone does find any; they keep it to themselves. In other words; they don't tell anyone that they have any and they most definitely do not use it out in the open where everyone can see them. The last I heard, if anyone did have any salt, they could sell it for equal weight in gold; ounce for ounce; that sort of thing. And salt is one of the things the human body needs. We can get a certain amount out of the foods we eat and other things, but without a ready supply, most people are salt-deprived or close to it. The best thing I can tell you is . . . don't admit it to anyone . . . including me. Understand?"

Gee nodded his head. He paid attention to the food that was on his plate. The stew was better, now that he had added salt, and the bread was a welcome treat for him because he got very little of it. Maria sat beside him and quietly nibbled at her food. For a girl that had seemed so very hungry just minutes ago, she seemed entirely too quiet. Then he understood that she most likely was feeling guilty because of the fuss she had unintentionally caused. He reached over and touched her shoulder gently.

"Doesn't feels bad;" he whispered to her softly; you din't know and I din't neither. I din't even know what it was; I jus' knowed it tasted awful good; both when I sprinkles it on my han' to taste it as when I puts it in my foods. And doesn't worry; this isn't alls I gots; but doesn't say anythin 'bout it 'cause it looks like it might cause a riot. An' I's had 'nuff 'citement for today. An' I bets you'se had 'nuff for todays as well." She raised her head, looked in his eyes and with gratitude clear in her eyes, nodded her head.

They finished their meal; he took the tab over and reaching into his pouch, pulled out one of the twenties that were sitting back home on his shelf. Mr. Forrest, with a grateful smile, handed him his change. In the next moment, in a very quiet voice, he whispered; "Gee; if you have any more of that salt, any at all, enough that you'd be willing to sell it; please, I beg of you, don't sell any of it to anyone but me. I've searched every source I can find and I can tell you as a matter of fact: no one has any; or won't admit to having it. Or if they do have any; the prices they demand would give a man a coronary. Please; I beg of you."

"I puts you t' the top of my list; Mr. Forrester, I promises, he whispered back. As he turned to join the others, the unliked man and his two guards moved up, and shoved some money into Mr. Forrester's hand. He counted it, made the proper change and gave it to the man. Or actually, to one of his guards as the man turned away and started walking out after Gee. Mr. Forrester shook his head. At least Gee had two patrol people with him; the man was unlikely to start anything with officers in plain sight. He was greedy, yes, but not a complete fool. Or at least Mr. Forrester didn't think he was a fool. Appearances can deceive at times.

Forrester's groceries was quite close to where one of the bomblets had hit; far enough to completely miss the store and the buildings nearby. Less than two blocks away, lay an area of near-complete destruction. Some buildings were utterly leveled, a few more nearly so. Perhaps a block from Forrester's stood an entire wall of one such building. It had been the site of a fairly large supply building that hadn't actually been in use at the time. The one side of the structure was facing south while the entrances had once faced west. The entire northern section had been blown away as had all of the west side and much of the east. It was a great brick section that looked much like a giant 'L' from the air, and was at least two stories high. People avoided it because it did not look like a healthy place to be. Gee headed just to the south of the site, back to the general area where he had met the two officers. The unliked citizen and his two men followed closely. The four stopped and the citizen and his two guards came up behind.

"Where;" the nasty man demanded with a cross expression on his face; "did you find that; where did you find salt around here? Well; don't just stand there, gaping like an idiot, tell me where you found it."

Gee gave an expansive wave; gesturing at all the buildings around him without actually indicating any one of them. "Looks around you, citizen, sees what they's to look at. Some of the buildings is hammered flat; not much to finds there. Some buildings only scratched a bit an' some's not hardly bang up at all. Manys of them buildings is still in use. Many more's maybe a little and somes not at all. I creeps and sneaks and pokes around the ones I feels is safe and tries to looks in places where others din't looks." He turned to the bombed-out relic that was almost directly across from them. "But I doesn't goes there."

"Why; why don't you want me to go there;" the revolting little man demanded; "are you hiding something over there?"

"No; and I din't tells you not to goes there. I say I doesn't go there; it be 'cause o' the squee-plop; I doesn't go there's because I'm scare o' the squee-plops; they's danger." And he shook his head and even though he was well away from the place, he gave a small shudder and backed up even more. Off in the southeast; once again dark clouds were beginning to gather; this time more of them and they looked far more ominous. But now they were much closer . . . it did not look good.

"You can't tell me what to do!" the man screeched at him. Turning on his heels, he headed that way. Gee immediately reached out and grabbed the man by an arm; swinging him around.

"No! Listens citizen! Squee-plops! I doesn't know the right word! But they's danger! A squee-plop get'scha and you's a deader: quick, fast and in a hurry!" He tried once more to pull the man back but he shoved Gee. He tussled with the man briefly and then backed off. The man, clearly irritated, yelled at his two men to follow and he headed across the street and disappeared behind the brick wall. The two men who answered to him started to follow but Gee grabbed both of them;

one by each arm. "Doesn't go;" he insisted. "'Death awaits without'; as my Da usta says." The two men, confused, turned slightly and looked at the two officers who just stood and stared.

Officer Taylor gazed at the two men and understood their indecision. "For whatever it's worth, was it me in your shoes, I'd obey Gee before I'd ever obey Mr. Coldbrick; any day; every day; every way. You just might live longer." The two nodded their heads as if controlled by a single mind and backed away from the standing wall.

Tom Coldbrick had his mind on only one thing. The boy had found something that he wanted. He had found it somewhere, and from his actions, the boy was hiding something. He based his opinion on the single fact that it was what he would do in the same circumstances: lie about everything and admit nothing. He stared around.

There was an unbelievable amount of rubble: broken bricks; busted roof girders; bits and pieces of roofing tile; and off away, half buried in the rubble, was the obvious outlines of an old safe. He chortled when he spotted this. "I got you;'" he screeched in fiendish glee; "now I know why you didn't want me to come here. And it's mine; all mine." He waded through the debris and with both hands, began pulling junk off the safe in the intent of digging it out and finding what was inside. He was not at all careful; in his greed and haste, he threw items every which way; bricks flew to the corners of the compass and some of them, too many of them, bounced off the rickety southern wall; knocking small chips off both brick and dried mortar alike.

Gee glanced towards the southeast. By now, the dark clouds were much closer, and the wind was starting to pick up; he nudged the policeman next to him. "Looks like some weather comin' our ways" he supposed, "prolly be some wind pickin' up purdy soon." The words were no more than out of his mouth when a gust came along and slammed against them, making all of them shuffle their feet about, trying not to get blown over. The gust struck the standing wall; the wall shuddered. Between bricks hitting in on one side and the wind on the other, the wall; brick rubbing against brick, gave an enormously loud 'squeeeeeee;' seemed to wiggle like a hula dancer gyrating her hips and then base and top separated, and not unlike a giant flyswatter descending up an unfortunate insect, the wall toppled over onto Mr. Coldbrick. And he was no more.

A massive cloud of dust and other particles were blown towards the northwest; clearing the view of the wreckage. Where moments before was a very large wall, perhaps twenty-five feet tall and at least sixty feet long, there was now little more than a humongous pile of broken and twisted brick wall; devoid of anything that looked remotely human or alive.

Officer Taylor's radio began to chirp; tweet-tweet-tweet; tweet-tweet-tweet. He picked it up; took a look at the dial and groaned. "Oh God, no, it's Lendl Holmes;" he moaned. He turned to Gee. "Somehow, he must know about that wall going down. That man would skin a flea for its hide and tallow; he'll want to know how many bricks were in that wall; how many . . . Gee made the gesture with his hand and thumb that meant "shut up" and stuck out his hand. The man handed the phone to him; an odd expression on his face.

"Hi; this be Gee. What's kin I doos for you today?"

"Who is this? What are you doing on a police radio anyway?"

"Talking to you's; what doos you want? It was you who calls me; not 'tother ways aroun'."

"Get off this radio and give me Officer Taylor! That's an order!" he snapped.

"Can't!" Gee responded. "Him an' the rest is off lookin' for th' citizen." He looked first at Taylor, then at his woman. He placed his hand over his eyes, as if shading them, and then pantomimed staring off in various directions. Taylor, already laughing, immediately duplicated the motion; closely followed by his mate. The other men, seeing what was happening, joined in. A single heart-beat later and Maria did it. Now all of them were pretending to stare in every direction there was. He nodded; pleased.

"Who is looking for what citizen?" the man on the phone demanded; his voice was starting to show the frustration he was undoubtedly feeling."

"Everybodys;" he announced. "Looks at it this ways; just a bit ago, they was seven of us here. Then one of us goes off and walks a'hind this tall wall. Then a big gust o' wind pops up and the tall wall fall and now we doesn't know where the citizen be. Be he under the wall? Be he six block over and still runnin'? We doesn't know. So's everybody be lookin' 'cept me. An' I'd be lookin' too 'cept I gotta stan' here an talks to youse! So's; why'd youse calls anyways?

Gee could almost feel the frustration of the man on the other end of the line. "I'm calling because there was a big crash sound coming from your direction and I want to know what it was and why."

"Why doos you want's t' know; you day to 'vestigate soun's? Lookit;' right nows we gots a missin' citizen. We doesn't knows where 'im is. Doesn't know he be under the wall or did 'im get traction under 'is foots and is now blocks away an' still runnin'. An' I still not sure 'zactly why you is callin' enneyways."

"Is there anyone else I can talk to?" the man demanded.

"Yep; hol' on a mo' and I'll puts her on." He put the palm of his hand over the receiver and turned to Maria. "Talks to 'im, but doesn't say anything but "hello." "Y'understands? Listens to 'im and whatevers he say, say 'hello' back." She nodded her head, blue eyes dancing in glee and reached for the phone. She placed it up against her ear and listened.

"Hello."

"Yes; this is Lendl Holmes. Can you tell me what is going on here?" he demanded

"Hello," she said again in her little-girl voice.

Chapter 5

"**G**et off the phone," Lendl Holmes bellowed. A moment later a deeper, more authoritive voice roared; "No! You get off the phone, Lendl! This is Captain Taylor and I've told you more than once about sticking your nose into things that are none of your concern." There was a muted 'click' and then relative silence ensued.

"Now then," Captain Taylor continued in a more reasonable tone, "can someone tell me what is going on? Gee, if you're listening to this and know what is happening; and I presume you are both; would you be kind enough to bring me up to speed?"

Gee was not one to do things by halves. He started with the trip to the diner and the minor flap between himself and Mr. Coldbrick. He made no mention of the salt incident. For the first; it had little to do with what followed, and for the second, he had no idea how many other people had radios that could listen in on this conversation and from what Officer Taylor had told him, it would be a form of suicide to let that bit of information out. He expounded on Mr. Coldbrick's part of the incident without saying exactly why he had become so obsessed in the first place. As it turned out, it didn't matter, the man was so erratic in his greed that the exact cause was incidental to the fact. In the end; Captain Taylor understood almost as well as if he had been present and had seen the entire fiasco himself. "You do give good reports, Gee, I'll not deny you that;" the Captain admitted.

For the present, things were settled down about as good as they ever got. The two men hung their heads and admitted that they had no place to go. They had lived with Coldbrick, almost as much as slaves as employees, for he kept them months behind in their pay and had they left; they would have had to leave as penniless paupers. What was worse; Coldbrick's home had one of the most advanced security systems that could be bought and only he, Mr. Coldbrick, had the needed keys to get inside. When Gee heard this bit of news he nodded and admitted that it didn't surprise him at all.

"Considerin' his ways, it figures," he admitted. "That kinda be the reason I hads that little tussle with him just afore he went ahind that wall. I expects what you'll be needin' to get inside is these;" and he reached inside his pouch. Maria had been watching and listening to Gee, almost from the very moment she had first laid eyes on him, and she had been paying attention when he was wrestling with Mr. Coldbrick. She had clearly seen him stick something into that pouch of his directly after the last encounter. Maria wasn't the least surprised when he held a large ring of keys with his right hand and a leather wallet with his left. The two men stared at the items and gaped.

"How . . . when . . . the pair stuttered.

"When he was wrestling with Mr. Coldbrick;" Maria said confidently. "I saw him do it."

"You was watchin?'" he demanded. "I'm gunna has to keeps my eyes on you, little missy, you jus' too smarts f' you own good." Then he smiled at her. She, in turn, beamed back at him. She liked him almost from the very moment she laid eyes on him; and just about every single thing she had seen and heard him do since only solidified her interest in him. He was exactly her kind of boy . . . and she knew it!

Once a major storm moves in, the police move out, of a given area. The general theory was simple. For the most part, people don't like to go outside when the weather is bad, they prefer to stay inside where it's at least relatively warm and dry. And the impending storm threatened to be a bad one. The group, as a whole, moved to the Coldbrick residence. The two men were well versed in getting in. While the man wouldn't trust anyone with his keys and other things; he considered it below his station in life to actually unlock his doors. That's what servants were for.

Gee looked around in awe. The home was huge by his standards, not only big, but filled with the very best of everything; furniture, drapes, rugs, and even art work in the way of statuary and various paintings; some of which were worth a fortune in and of themselves. The two men led Gee and the rest around the mansion; showing them what there was to look at. They ended up in the Master bedroom, where all of Mr. Goldbrick's personal effects were, including a massive floor safe that almost looked like it would be more at home in a bank than a personal dwelling. Gee walked up to the safe and stared.

He reached out and touched the knob in the middle of the door. He spun the dial clockwise three full turns to reset all of which he now knew to be tumblers. Then slowly but surely he turned the knob to his left; turning carefully just so far. He stopped, turned it to his right, and repeated it. He did this four times and once he quit, he reached out, grasped the door lever and pulled it down and the safe opened wide. There was a king's ransom in there in the way of gold and silver; money in paper form as well as metal; more paper and documents than he could imagine; and a number of guns and some ammo. He spotted one in particular. It looked very much like the one Chief Taylor had showed him. He reached in and pulled it out. He opened the cylinder like a pro and looked inside; it was empty. He turned to the two officers and showed the gun to them. "What does you thinks of this?" he asked politely.

It was a man's gun; much too massive for female interests, but even she admitted she'd never seen one more beautiful. He picked up one of the ammo boxes that lie just below where the wheel gun had been; he stared at the end of the box. Slowly, because he couldn't read very fast, he read the letters: 38 Spec. 125 gn +P. He turned to the two men who watched his every move.

"I gots no use for such," he admitted; "an' I doesn't want any pay f' heppin you boys. You needs more; you knows where to finds me. But I wants these f' Captain Taylor; he tells me that this ammo is very hard f' hims to get ennywheres. It be Mr. Coldbrick's contribution to the police. Be this well with you's?

The pair immediately nodded their heads. "But what about you; Gee; what are you going to take for yourself?"

He smiled and slipped an arm around Maria's shoulders and gave her a very gentle hug. "I has already taken the bestes prize f'myselfs." he announced with a broad smile.

Under normal circumstances the four would have had to make their own way back to the police station, but Patrolman Trent thought that under the circumstances, the police could provide him transportation; which was his next intended stop. Once Patrolman Trent explained the circumstances to his Chief; the ride was not only guaranteed; it was personally chauffeured by the Chief. By the time they all got to the station the Captain was all but drooling.

"My people tell me you cracked that safe your very first try;" the Captain chortled. That's astounding. My hope is that you can open this other one for us equally easy. I've no idea what is inside; if anything. But it's been a thorn in my side ever since I was saddled with it, and if you can pop it open as easily as you did the other, it will be a load off my back. And that doesn't even begin to express how delighted I am with the revolver and ammo. It's the exact ammo I've been looking for the past few years; it's even my favorite brand. I can't begin to say how pleased I am."

Gee smiled and nodded; his mind was already on his next project. And not so oddly; his mind was increasingly on getting himself and

Maria back to his own place. The storm that had been threatening for days was in the process of arriving; once it did, it looked to be a bad one; one that would be many days in leaving.

They were now in the chief's office; the safe was off to one side. It was a very large one; something that would take at least three or four men to pick up and bring in. And even then; they would need a dolly of some sort. He turned his head to look at it, and in the same instant, a buzzing took place in his forehead and he staggered.

"Gee; what's the matter; what's wrong?" Captain Taylor demanded when he saw Gee react.

"That safe; it gots, gots, gots, I doesn't knows the words!" Patrolman Trent immediately grabbed Gee by the arm with one hand, his superior with other and dragged both of them from the room. At the astonished look on his Commander's face, he said: "The last man he said those words to; 'I doesn't knows the words,' is now MIA and presumed dead. As in, squashed flat, like a bug under a truck tire." The Chief wanted to sit down in his chair, but at the moment his chair was in the same room with the safe, and he didn't know what to do.

Gee got himself under control before the adults did. "I doesn't think it be danger as it be. I thinks the danger only be in openings it; or maybe not openings it, but removing anythings from it. That make more sense; did someone want to set suthin' like this up, they's wouldn't wants to hurts theyselves."

"What kind of danger; do you know that?" Patrolman Trent asked.

"Not real sure. I sees a pop; a real big, bad pop."

"An explosion?" the Patrolman demanded.

"Not sure; I not heared that word afore; what be 'splosion?"

"A very big, very loud and powerful 'pop,'" Patrolman Trent assured him.

Gee thought a moment and nodded his head; "that be it then; 'splosion."

"Best get a demolition team up here; Stat!" Patrolman Trent said. His chief looked him in the eyes and immediately nodded. He started to take a step, stopped and turned to Gee. "Is it ok if I go into my office and make a call?" he asked.

Gee nodded. "Yep;" he said. "I now thinks it more sane to b'leve it only danger when suthin' be took out. Other way-wise, why would ennyone's put such in there's in the firstest place?"

The buzzing in his head had died out to a faint, almost harmonic hum; one that wasn't remotely threatening. He walked confidently up to the safe, crouched down and spun the knob clockwise three times. He stopped, stared at the knob and as he had recently done with the Coldbrick's safe, he did with this one and almost before the viewers were prepared; he moved the lever down and opened the safe. There was no explosion; not as much as a pop. Everyone moved around to the front, keeping a safe distance, and looked in.

There was a tray of sorts across most of the top; the rest seemed to be a great number of documents; something that might have been in a business man's or attorney's safe. There didn't seem to be any money or anything else intrinsically of value; it seemed to be in all ways a very safe . . . safe. Sometimes; appearances can be deceiving.

Gee squatted down on his heels a discrete distance and began staring into the safe. First was the tray, which seemed to be made of an expanded metal, one with more holes than metal, and it held a number of papers; underneath were file holders, thin wire forms made specifically for holding documents and other such things. Hanging from a hook dangling down from the tray, was an almost transparent, thin thread that ran towards the back. And somehow; in the foreground was the face of an animal, perhaps a very big, black dog and the animal had its teeth bared; It did not remotely look like anything anyone would want to reach in and pet. He stared for a few more moments but didn't see anything else that seemed out of place. He rose up easily and moved back a few steps.

"Does not try and reaches in there;" he said needlessly. One could not have hired anyone in the room to try and do so.

Gee looked around the room, trying to see if anything might catch his eye that might help. Off to his right; a fairly large mirror hung from the wall. It, reasonably, was used so that one could stand before it and make sure that their tie was straight and hair combed and so forth. He got up from where he was squatting and went over to the mirror. It was not directly attached to the wall but merely hung from the head of a nail that stuck out from the wall by perhaps a quarter of an inch. He grasped the mirror and lifted it off the wall and carried it over to the safe. He set it on the floor perhaps four feet out. He turned and looked about. "Wills someone brings that chair over here; please," he asked politely. Someone immediately did so.

He placed the mirror on the floor just in front of the chair and leaned it backwards against the chair, but the chair had very little weight and the floor was smooth and fairly polished and it wouldn't stay put, but slowly slipped away from the mirror. He looked about. Off in one corner someone's jacket was tossed carelessly across yet a different chair. "Brings me that coat;" he asked. It was; promptly. With mirror and chair both setting on the coat; the slippage ceased. He gave it his best shot and then walked around behind the safe and stared.

"Moves the mirror bottom a squinch closer to th' chair," he asked politely; it was quickly done. "Makes that a squinch and a half," he added. This too was done. He stood, looked into the mirror and saw the inside of the safe very clearly. He moved first right and then left, then raised his head up and then down. The view inside the safe also shifted. It was about as good as he was going to get it. Before he could do anything else, there was a knock on the door and three men entered the room; all were wearing blast suits and each had a heavy helmet with ear protectors attached. The leader of the group stopped and stared at what Gee had done.

"Now that's just plain sweet!" the leader exclaimed. I've checked maybe a half-dozen things like this and I never once thought of the obvious. My hat's off to you; sir," he said with a slight bow. Gee looked at the man and nodded.

"So; what's the score so far; are we tied, ahead, or so far behind we'll never catch up?" Gee grinned up at the man. He only understood perhaps half of what the man said, but what he did understand, amused him.

"Maybe-so a bit of each;" he admitted. "Comes here and says what you thinks." He led the man over behind the safe and then began to describe what he saw and thought. But the hook was very small and the thread mostly transparent and he couldn't see what Gee described. The man pulled a small cylinder out of his breast pocket and showed it to Gee.

"This is called a laser-pointer;" he began; "just point it at where you want me to look and maybe then I'll see it. Do take care and not look directly into it and don't point it into anyone's eyes as it can easily cause retinal damage." Gee had no idea what a retinal was, but he believed almost anything that people told him, and if the man didn't want him to do something; then he wouldn't. He pointed the devise at the mirror and held the button down as he'd been instructed. In a remarkably short period of time he'd not only shown the man the small hook; but also the line that appeared tied to it. "Good job, m'man, well done indeed. Do you ever want to go looking for a job; look no further; I'll put you on my crew any day of the week."

"It looks t'me," Gee began, "all's a man'd has t'do, is reach down and unhooks the hook f'm the tray. Logic; th' man what done this woon't want's to blows hisself up; jus' somebodies he was mad at." The squad leader nodded his head. "Then what's we needs t'do is lifts the hook up 'n' the tray'd slide out nice and easy. "Er 'so it says in the fine print'; as my Da useta say."

"Smart man; your Dad; and that's a direct quote; I used to know him; even took some of his classes. It's a sad thing; how and why he died. And damned heroic how you managed to repay the ass-wipes who murdered him. My hat's off to you; sir; or would be if I was actually wearing one. Let's see if we can't just snip that little thread there. According to all I understand of such, that should eliminate the problem, provided we don't manage to pull that thread."

It took a surprisingly short time to do exactly that, and in the end, they had the safe completely empty of all the paper folders and the only thing left in was an Improvised Explosive Devise of unknown origin and power. They got the devise out of the safe and into a blast-proof holding case and two men carried the case between them on a pole. They took it off to an area reserved for just this purpose. Once everything was set up properly; Gee, behind a cement bunker, gave a cord a quick hard pull and the devise went off with a thunderous blast; anyone caught in such would have been instantly killed.

With that out of the way; Gee's mind turned towards home. The people were all busy; trying to get things done before quitting time. He gave Captain Trent and other goodbye hugs, and waving off offerings of a ride, he took Maria by the arm and both headed east. The storm was almost upon them; threatening rain at almost any instant. Maria didn't like thunderstorm in the first place; to be out in one, getting wet, was not remotely on her 'to do' list, and she started telling him so.

"I understands," he admitted. "I doesn't like getting rained on much neither; but we's gunna be home almosts before you can believe. Just this next turn and we'll be insides; safe and dry." She wanted to argue. She had come in this way and there wasn't anything on the other side of the corner except a very large parking lot. Before she could vent her thoughts they turned the corner . . . and in the next instant they were indoors, inside an apartment, and a grey hairball hissed at them and promptly swapping nose for tail; vanished around the corner and out the door. She stopped and stared about frantically; missing the little animal's theatrics.

"Girl; they's a great many things abouts me that you doesn't know; things I'm not sure I can explains in words. But maybe-so I can at least shows you some of them. F'instant. We just jumped some blocks away faster 'n you can blinks you eyes. Don't knows I can 'splain; but I'll try. But firsts; I gotta goes to the toilet; my bladder is about to pops."

"Me too;" she wailed. He led her in the right direction. Being the gentleman that he was; he let her go first. That was almost a mistake. Either she didn't have to go as badly as she said; or spent too much time exploring the room. Finally he yelled at her; she scooted out and he scooted in . . . none too soon.

By now; the storm had decided to arrive. It announced its presence with a clap of thunder that rattled the windows and made her jump. Just out of the corner of his right eye he saw three little furry critters coming on the run; in the next instant they shot through the slightly open door and squirted behind the couch where they felt a greater measure of safety. A moment later another bolt of lightning lit up the sky; shortly followed by another loud rumble.

Looks like we gots home jus' in time; he said cheerfully. "Tells me; d'you like surprises?" From her reaction; she did. "And what if the surprises are 'bouts little furry aminals that scampers 'round?"

"What kind of am . . . animals?" she demanded. He beckoned her over; then carefully turned her around and pointed at the near end of the couch. There, next to the wall, was perhaps a third of a kitten poking its head out; trying to see exactly what was going on, and more importantly, if it was safe to come out and go to her food dish because at the moment it was empty and she was very hungry. Maria squealed and tried her best to scoot forward but Gee kept his arm around her and held her back.

"Stops!" he commanded her. "Stops and listens to what I gots t'say. They's three little kittens, and I dunt knows they's lost they mittens, but they's new here and nowise tame. You can't remotely goes and picks 'em up or touches 'em; cos' they's still mostly wild. I's only been here f' a few days and they showed up the very firsest day. They will comes to me but only if I'm bein' still. An' then; they comes to me on they terms and not mine. They is very small and has they a mother I's never seen her. I 'spects they's really hungry. I've been gone 'most o' the day an' I can't recall did I feeds 'em afore I left. As you prolly already knows; I left fast 'coz I had an itch inside to go and do; an' that itch was 'cause of you.

"Now you knows; lets works together and sees if we can first feed 'em, and secondly, sees if they'll come to us. They mights not. I actual doesn't know, but thus fars, does I be very slow and stops often; better yet, sits down with some cat's food, then they feels safer and maybe-so they comes. You unnerstan'? Y'gots to doos it slow and easy or they'll cut and run."

Maria nodded her head. From the expression on her face and her body language, she was all for dashing off and capturing the little creature in a rush, and he knew that would not work out to either's advantage; hers or the kitten's.

He took her by her upper arm and led her over to a wall, more of a neutral zone, and with his gentle urging; both sat down. He reached out with his left hand and a moment later he was holding a cat-food box in his left hand. "How do you do that?" she demanded of him.

"I honest doesn't know;" he replied, "but what's most important nows; askin' questions or learnin' 'bout kittens?" She was human and curious about everything in her world, but at the moment, nothing was more important than kitties. She nodded her head and applied herself to the task. She was, by nature and inclination, impulsive; partially from being young and mostly from being female. But she could at times understand that she needed to control her impulses; that she could satisfy the need to learn and still be a part of everything. She focused, nodded her head, and applied herself to listening.

He opened the box and poured out a generous palm full of kitty kibbles. At the sound of the kibbles rattling around in the box, a second kitten came scooting out from wherever it was, closely followed by yet a third. Maria nearly had a coronary at the sight of three little animals zipping about, but remembering Gee's words, she controlled herself . . . only barely. He handed her a generous amount and then serving an example; began gently tossing individual kibbles in the general direction of one small animal or the other. Maria watched him for a moment; then she also began to toss the small bits of kitty food towards whichever seemed ready next. They, in turn, became predators and began stalking and pouncing on their prey; only to gobble it down and moving on to the next.

Feeding the young and hungry is a facet that comes easily to females; as it is part of their very existence. Maria applied herself to her self-appointed task and slowly she began to understand that if she threw the little bites of food ever closer to her; the small animals would gradually come nearer. Not remotely close enough to touch or catch. But watching Gee, she came to understand that some things in life have to be taken in slow steps, and not running full tilt at it. In time, the little animals became full and in so doing, gradually stopped coming so close to the humans.

Gee, understanding Maria very well, told her to stay where she was and carefully got up and went and got their water dish and carried it over to the sink and filled it with water. The three kittens moved to a neutral corner and watched out of yellow eyes to make sure that what was happening was what they wanted and needed. He carefully put the bowl down at the proper place and moved off. At first hesitantly and then with more trust, the three came out and sticking their faces into the water, began to lap thirstily. He moved over and extending a hand, helped Maria to her feet. "I bees no expert on such, but so fars, I's found the best way of gettin' along with the critters is t' kinda ignors 'em. They's moves about, watching to see if I'm watchin' them. Apparently in the cat worl'; being continually watch is not a good thin'."

"Now we gots that took care of . . . how 'bout you; is you's hungry? It turned out that she was for she immediately forgot about feeding kittens and wanted to feed herself. "Well; I got's some really good news. While first snoopin' 'round here t'other day, I finded somethings I never et afore nor even smelt, and it's the bestest tastin' thing I ever put into my mouths. Does you want; we'll go over and makes some now." This; she was more than interested in.

He led her over to the kitchen and opened the 'fridge and pulled out the remains of the can of Spam, along with the cheese. He dug more crackers off the shelf and made up some of the small sandwiches and gave her one. She took one bite and promptly went ballistic. "Oh; this is the yummiest thing I've ever eaten . . . but we need to microwave it so it's hot and the cheese is melted."

"K" he said. "Zactly what be a . . . whatever you said?"

"Behind you; right there on the shelf. Don't you know what a microwave oven is?"

"Nope! My Momma was a country girl; she consider a 'lectric stove almost sinful; she were raised on wood stoves and if suthin' weren't cooked on a wood stove . . . it weren't cooked; not 'cording to her it weren't."

Between them, they made another dozen of the little sandwiches before they ran out of the meat they were using. Maria laid them out on a ceramic plate she found and tucked them into the oven. Gee watched with skeptical eyes. The appropriate number of seconds ticked by and she pulled them out of the oven. To Gee's surprise, not only was the meat in the small sandwiches hot; the cheese was mostly melted. With the small sprinkle of salt he had put on them before sticking them into the oven, they were the tastiest thing he'd ever put into his mouth. Not only that; the smells that drifted throughout the room brought every kitten in the place out of hiding and three little noses were lifted up into the air, sniffing as if their lives depended on it. Gee shoved the last morsel into his mouth; leaving nothing for the kittens.

"That's mean;" Maria said with a giggle.

"Nope! I just 'membered; zactly where I gots the kitty kibbles from, there be a case or three of little cans that have pi-turs of cats on 'em. I bets almost anythin' they is cans o' cat food. And 'cause they's pictures of fish on 'em alsos-too, think they must be made up of fish guts and other parts. Yuck to human mind, but to little aminals like these an' I bets they goes down jus' fine. Jus' a mo' and I'll gets some; you waits; them kittens gunna lose they mind." He reached out and seemingly plucked a small can of something out of the air that did have tiny little fish shown in the paper around the can. He popped the lid and pulled it off. A few moments later and even the humans in the room could smell fish. What it did to the kitten's minds is best left to the imagination; they went berserk.

All three were mewing their little brains out; their paws carrying them around in mindless circles while their mouths were crying piteously. He picked up the plate that had recently held small sandwiches and dumped the contents onto the small plate. He carried it over to where their regular food bowls were, all but tripping over three frantic little animals that no longer had any thoughts in their tiny heads but what was on that plate. He beckoned to Maria and she closely followed. He set the plate down and in the next instant, three furry little faces were down in the plate, each trying to eat it all up and at the same time force the others to go away. He waved Maria over closer; soundlessly motioning that she would be very quiet. She knelt down beside him. He took her small hand by the wrist; and ever so carefully drew the palm of her hand down the back of the nearest kitten. This; the animal did not like. But it wasn't about to abandon anything that smelled so yummy. It tried to move. On her own; Maria found a second animal and gently petted it as well. Given the choice between eating the best-smelling food they ever found and being touched; or running away in fear; once again the stomach decided which was wiser and by the time the little animals had licked the plate clean, each and every one had received several pettings from each human, and had independently decided that being touched wasn't all that bad after all.

Gee put his hand on Maria's shoulder and pulled her gently over to the sofa, where they both sat down; he looked her in the eyes. "Now then, pretty little girl, why doesn't you tells me why youse dun't mind being touched on the shoulder, the sides or even front, but the moment I touches you back, you pulls away?" She shook her head and tried to back off but his arm was around her and he easily pulled her next to him. They were mostly facing each other. He reached up with both hands, put his fingers to the back of her head and in a moment had divided her hair into two halves and pulled the two over her shoulders to lie on her chest. Maria began to weep. Not little; polite whimpers but in deep, encompassing, soul-searing sobs. She hung her head and would not look at him.

He took her by her shoulders and turned her gently around. He was reasonably sure of what he would see; what he was no way prepared for was the number of dark streaks across her back, nor the sign of still-fresh blood.

"Arright" he said as he stared at her back. "We comes back to this later; rights now; we gunna takes care of you back. The peoples who actual own this place left mebby some eight year ago. As I recalls; the attack comed on a Christmas night, somewhere 'bout 10 in the evening, when most folks was in bed. Thing was, bein' Christmas, a great many folks was outta town and in other places; havin' Christmas with they folks; that sorta thing. So fars; I've only looked inta two of the 'partments here, but in both cases, they was no ones home when the missile struck, destroyin' everything. Did anyone's come back from where they was, and a great many din't cause other cities were 'tacked at the same time, they woun't be able to gets back in. The onlyest ways I knows is hows I gets in and out, and I dun't knows how I does it; I just does. Bottom-linin' it; whilst lookin' 'bout in here, I finded a bunch of first aid things, and first aid is suthin' m' pa taught me. And they's a big box of such right here in this closet right here.

He got up and taking her by the hand, led her over to the closet and opened the door. In part; Maria was afraid of what was about to happen; in another, she was young, female, and very curious about everything about her. In the end, curiosity won out and she willingly went over to the closet, watched as he took down the plastic box with the big red plus sign on it and with very few false starts he selected the exact things he wanted. He led her into the bathroom and completely removed her blouse; draping her hair over her front.

Her back was a mess. "I be sorry, Maria, I truly be; I wisht it were me being treated 'stead of you. Here; there's a tongue depressor; it s'posed to hol' the tongue down when a Doctor or Nurse look down you throat. Turns it sideways and bites down on it. Don' know how much this gunna hurt; but thisaway you won't be biting you own mouth by mistake. Understands?" She swallowed; then nodded her head. She took the depressor and placed it crosswise in her mouth and bit down.

Gee had a small bottle of hydrogen peroxide; something he knew of and understood from the things his father had told him and showed him. It wasn't pretty, but it wasn't nearly as bad as he feared. Either it didn't hurt nearly as much as he thought; or she was a very brave little girl. In time, her back was properly cleansed, and all of the crusties that had formed around the cuts in her back were gently wiped away. Next; he took a green metal cube out of the first aid box. This was something else he was aware of. The metal box was still sealed with the plastic that ran all around the lid. He got something sharp out of the box, cut the plastic and removed the lid; a very pleasant scent arose within the room. "Here's. Hol' this; smells it if you wish. M'pa said that it has eucalyptus in't and that's why it works so well. Holds it and smells it as you wants; it might help you forget what's happening ahind you."

She held the metal box and did smell it regularly; he was right, it did have a very nice aroma to it. He worked as quickly and gently as he could and in time he was done. He put the lid back on the box and set in on the shelf next to the sink. She turned and looked up at him, a smile on her face. "You do good work, Gee," she told him; "you hardly hurt me at all. And now, my back feels so very much better. Thank you." She leaned over and gave him a small kiss on his lips. He smiled.

"An since you'se been such a good patient, I has a surprise for you. The folk who once lived here seemed to have a daughter; maybe-so a girl about your size and age. The other day whilst lookin' through the rooms, I finded somthin' I thinks you'll be interest in. Waits right here an' I'll be direct back."

He turned and left and she picked up the green box and started reading. There was a list of ingredients on the can, but as she read, she found nothing that mentioned eucalyptus. Before she could form an opinion Gee returned with two objects in his hands; one fairly large and bulky and the other quite small. He handed the smallest to her first. "Here; this be a t-shirt; kinda like boys usual wear. I thinks it be soft on you back and will help keeps this cleaner. And he exposed the other thing he held.

Maria froze. Her eyes darted over the object in his hand. Stared, swept it again and stared once more. "What is it?" she asked; wide-eyed.

"I thinks it be a bunny suit;" he admitted. Somthin' a little girl would like to wear to bed when she sleeps at night. I finded it under her pilla when I wuz lookin' through there t'other day." He unfolded it before her; that was exactly what it was; including a fuzzy little tail on the backside and a hood that could be pulled over her head; complete with long, floppy ears. She took one look at it and burst into tears; not little tears that trickle down a child's face unheeded but a full-lung wail of grief and despair. He dropped the cloth to the floor and immediately pulled her into his arms and hugged her. Very gently; considering the mess her back was in.

Chapter 6

ow what?" he thought to himself. His little sister could be moody at times but Maria seemed able to take it to new levels he'd never encountered before. "What's the matter; why are you crying;" he asked of her: he was most confused.

"Why are you so nice to me?" she wailed and collapsed into heart-broken sobs.

He took her in his arms, and careful not to touch her upper-mid back, pulled her close and cuddled her. "I believes we s'pose to be nice to each other. M'Da usta reads to me outta the Bible. He told me 'bout the Fall an' how the Devil usta be a good angel and now him's bad. We humans 'spose to be good one to another; some of us is; 'tothers ain't so much. You problem is that too much of the time yous been 'round the bad kinda folk; the kind that ain't nice; and since you mostly been roun' th' bad kinda peoples, you gets confuse when you be treated as you should be treated all along. It be differn't, an' the different confuses youse. Just trusts me, and after some times has past, you'll sees the difference and unnerstans better. Honest!" She nodded her head, and deciding to try it his way, cuddled closer to him.

They stayed this way for some long minutes, and once she calmed down and had recovered at least most of her poise, he reached out and gently stroked her face. "Now thens;" he said softly, "lets start at the beginnin'. What happens they beats you so; do they doos this alla time er wuz it just this onct?"

She curled up into a miserable little ball and said nothing; then, slowly, she began to unwind, backed up a bit and looked him in the eyes. "It was later in the evening. They were cuddling, kissing, and that sort of thing. He couldn't get it up."

"Get whut up?" Gee asked; perplexed.

"I'm not sure," she admitted. "She, the woman, made me put on some things; there wasn't much to them. Then I had to dance around, kind of wiggle myself around, and then bit by bit I had to toss my clothes off and then writhe around like a snake or something. And they were drinking something and getting rowdy and then she got mad, jumped up and grabbed me and beat me with a belt because I wasn't doing it right. And I tried; I did the best I could because she's done it to me before; me and others before me, and I just couldn't do it right and they both were drunk and then she beat me. She beat me bad; wouldn't quit, then sent me to my room and wouldn't feed me or anything."

Inside; Gee was boiling. He only understood part of what she was saying, parts of it made no sense to him at all, but the part where the woman was beating Maria came in clear as a bell. A seething rage came over him and for a few frantic seconds he only wanted to get his hands on this woman, someone he'd never knowingly seen, and kill her; exactly like he'd killed the four cannibals. His mind could see no other fate than the dead body of the woman lying on the ground before him. He carefully pushed the raging monster inside him back down, assuring the beast that in time, they would take care of that particular person.

"I thinks I understands. I wants t' kill this woman buts I b'leve we gots to leaves it to the p'lice; that's what they's there for in the firstest place; to enforce the law. Jus' soons as this storms pass and we kin gets out, we's gunna go the p'lice station and tells Capt. Taylor; even shows you back to 'im so's 'im kin understands. That's the proper way o' doin' it."

He got her tears dried, and then with only the least amount of adjustment, got the little bunny suit on Maria; she was the cutest little bunny the world has ever seen.

The storm that had raged inside Gee also raged outside and it was a toss of a coin as to which was more violent. True; lightning flashed and thunder crashed and rain like coming out of a bucket fell on the city but the two were snug and comfortable in their apartment. He made sure he treated Maria's back at least twice a day with Bag Balm and the improvements were noticeable. In time, all such must pass, and by the time three days had passed into oblivion; the storm was only a fading memory. On the first clear day, the two of them got their things together and stepped out. One of the first things Gee did, once he'd gotten the monster inside at least partially placated, was to go to his supply of salt (and there was a surprising amount of it) and picked out the biggest container and stuffed it inside the backpack; which still actually belonged to Mr. Forrester. The two stepped out onto the area just outside his sliding door and in the next eye blink they were standing in his favorite spot.

The walked, hand in hand, heading first towards Forrester's Groceries; they walked through the door and spotted both Mr. Forrester as well as William; both were helping customers. Gee and Maria moved off towards where the fruit was and started looking at the apples, because as it turned out, Maria loved apples. She didn't just like them, neither did she obsess over them, as Mr. Forrester's wife did over chocolate; but she was into apples. In his left hand he held the back pack he'd borrowed from the grocer; now nearly seven days past. Maria was looking the apples over. She would pick one up; smell it, gently run her hands over it, and smell it again. And then select another. Gee wasn't sure if she was particularly picky or just enjoyed the texture and scent. Mr. Forrester finished with his client and with a broad smile he walked up to the pair.

"It's been several days since we've seen you; Gee; what have you been doing besides ducking raindrops?"

"Mostly stayin' inside and stayin' dry;" he admitted. He handed the backpack to the grocer. "Here's the backpack you lended me t'other day; thanks; it comed in handy." As he handed the backpack to the grocer he leaned over and spoke very softly. "Be sures you doesn't look inter it 'til you gets inter you back room; they's suthin' in there's you's gunna be right happy to sees; jus' makes sure nobody sees you with it. And that goes for William; toos. The less folks knows about this; the safer I'll be. An' I needn't tells ya t'keeps you mouth shuts 'bout it." Mr. Forrester groped the packsack, felt the size and weight of what was in it and his face all but turned white.

"Is this what I think it is?" he asked hoarsely.

"No questions;" he whispered back; "'Loose lips sink ships' an' all that stuff." Mr. Forrester took the pack and without further talk or even looking around he hustled himself into his back room. He was there fairly long and when he finally did come out he looked like he might be in shock.

"That sack has five pounds in it, Gee, where in thunder did you get it?"

"No questions; no lies," he returned softly. Then in a louder voice, said, "Me 'n' baby gots to go sees the p'lice Captin'. Hasn't seen him in three days; been wonderin' how he's doin." He nodded to Mr. Forrester and William, who had just then finished with the customer he was helping, then turned and slipping his arm around Maria's shoulders he headed out.

The two walked. When it felt right for him and he was sure no one was watching, he jumped, and in the next instant he was perhaps a hundred feet from the police building. People were coming and going but none were looking in their direction; the two of them walked in as if they belonged there.

They hadn't gotten more than a very few steps when someone spotted them. "Hey!" the person yelled; "They're here! Gee and Maria just walked in." In a blink it seemed that half of the precinct turned and came towards them; everyone seemed overjoyed seeing them. A moment later, Captain Taylor, hearing all the noise; came out of his office to see what was happening. He took one look at the two and with a huge smile on his face; came towards them.

"Son; when you decide to make a flap; you make a flap;" he announced. I've been getting calls from her parents ever since you two disappeared and the storm hit. I wouldn't be surprised but what it's ringing right now. Come on inside; come on in and tell me what news you have for me."

"We gots news for youse; an' it ain't good. It 'specially aint' good for them's; and it be best if they dusn't know just how bad the news is 'til they gets here. You ain't gunna likes this; I knows for a fact coz' I dusn't like it one little bit. P'haps we best goes inter you office f' this; us, and at least one female-type officer: this ain't purdy and I isn't gunna sugar coat it." The Captain stared at Gee and the welcoming grin on his face slid away. He nodded and led the group in; beckoning one of the female officers to follow. His usual two were not in the office at the time, and were presumably either out on patrol, or perhaps this was their day off. The Captain closed the door behind them.

OK; Gee, what's this all about? You aren't one to make statements like that unless you mean them."

"Arrites; please stands in a group just there and faces us. Now, love, turns 'round to me and puts you arms 'round me. But first; lets me part you hair. That's the girl. Now gives me a hug." She put her arms around his chest and buried her face between his chest and neck and just stopped moving. Moving as carefully and gently as he could, he pulled her blouse up and over her head until her entire back was exposed to the group; the female officer took one look and screamed.

"Oh . . . my . . . God!" Captain Taylor said with a moan. "Gee, tell me, what happened!"

Gee looked the Captain in the eyes and without further theatrics, gave the group both barrels, telling them everything he knew. "Maria sed the woman gots mad 'cos the man couldn't 'get it up;' whatever that mean. The woman made Maria puts on somethin' then dances, wiggling herselfs 'round and takin' clothes off til she had nothin' on and the man still couldn't 'get it up' whatever that is, and the woman goes and gets a belt and whups her bad and puts her in her room and wouldn't feed her. Maria also says they was drinkin' and that she wasn't the first girl this happens to. And mebby worser of all . . . as I walks up, the man who was sellin' her had a roll of money in him hand and was tellin' the other man; the one I kills firstest, that it better all be there and that the last had 'funny money' in't; and Maria tol' me t'other night that she wasn't the first. I not sure what she means about that 'cos I din't ast her; I was to busy tryin' t'get her patched up an' not hurtin' so much."

Captain Taylor looked Maria in the eyes; his own eyes gentle and concerned. "Honey; can you explain that; what did you mean that you weren't the first?"

"When I was first moved into that room and I was trying to get used to it; I found a blouse stuffed up under the bed. When I pulled it out; the back side had dark streaks on it. I didn't know what it was but I didn't actually like the streaks or the blouse so I just stuck it back where I found it. Then later, I found some writing, something written by a girl named Ann Willits. And there was another piece of paper with writing on it by a girl named Robin. If she had a last name she didn't write it down. I put both of them back where I found them because I didn't want to be there in the first place; the woman gives me the 'willies' when she looks at me."

"Thank you, Maria; thank you, Gee; there have been some questions about those two in the past, but they've always seemed upfront about things, nothing to get too worked up about and we always put it off to neighbors just trying to cause trouble. These people are fairly wealthy and that often makes the poorer neighbors jealous. And that can lead to false accusations."

The phone rang. Captain Taylor picked it up, answered and then listened for a moment. Next he put his hand over the receiver and mouthed to Gee: "It's them! They're demanding the return of their daughter . . . (he listened carefully to the phone) and from the sounds of it, they want your head on a platter. And they're demanding we bring her back to them!"

Gee pantomimed covering the receiver with his hand; the Captain continued to do so. "You bees a police department; not a delivery service;" he said. "Tells 'em iffn they doesn't get down and picks the girl ups, by law you gotta take her to a health center where they gives her a total physical; an' then she's put up f' 'doption."

"Oh; that'll put the old girl's undies in a bunch!" he exclaimed. In the next moment, he repeated Gee's words, verbatim. He listened to the other end, then injected, "It's the law; madam; we enforce the laws; we don't write them. If you don't want the girl back; then tell us so. She will go to a health clinic; they will give her a full physical; from head to toe, from front to back, and from the skin in. If she is healthy enough; she will be put up for adoption. If she has health issues of any kind; she will be put in a clinic until she is healthy enough for adoption. There are no other ways." He listened carefully. "Very well, then; we'll see you within a half hour. Otherwise; she must go to a health clinic; it's the law. And we enforce the laws; we don't just make up things for our amusement." He listened for a few more moments. "Very well then; I'll give you a half hour to get here; and a good day to you." And he hung up.

The Captain gave Gee a long stare and a bigger grin. "I just wish you could have heard that old crow; I thought she was going to have a coronary when I said Maria would go to the health clinic for a physical. As if she would dare risk something like that."

Gee nodded his head, and then bowed it in thought; he held it for a moment and then looked back up. "Gotta question t'ast ya; Capt'n. Do's the Judge knows about this? D'ya thinks he otta be call and fill in on the detail?"

Captain Taylor gave Gee a single, long look, and all but erupted. "My God, Gee, you've done it again! And, no, he doesn't know about this. And yes, he's gonna find out about it, just as soon as I get him on the phone."

It didn't take long. The police center and the city courtroom were all in the same great building. By a twist of fate, or perhaps the Hand of God, the buildings were entirely spared by the bombing; not even any of the parking lots had been hit; though many surrounding buildings had been hit with many being demolished. Chief Taylor got the Judge on the third ring. By the time he'd explained it; three times, because Judge Clark was a thorough man, the Judge was at least as angry as the Chief. "Don't step foot outside your office, Chief, not until I get there. I want to see this for myself. If even half of what you say is so; I'll hold an impromptu trial on the spot. And if it's true; this woman and her man are not going to like it one little bit."

Chief Taylor relayed the Judge's commands and the group waited. By a twist of fate, perhaps , the woman and her man walked into the Chief's office no more than a few steps ahead of the Judge. She, taking one look at Gee, walked up and slapped his face as hard as she could. Or at least; that was her intent. Gee flicked his left arm out, blocking the blow, and then with uncommon finesse in one so young; his right fist shot out and tagged the woman on the point of her chin and her knees buckled and she went down in a heap. A moment later there was the sound of a single person clapping their hands . . . it was the Judge.

"Well done, young man; very well done." He turned to the Chief and nodded. "And may I presume that these two are the defendants you spoke of?" he asked the Chief. He, in turn nodded his head.

"Very well; this court is now in session."

"You can't do that;" the woman screamed; "you can't just walk into a room and start a trial!"

"Your ignorance of the law is matched only by your homeliness;" the Judge calmly informed her, specifically, and the room at large. "The courtroom does not make me a Judge when I enter it; I make it a courtroom by entering. And that goes for other places as well; including this office. This court will now come to order. Chief Taylor; will you please read off the list of charges against these two?"

It was not something that could be done in a matter of minutes, but in time, all of the charges were related. Gee told of his part; from waking with an uneasy feeling to getting her back to his place (without going into details about that); explained how he noticed that she didn't like being touched in the mid-back and what he had uncovered when at last he got her blouse off. At this point, and Maria knew it was coming, he turned her around to him and held her close for a few moments, then dividing her hair and bringing it around to her front, he lifted her blouse and exposed her back for all to see. The woman, weeping softly, burst into loud wails; not in sorrow for what she had done but in sensing what was going to come next. The Judge stared and his jaw muscles flexed and the expression in his eyes and face did not bode the couple well. He even mentioned the "getting it up" comment and then admitted he had no idea what it meant. But the adults did and the stares they shot at the couple were not nice. At last; Gee ran out of words. "As you can sees, I clean her up best I could, and put what med'cins I had; on her. She looks heaps better'n she did when first I uncoveres it."

The Judge turned to the woman and her mate and the muscles in his jaws flexed. "Of all the cases I've ever seen . . ." he began. Gee cleared his throat. The judge turned and stared: "there's more?" he demanded.

"Th' worser parts maybe;" he admitted. He then covered what he had heard the man say to the one he first killed; about "all of the money better be there" and the "funny money" comment, and then told them about the letters and stained blouses that Maria had found hidden in her room. "Nows I believe I's said it all," he admitted.

The Judge stared at the couple. He was so angry he couldn't talk at first. After a few moments he got his own raging tiger inside calmed down enough that he could be coherent and at least moderately composed when he faced the two. "Son; you just may be the sanest one here right now. What do you think should be done with these two?"

"F'one; the woman's home be taken away from her as well as, whut's th' word, assets; I thinks that the word I wants. Further, I thinks since Maria be the last known in a line of victims, I thinks she should be give the place. Since I'm purdy sures she don't wants to lives there anymore; 'least not jus' yit, I thinks she should be able to rent it out. Because the place be right at one of the hot spots 'round here, I thinks the p'lice otta rents it from her, for a very reasonable price; and puts some of they officers in't; peoples they can trust. With police living right there; a lot of the trubble thereabouts otta slows down.

As f' them . . . I doesn't b'lieve they should be permit to live. Ennybodys who'd kill innocent little chil'ren don't deserve to live one minnit longer than it take to ties a rope 'round they necks and hang em. The sooner dirt be shovel in they face; the better f'everone."

With these words the woman screamed and began to weep and wail and no amount of talk could shut her up. In a few moments someone found a large cloth of some sort and shoved that in her mouth. That didn't stop her completely but it did reduce the noise level down to where others could talk and be heard and understood.

Captain Taylor, followed by the two youngsters and several officers, began to get ready in his office. He got his small revolver and tucked it into his belt; getting ready to go. For a moment, there was a doubling in Gee's vision; he saw the Captain holding the small revolver; in a blink, he was in the same position as he was at first, but this time he held a gun that was much bigger, and silver; like the stainless steel version he'd seen earlier.

"Um, Captain," he began. The officer stopped what he was doing and looked at him. "I doesn't thinks you wants that little gun; you wants the bigger gun. You tol' me iffn you had to shoots a perp, it were past time f'talks an' did you has t'shoot 'im, you din't wants him t'ever gets up again. Never!

The Captain stopped, looked at Gee, then reached into his desk and pulled out a stainless steel revolver with a 4" barrel on it. "This one?" he asked.

Gee shook his head. "Nope. I sees a much bigger gun; bigger and longer barrel on't."

Captain Taylor went over to a closet, unlocked it and reached in. He pulled out the biggest handgun Gee had ever seen; it was stainless steel, had at least an 8" barrel and it was in a shoulder holster and obviously ready for use; should the occasion demand it.

"That be it," he agreed; that be th' one I just seed in m' head."

"I'm not even going to ask you how;" he admitted, and removing his jacket, he slipped the behemoth on. He opened the cylinder, checked it for loads and then gently pressed the cylinder back into place. He put the gun back into the holster and removed the snub nosed revolver that was just held in place with a clip. He got his jacket back on, and with a number of bemused and confused subordinate officers watching, headed for the door.

Three police cruisers headed out; one after another. It wasn't actually that far of a drive. As they pulled up to the house, they saw two of the local people carrying something off the grounds while a third man followed along, apparently giving directions. The officers got out of the cars.

"Stop in the name of the Law!!" Captain Taylor bellowed at the three. The one man, the one who was only following and not actually doing anything, didn't ever slow down or turn his head; he just raised his right hand as high in the air as he could get it and extended his middle finger.

"Stop I say; stop in the name of the law." Again the middle finger waved boldly in the air. Captain Taylor drew the large revolver out of its holster.

"Th' one with th' finger. Gives him one more yells and if the finger come up again; shoots him. Y'don't want him getting' up again. Never!"

"This is your last chance; stop in the name of the law." Again, the finger waved boldly in the air. The two men carrying off whatever they had; began to laugh. Captain Taylor thumbed the hammer back. Maria was directly next to Gee. He turned her around and cupped both hands over her ears. In the next instant there was a small flash of fire at the muzzle of the weapon and a loud noise and the gun reared up like a stallion. Seeming in the same instant, the man with the finger went down onto his face. The bullet struck the perp in the center of his back, severed his spine completely, punched a hole through his heart and came to rest against the back of his sternum; a textbook mushroom shape on its front. They walked up to the group; the two men were no longer laughing. Their faces were white and they were staring down at the ground at a man who had gone down as if he'd been hit with a hammer. And so he had.

"When a police officer gives you an order to stop; you obey!" Captain Taylor told the two. "One way or the other; you *will* stop. The sooner you recognize this simple fact; the longer you may live."

The gunshot turned heads all over the area. This not only was unusual, it was unheard of, they always flipped off the cops and walked away. All of a sudden, the rules had been changed, and in a way that many of them did not like.

The item the two were packing off was an ornate set of outdoor shelves that might hold potted plants. Gee stared at the two men who had been packing it out; it was neither small nor light; it obviously took both of them to carry it. "Picks it up and puts it backs where you finds it. And then comes back; we may not be done with yous yet."

Other officers were still arriving in their cruisers. One of them gestured to the pair; they picked the item up and carried it back to where they had found it shortly before. Within a few minutes the two men were back. By this time more officers were arriving. All around the area anxious faces were peering out of windows and from behind bushes. The cops rarely came around this area and never in force. This was not only unusual; it was frightening.

Gee looked at the two men whose faces were now ashen and showed signs of being in shock. "News flash; cops be movin' in next door. All the bad thin' folks been doin' 'round here gotta stop so's the good folk who also lives 'round here can goes to bed at night without being afraid of wakin' up dead or all they has be stolen at night. The bad folk better plan on movin'. T'some other city might be best; talks about it 'mongst youselfs.

He turned to Chief Taylor. "Y' gots the keys?" he asked. The Captain nodded his head. "Then I s'pose we best goes inside and sees if them items Maria seed is still 'round; or did they be foun' and did away with."

A meat wagon was summoned for the deceased. As they were moving the corpse around, putting him on the stretcher, someone snagged his upper lip on one of the tie straps. As the strap was tightened, it pulled his upper lip back, exposing teeth that were exceedingly sharpened; these weren't just chiseled but came to tight points at the top of each incisor. The men stared, turned, and went for Captain Taylor.

Gee, along with the others, stared at the pointed teeth. They were filed so sharp that it was a wonder the man could eat anything without drawing blood in his own mouth. "Musta been t' chief er suthin';" he supposed. "No wonder them other two was doin' what he sed'; they was prolly scare green o' 'im."

With the recently deceased tucked safely away in the back of a meat wagon, the others walked up the front steps and up to the door. The house was a two-story with a modest attic on top; and existed on an acre of ground that was mostly fenced, with the exception of holes that had been cut into it by others. Some of the holes had been mended after a fashion; yet others looked to have been cut quite recently. Captain Taylor pulled out the keys he carried and after a few false starts, located the correct key and one after another they all trooped in. Maria looked around, wide-eyed and moved closer to Gee. It was a very beautiful house; well taken care of both inside and out and looked to be exactly what it was; the home of wealthy people.

"Maria; althin' consider, I'd likes you and the two officers t'go ups to your room; shows 'em the thin' you was talkin' 'bout as well as lookin' f'other thin's that might incriminate. 'Special looks f' annathin' as can be used 'genst 'em. I dusn't no this State still has a death penalty, but do it, I want's to leave no stone unturn to sees they gets what they's deserves."

Chief Taylor watched the youth with growing pride. Here was a child that didn't quite come up to the chins of those around him; yet he gave out orders he obviously expected to be obeyed; orders that were clear, intelligent, and logical. In a very few more moments the two were alone.

Gee turned to the Chief and looked upward into his eyes. "I been wantin' t' gets y' alone; I gots thin' t' say I thinks y' needs to hear. F'one; I kin do thin's I can'ts explain. I hasn't allus been able; er, maybeso I din't allus knowed it. An' I doesn't gots t'words t'explain it. M'Mom was of the Deep South and had a accent y' couldn't cut with a knife. She was also lazy of speech and most prolly not all that bright; but Da loves her with alla his heart and soul and that was all that matter. Bottom liniin' it; theys a lot o'words I just doesn't know. So's I just gunna blunder 'long; does you get lost, stops me and asts me t'try 'n' says it different. Be that good with you?"

Chief Taylor promptly nodded his head. This child intrigued him on levels he was not ready to explore; that he began the conversation on his own was a Godsend; as far as he was concerned.

"I 'members thins that seems impossible. I can sees thin's that other's can't. Jus' for examples; looks over there at that wall there; what do's you see?"

"Just a wall, Gee, what else is there to see?"

"A door; a hidden door; an' I sees stairs goin' down. 'Most o' the land hereabouts is purdy flat; not much rise or fall. Just heres be there a hill an' it ain't a big hill 'er a fast hill: comes up; maybe-so six er eight foots above the rest. Might be natural; might be made by man. An' when I looks down, I see floor joists and 'neath that, there be a room; a room full o' thin's that look suspiciously like guns 'n' stuff. From what's I unnerstan,' the folk who lived here now, din't make this house; they buyed it at auction when the feller what builded it died unexpected. And I'm purdy sure the folks here dint knowed 'bout the room beneath the floor."

"A door?" Chief Taylor demanded. He walked over to the wall and began to run his hands over it. It looked like any other wall; built like most other walls and nicely paneled with wood paneling that was most definitely not something that came from a cut-rate hardware store. He felt only premium wood panels. He turned to Gee.

Gee walked, not toward the wall where the Chief stood, but to a place that was more to the Chief's right. Along the edge were burnished aluminum bars set into the edge of the wood. Each bar was perhaps six inches long and half an inch wide and no more than an eighth of an inch thick. They formed a pattern of perhaps six inches of aluminum with the same distance prime wood paneling and repeated; from the top next to the ceiling and continued all the way to the floor. This was something that would have taken master craftsmen time to complete and actually looked very nice. He reached out and carefully pulled one of them off the wall. It now was a long, thin bar with a sheet of extruded aluminum perhaps three-sixteenths of an inch thick and three inches square sticking out. He took the odd devise, moved over to a place where the panels were jointed, and slipped the flat part that stuck out into a hidden slot in the wall. He pushed gently, and an eye-blink later an entire section of wood swung away, revealing a hidden niche and stairs leading downward. He pulled the bar out of the wall and put it back where it was. Chief Taylor stared in disbelief; then remembered to close his mouth.

Gee looked about for a moment, then finding a light switch, flipped it on. These were not the older incandescent that had been in use for so many decades, but the newer LEDs and the light filled the room with the closest thing to real sunlight that Human has yet been able to devise. The two moved downward; into something that might have been lifted directly out of a sporting goods store somewhere. There was one wall that had a long row of shoulder arms; ranging from shotguns to hunting rifles to weapons that would have looked more at home on a battle field. Another entire display showed handguns of every sort; from single-barreled target guns; through autoloaders to wheel-guns like those favored by many police. Off to the right, as they stood and looked, was a massive wall-safe.

Chief Taylor walked in, his eyes trying to take in everything in a single glance. While that wasn't remotely possible; he gave it his best. At last, his roving eyes landed on the safe and stayed there. "Gee; a safe. Gee; too bad we don't have someone here to crack it. Gee; I sure wonder what's . . ." Gee hissed at him and clapped his hand over his own mouth. He looked up at the door that still stood ajar; in the next moment it softly swung shut. Gee put his hand on the Chief's wrist and the lights blinked out. Before Captain Taylor could adjust, they were both once again standing in the living-room and from above he could hear the sound of weeping and small feet tripping frantically to get to the bottom of the stairs. It was Maria and she was wailing in grief.

In the next blink Gee was there. His arms reached out and caught Maria and she wrapped herself around him, arms and legs, and wailing she buried her face in the crook of his neck and dissolved into a sea of bitter tears. The officers who had accompanied her upstairs were not much better. The man looked like he could cheerfully kill and the expression on his mate's face was of the most bitter hatred the police chief had ever seen.

"Goddamn them; Goddamn them to the burning Hells;" the male bellowed. "Four of 'em; four innocent little girls these . . . I can't think of a word foul enough. Four of them; these people had and four of them they beat, raped, tortured and eventually, to cover their own crimes; sold to people they knew were cannibals and knew that the children would be murdered; cooked and eaten. God damn them both to Hell!"

Captain Taylor immediately went over to his officers; "Show me; show me what you've found!" he demanded. The man handed his Chief a handful of children's clothing with dried blood on it; and pages and pages of papers where young victims, who had no chance in life, recorded their ordeals at the hands of people they'd fallen prey to. By the time the Captain was done; he was as nearly livid as his two officers.

"Oh yeah; oh yeah; the Judge's gonna get an eye-full of these. I gotta admit; that war took away a lot of innocent lives. But to add more to the tally; that's the limit: it doesn't go further."

They had done what they'd come to do; done and managed to cover things they couldn't have foreseen. They left several officers to run a loose patrol around the area; in part; to get people used to seeing police where they hadn't formerly come. Then they headed back to the precinct.

Maria was very quiet. Logically; revisiting the place that had caused her so much pain, both physical as well as emotional, was about as much as she could take for one day. The two talked quietly between themselves and when Captain Taylor asked the pair what they wanted to do next; both admitted that they wanted to go home. The weather had mostly cleared off and Gee, especially, wanted to stop at Forrester's; they walked away, headed in the general direction they usually did and then when conditions were right, he popped into the area where the grocery store was and both walked in.

As it sometimes happened; when they walked into the store they found quite a few people inside; some were being helped, a few were walking towards them with their packages in their hands, yet others were either waiting to be served or nosing around to see what there was to look at. Gee and Maria joined the latter group. It was no surprise to Gee when Maria walked directly over to where the apples were and started feeling and smelling them.

"Dirty little urchins; who said you could come in here?" a middle-aged woman sniffed disdainfully.

"Captain Taylor say so; Ma'am;" Gee replied politely. I gots a jobs with him and gots some pay-money; we's come to find some eats and takes 'em home with us."

"Little liar," she snapped, "you don't have a job with anyone."

"Actually; he does," Mr. Forrester assured her as he came up from behind her. "Not only does he do little odd jobs for me, he also helps out our Police and Fire Departments as well as a great many others. He's a finder by trade and quite often locates things we need."

He turned to Gee and Maria; "now then; how can I help you two today?"

"We jus' stopped by to sees what you gots f' dinner t'night. From the way Maria be sniffin' 'round the apple bin, I 'spects there better be's some apples in there alongs with anythin' else we finds." Mr. Forrester nodded his head and laughed softly; "She does seem to have a thing about apples; doesn't she?" It didn't take long and the two had completed their shopping. Gee reached into his pouch to get some money but Mr. Forrester quickly waved him down. "Your money's no good in here, my little friend," he whispered softly. "What you brought me in that backpack will take care of your needs for at least the next few months; if not longer."

Chapter 7

Gee and Maria both walked out of the market and turned, headed east. He glanced carefully in every direction as they walked. In the day and age, walking along with food in hand was nearly as dangerous as having a conspicuous amount of money for there were always hungry people around whose habits tended towards stealing what they wanted and needed rather than trying to earn it honestly. They walked the proper distance and once they rounded a corner, winked out and instantly appeared within their own home. As usual, several kittens hissed at their sudden appearance, but what wasn't quite as usual, the little animals recovered their poise almost as soon as they'd lost it.

The two of them went into the kitchen and put their purchases into their proper places and then went to take care of their kitties; this, the animals approved of completely. They filled their food bowls and made sure that the water dish was full and then cleaned out the sand box of solid waste. Then they went to the kitchen to see about their own bellies.

With that taken care of; both went into the living room. Maria was getting more interested in the giant TV that took up much of one wall. Gee had never experienced such and was therefore unsure of what to expect. She poked around a bit, when suddenly the big screen came on, flooding the room with white light. Gee looked at the screen with mouth agape. By this time in the history of such things, batteries had become so long-life that as long as they weren't used up, their shelf life was almost indefinite; as were the lifespan of the rechargeable. She poked through some Blue Ray discs and chose one she was familiar with and liked. And for the first time in his life, Gee got to see a movie, on TV or anything else. He sat there with his mind all but blown; watching the movie called Bambi. It was almost a life-changing event for him for there were shelves full of different movies; none of which he had ever seen. "What a glorious time-waster;" he chortled in joy.

Several days passed peacefully by. The two took their time getting to know each other; their likes, their dislikes and all the things that young couples need to do to finally learn to function as a duo, rather than in single mode. Gee still hadn't gotten his hair trimmed; this was something that was getting more obvious as time went by. After awhile; Gee decided that it was time for him to get a trim. He would have gladly let Maria take a try at it but she wouldn't consider it. Finally, one bright morning, the pair got themselves ready. He took yet another twenty dollar bill and stuffed it in his right front pocket. Holding hands the pair winked out, and in the next instant, were standing in his usual place.

They turned, and holding hands, headed towards Forester's place. They had not been there for several days and both were looking forward to going there; they didn't quite make it.

"Gee; hey, Gee," a voice bellowed out. The pair turned, just in time to see two of their favorite officers come sprinting up. "Where in the devil have you been? The Captain's been asking about you every day now; several times a day in fact."

"We kinda been layin' low; mostly just getting to know each other. Maria's been workin' with me on my talkin'; tryin' to get me more civilized; that sort of thing. I think that females just not happy lessen they gots a male to boss around." Maria whacked him on the shoulder; he pretended to be injured. The two men nodded their heads and laughed softly.

"Captain Taylor's been asking about you daily;" one of the two repeated.

"Several times a day," the other injected. "He's got some questions he wants to ask, and while I'm not sure I'm supposed to be saying this, I think he's got a problem he can't figure out and is hoping you can help him.

"Wull; gets him on the line and sees . . . I mean, Well; get him on the phone and ask him what he needs." He glanced at Maria; she whacked him on the shoulder with a play-swat that females often use. He pretended to be injured. The two men laughed and nodded their heads. Both had wives at home and both understood and identified with him; a moment later one of the men's radios came on.

"Hello; this is Captain Taylor; have you found Gee yet? Over."

The officer didn't even try to answer the radio; he just handed it to Gee. "Hi; Captain Taylor; this be Gee; what's up besides the sky?"

"Enough with the wise cracks, Son, where've you been the last three days; we've been going nuts trying to find you."

"Captain Taylor; I'm surprised: has it been that long since you was on you honeymoon?"

"Your honeymoon," Maria sniffed softly; but not so soft that the two-way radio couldn't catch it. In the next instant Captain's roaring laughter came over the air.

"She's got you broke to the halter already; does she? He laughed with glee. "Good for you; honey; someone needs to trim that boy's ears back.

"Speaking of trim . . . do you know where I can gets a haircut?" Gee asked. There was silence on the other end. After a moment; the Captain spoke again.

"Did one of you men tell him what's up or is that just another of his lucky guesses?"

"Not I, said the cow," Officer Trent admitted.

"I doesn't . . . I mean, I don't know what is up, Captain Taylor. When I walked up I mentioned to Officer Trent that I need a haircut. Things were just starting to proceed when you called. Why; what's happening?"

"I'm not sure I can explain this unless you are here; not only because of the content; but because of the content . . . if that makes any sense to you.

"Nope; not a bit," he admitted, "best wait until we get there. Gee; out." He handed the transceiver to the man who had it first. He took Maria's hand in his and the two headed towards the police station. Just as they rounded the corner he made his jump and in that precise instant he rounded the corner leading to where Captain Taylor waited; nearly at his wits end. The pair walked up the steps and into the big building that housed both the police station as well as the court room, turned right, and moved down the hallway to where Gee knew the Captain's office was. They walked into the police department, only to find a woman wailing her soul out, full volume and broken hearted. Around here were several officers; both male and female and a very distraught Captain.

Gee walked up to the woman, grabbed her by both shoulders, lifted her bodily up from the chair she was sitting in and slammed he back into it. "What's you wailing 'bout?" he bellowed. You want's reason to wail? I gives you reason; somebody, you, gives me you belt;" he commanded one of the man standing nearby. He, without hesitation or question, immediately pulled his belt off and handed it to Gee. Gee doubled it over and stuck it before the woman's face where she couldn't possibly miss seeing it. She gave a half-wail and in the middle of which she saw the belt and instantly stopped. The silence was almost deafening.

"Tha's better;" he admitted. "Now then, without you starting to weep and wail again, tell's me what the problem is. Starts at the beginning, and when you get's to the end, . . . stops."

"M, m, my hair;" she sobbed. She had a scarf pulled over her head and tucked under her chin; Gee couldn't see her hair.

"Arright;" he said, "lets take a looks at you hair. C'mon now; you among friends. We not gonna laugh or makes fun but we needs to see what you problem is; elsewise we can't help you." At first slowly and then with increasing speed she slipped the scarf off. Several women in the group gasped; and even moaned. "Omigod," one woman wailed. The woman began to weep. This time; Gee didn't reach for the belt he had already handed back to the man who owned it. This time he reached out, and taking her by her shoulders, pulled her up against him. "That's alright, Dear, just lets it out; goes ahead and weeps does you needs to. We understands." The woman dissolved into a clot of misery and taking Gee at his words, buried her face on his shoulder, and burst into a torrent of tears. He held her gently. At first slowly, then starting with Maria, and spreading to every female in the area; they surrounded her and held her and she managed to weep on every one of them. In time; even her supply of tears was used up. One of the female officers, understanding exactly how these things go, went and got a large cup and filled it with water and brought it over. She handed it to Gee; he in turn helped the woman hold it, she drank it down greedily, as if she couldn't get it into herself fast enough. She drained the cup twice again, and then finally getting her fill, started sitting more upright.

It would be, perhaps, a misnomer to say she had been butchered; but her hair was aggressively cut and unevenly with some spots almost bald with areas abutting where several inches of light auburn hair jutted out in different directions. Several female officers were quietly weeping at what they saw.

"This; my Da tol' me when I was younger. Men an women don't looks alike on th' outside; 'cos we be different alsos too on the insides. One of the difference bein'; women has way more chemicals and hormones than men. This, because it is women who gots to make the babies, that becomes the grownups of tomorrow. Because womens has to have babies; they has way more hormones and chemicals inside they bodies. These chemicals and stuff is need for makin' babies; but sometimes they messes with the female mind. Women understands feelin's in ways men do not; mostly men understand logic. Female understand logic toos, but only's to a point. Thereafter; they's understand emotion. When a female gets too emotional, Da says it a waste of time to tries logic on 'em, y'gotta use emotion. Fear is emotion; one of the strongest of all. That ways; does a female get so inta one of her emotions that logic can't covers it; y'gotta use a stronger emotion. Fear; fits the bill. And that's why I threaten you with a belt; t'gets you inta a emotion stronger than you was in. I wouldn't actual hit you, lessn I had to. Even then I wouldn't do mor'n I absolute had; coz I doesn't like violence and I doesn't like violence to a female. Does you unnerstands?" She sniffled a bit and nodded her head.

"Now then; when did this happen to you; was it today you got your hair cut?"

"No;" she said softly, "it was almost two weeks ago. I went in for a light trim. Somehow, and I'm not sure why, they thought I wanted it all cut short. Before I could stop the woman doing it; she had whacked off a large chunk of my hair. I tried to make her stop but she said I had told her that I wanted a 'fairy' cut; one where my hair would be much shorter. We argued and she kept cutting, and before I could get her to stop, she had whacked off my hair and I was left with bald spots and short pieces like you see. And they said that it was my fault because I didn't make myself clear. I went home and cried. Then, earlier today, I was out, trying to do so shopping when I saw Mrs. Topperwien . . . and she was wearing my hair!" Again; she began to weep.

Gee looked up, first at Maria and then at several of the female officers; a very confused expression on his face. "What do she mean; 'wearing my hair?'" he demanded.

One of the female officers turned to him. "There's something called a 'wig'. It can be made from a number of things; but the best and most natural would, obviously, be human hair. If the hair is long enough, it can be fitted into a form that will slip over another woman's head, making it look as though it is her hair. This wig is often used by women whose hair has either fallen out from the woman's age; or even disease or just to cover her normal hair. Evidently; her hair was made into a wig and sold; and Mrs. Topperwien bought the wig and was wearing it."

Gee nodded his head; then turned to the woman. "An' you recognized you hair on her and knowed that you hair that was cut off had been bought by someone else an' was bein' worn by someone else. Be that right?" The woman nodded her head and began to pucker up for another run at tears. He moved in, hugged her gently, and caressed her face gently.

"Tells me, Ma'am; what most important to you right now? Stirring up another tear-storm or gettin' even with them what treated you so badly?" She was on the thin edge of doing exactly that; stirring up another storm, but at the words "getting even" she stopped, sniffled once more and stared at him.

"What do you mean; 'getting even?'" she demanded quickly.

"As I sees it, they did you dirt, real bad dirt. So bad; there gotta be a law 'gainst it. About the best 'getting' even' I can thinks of; would be to get the woman and them who's also involved and tossin' 'em all inta jail." He turned to Captain Taylor and looked him in the eyes. "What does you thinks; be it crime 'nuff to toss someone's backside into jail?"

"Absolutely;" Captain Taylor said.

As it turned out; the shop where the crime had taken place was located right on a dividing line between Captain Taylor's precinct and the next one over; and it was an ongoing debate as exactly which department controlled what part of any specific street in the area. The Captain decided that since the injured party was from his precinct; the control of the given shop was his to handle as he saw fit. He, Gee and a generous number of other officers of both sexes worked out different scenarios. When they found one they could mostly agree on; they got the proper people programmed for the parts they were going to play, and then one by one they were wired for communication, so Captain Taylor and his group could hear what was happening but he could not contact them. Once everyone was in their place; the first female officer, dressed in street clothing, stepped out and headed in the right direction. It wasn't far; not quite two blocks to their south and the shop was about half way down on the left side, or east as some thought of it. She walked in.

There were four chairs but only two people styling and cutting hair. A row of chairs lined the wall opposite and two women were working on customers while a third one sat, looking though a very old magazine. One of the women stopped what she was doing and looked at the person who just came in. "I'm sorry, honey, but you're going to have a wait; I just got started here and there's one ahead of you."

"Take your time, dear, I'm off for the day and my husband's at work. I just thought I'd zip down here a get a light trim. I was talking to one of the other ladies that I work with and she recommended you so I thought since I have some time I'd just come over and try you out. And I've got a new eBook I've not read yet; this gives me a chance to do two things at once." She reached into an oversized purse and pulled out one of the many such that still were in people's hands; she sat down, lifted it up close to eye level and turned it on. What many were unaware of was that many of the eBooks could also double as recorders and with a tiny push of a single button she could switch it from what she was reading, over to scan: and thereafter; record both audio as well as visual. She started to read; just in case someone got nosy. Perhaps five minutes passed quietly.

The door opened and Gee and Maria walked in. Gee looked shaggy and in dire need of a haircut. Maria had all of her golden hair carefully coiled atop her head by half of the females in the department. It didn't actually take that many to do the job, but the child's golden tresses were too big a temptation for many of the women there, and they all wanted to run their fingers though her hair. A stylish hat covered the hair without even a single golden strand hanging out to give her hair away. The same woman turned toward the two.

"I'm really sorry, but we've got a backlog; it's going to be at least an hour before I can get to you;" she apologized.

"S'alrite;" Gee admitted, "I gots lots'o time. Me'n baby just sits over here and looks through this book I got. I can't read none too good and she reads lots better and she's help'n me learn. I don't mind waiting." The pair moved over to some seats that had no one close to them and sat down. He reached into an oversized pocket and pulled out a book. It wasn't precisely a first-grade reader but it wasn't much more advanced than that. They sat close together, side by side, and he began reading very quietly while she helped him along with the words. The two did their best to be inconspicuous but their soft voices kept turning eyes towards them. It was during one of those brief moments when Maria, at a slight nod from Gee, pulled the hat off her head and her golden tresses cascaded down her neck and back like water running down the side of a mountain. In that instant all action and sound in the shop came to a sudden and complete stop.

"Oh my God;" the woman who had been giving instructions just moments before shrieked. "Oh my God; how could you let that child go out like that? That would have to give her terrible headaches."

"I don't have headaches," Maria said.

"Of course you do, dear; here, just let me cut that off nice and close to your head; we'll give you a nice elfin hairdo; it will look so cute on you." The woman advanced toward the two with a large pair of shears in her right hand; held, not as one should hold scissors, but like one would hold a knife they intended to stab someone with. Gee jumped up between the woman and Maria.

"Back off;" he warned the woman; "backs off or I'll levels you." The woman kept coming. Her eyes were of the demented and she kept licking her lips like she tasted something only she could savor. She advanced almost within reach and pulled the shears back. The door banged open and first Captain Taylor and then other of his officers charged in. She started to stab at Gee. He batted her right hand out of the way, avoiding what would have surely been a wicked wound at minimum, and in the next instant his right fist shot out from somewhere between his shoulder and chest. Before anyone could finish blinking; his fist exploded on the woman's unprotected chin. Her head jerked back, her legs crumpled at the knees, and in the next moment she lay in a wadded up pile on the floor looking only vaguely human; much less female.

For the next few moments pandemonium reigned supreme and the three women who were either being worked on, or were working on someone, all shrieked in three-part disharmony. It actually didn't take long but for some of the people involved time seemed stretched out in ways that were improbable; if not impossible.

"Enough!" Gee yelled and in an instant; relative peace descended upon the room. One of the female officers walked over to the woman on the floor that was beginning to move about. Gee hadn't actually hit her hard enough to knock her all the way out; nor did he intend to: he just wanted to get her stopped before she hurt someone. The officer got the woman's arms moved around behind her and cuffed her, and then began to read her, her rights.

"What about me?" demanded the woman who was being worked on before the beautician abandoned her to attack Gee and Maria. Gee pointed at the other female officer who at the moment was just standing; watching. "Hi; my name is Carol Donovan," she admitted. "Before I went into police work I was a licensed beautician. One of the reasons I came along was in case there were people who were not done. If you permit; I can easily finish you up." The customer looked around, seeming confused, and then nodded her head. The officer moved over to the woman and began asking her questions as to exactly what kind of style she wanted and before long the two had established a relationship that would at least get the customer out the door and reasonably happy. As it turned out; the second woman cutting hair wasn't involved in the wig scheme. In fact she was absolutely against it. But like a great many others, she needed a job and in order to keep hers, she just kept her head down and mouth shut. Very wise; under the circumstances.

In time; the paddy wagon came and hauled off the woman responsible for the problem in the first place. With the help of her former co-worker; they discovered that not only had she chopped the hair off of a number of victims; she also was the one who created and sold the wigs. In her inventory they discovered not only the hair of a number of different women; they also found another wig made up of the hair of the woman who had come to them with the complaint in the first place. Since she was the injured party; they confiscated the wig in order to return it to its original owner. This way; she could go out with her own hair in place until her hair grew back out enough that she wouldn't feel ashamed. Gee waited until everyone else involved was properly taken care of, and then he seated himself into a chair, and for the first time in his entire life; got a proper haircut from someone who actually knew what they were doing. The difference was remarkable. Maria walked around him several times; looking him over. "I think I'll keep you;" she admitted. He grinned; "Just tries to get rid of me;" he replied.

Rather taking a ride in one of the police cars, the pair just walked back; it wasn't that far and both were still quite young and enjoyed walking and looking at what there was to see. In time they got over to where Forrester's Groceries was; the place they wanted to go in the first place. For one; both liked the two men who worked there and enjoyed just talking to them. For the second; they were getting low on some of their supplies; and Maria especially was interested in getting more apples if they were available. They were. There were quite a few people already in the store when they walked in. The two nodded at the grocer and his helper and began to wander up one aisle and down another, checking out different products. Evidently, to at least some of the people in the store, two kids of their age didn't belong in the store; several even began to complain about it between them. Mr. Forrester, hearing the murmurings, turned around and spotted them. "Hey! It's Gee and Maria. Just as soon as we're done over here we'll be right over." Gee was sure the man said that in order to let his other customers know that he was both aware of their presence and that it was well with him.

In time, the others got their purchases and one at a time left the store; soon, it was only the four of them there. The two men came up; grinning. "Well; I've got some interesting news for you; my little friend;" Mr. Forrester began. "You wouldn't believe the flap those golden dollars you left me a week ago has caused. Now; everybody who comes in here wants their change only in them. I had to tell them that my supply was very limited and that I'm only giving them out one to a customer and for at least now, the next time they come back, they can't have any more. Speaking of which; do you have any more? I'll take as many as you can spare. Oh; by the way; I really like your new haircut; it looks very good on you. Where did you get it done?"

"Couple a' blocks away," he admitted. "And far as the gold dollars goes; I don't know for sure exactly how many of them I has. As I tol' you afore, I saw ten or so boxes what was lettered dollar sign two five oh an' I took several of the boxes. The rest I just left 'cause I din't have room for them. And thems . . . "he took a side glance at Maria and corrected himself. "I mean that I didn't have room in my pouch for them and I know where the rest be. . . are." He glanced at Maria and she just grinned up at him. She had gotten better at not correcting his errors and he was getting better at not making them. Between the two; he was making progress: slowly, that is so, but even an inch is that much closer to the goal. The two men watched the antics of the two children and laughed softly.

William stood listening carefully; "I make it around twenty-five hundred coins." Mr. Forrester admitted that sounded about right to him.

"I believe I can scare up two more rolls; will that be enough for now; Mr. Forrester?" he asked politely. He, in return, began to nod enthusiastically.

"That's more than I dared hope for," he admitted. A moment later he turned and headed for his cash register to pull some bills out. Gee reached into his pouch. His hand appeared in his safe and closed around two rolls of the golden dollars and promptly vanished. He pulled the rolls out of his pouch as if they had been in there all along. Maria watched him carefully. She was affectionate by nature and this specific boy brought all such out of her and she knew from personally cuddling him and touching his belly that there were no coins; nor anything else on him. Like so much else about him; it both confused and intrigued her on levels her mind was not prepared to address; much less hope to solve.

"With that taken care of, I'd like to cover something else;" the grocer said. "The news has leaked; exactly how I'm not sure, but at least a few people either know I now have salt or perhaps more accurately, are hoping I have some. In either case I'm getting multiple requests every day now and some of the requests verge well into the range of being demands and even threats. People want salt. They need salt and they're determined to get salt; as much as they can and as fast as possible."

"I think maybe the problem is; we started using some of the salt you gave us, mixed in with the food we sell, especially in the stew that we make;" William volunteered. "People can taste it and they want more. Our stew, which used to only be one of the things we sell, is now almost the only thing anyone wants to buy. Our question - and our need - is; can you scare up any more salt; enough that we can repackage it into smaller containers and sell to at least a few of the people? We'll be more than glad to share the proceeds with you. What are your words; can you do this?"

Gee's eyes traced back and forth between the two men. "My answer is; yes and no. Yes; I do have some more salt I know of; quite a bit, in fact: but not nearly enough to supply this part of the city; and specifically, not enough for the entire city. And I hopes you understands that if it ever gets out that I'm remotely part of this; folks might storm me in such numbers that many people could get hurt; including Maria and me. Even under the best of cases, I can't supply the whole city for years to come. Some place there might be a lot more; as much as I've looked around, I've only 'scratched the surface', as my Da used to say. But that's only a 'maybe' at best, and even then it is very limited; both in amounts as well as how long I can keep supplying. About the best I can suggest for now is to cut the amount of salt you put into the stew down to the very bare minimum; maybe so they'll stop tasting it and think its run out already."

The two men nodded their heads, and with all the necessary things done, Gee and Maria once again did their shopping and once again when they tried to pay; Mr. Forrester refused their money.

The pair walked out the door, and then to Maria's surprise, they headed more towards the south, instead of easterly as they normally did. She glanced up at him. "I'm feeling somebodies watchin' us;" he admitted. "Might be so it's only scaries on my parts, but I thinks they be someones' awatchin' us and I didn't want to go the usual way. This way, if they be folks watchin', maybe-so they'll think we lives out this way." As was usual for them now, just as they rounded a corner they winked out and immediately appeared in their own place. Two of the three kittens started to dart off; the third one opened sleepy eyes, watched them for a few moments and then its eyes sagged back closed and it returned to its nap; a thing all cats are so very good at. The two put the groceries where they belonged and then took care of the kittens needs as far as food and water and sandbox was concerned. Then they washed their hands and started in on feeding their own bellies.

Once they had taken care of their inner needs and cleaned up the resulting mess; Gee turned to Maria. "I guess the best place to begin is at the beginning;" he said. "I finded . . . found this place while escaping the Brandon boys. Come with me and I'll show you exactly what I mean." He led her out of the front door, a door she had not as yet been through and showed her both the other two doors that led into other apartments as well as the humongous mess in the lobby; and finally, the exit door. He opened it and let her look outside. She showed no sign of wanting to step out onto the rickety-looking platform. She contented herself by looking outside, while holding onto him, using him as a security blanket. By the time he was done; she understood as clearly as if she had witnessed the entire event. "Before this, I either couldn't jump this way; or perhaps more accurate, I didn't know I could. In a way; they helped me more than they'll ever know. Not that any of the three knowingly ever did anything good for anyone in their entire lives. Now then; move over here and look down." She did so. It was very clear that there was an entire floor under theirs, each with individual doors and presumably, yet other apartments. "What I still do not know is whether there are more apartments on the bottom floor. All the junk piled up in the middle totally covers the walk way and maybe-so even if there are apartments down there one would not be able to walk out the doors because of all the junk laying around. If you've seen enough and if you want; we'll go back inside and go out through the other door and take a look-see. Right now; I don't know any more about what's down there than you do; I've never been that far. I was going to, but I woke up with this itch that morning and had to go and rescue a girl, and I haven't had the time since."

"And which girl was that;" she asked.

"Oh; the sweetest, most beautiful and nicest girl one could ever meet. But I couldn't find her so I rescued you inste . . . Hey! Ouch! Watch it;" he yelled and jumped back as she took another swat at him. A moment later he reached out and under her swinging arm and tickled her ribs; she squealed and jumping back, clamped her elbows against her lower ribs. In the end the two walked back through the door and with arms around each other, through the apartment and out the back door. They turned to their right and walked down to the next pair of glass doors. He had locked the sliding doors, returning them to the same way he found them. It didn't take more than a very few moments and he unlatched the door and slid it aside and the two walked in.

It was exactly as he remembered; nothing had changed nor did he expect it to have. The two wandered around the place; finding a few things they wanted which Gee immediately sent to their own apartment, then nosed around in the two bedrooms. The adult bedroom held things that were very useful for a great many people in the way of clothing and such, as were the boy's rooms. But Maria found nothing therein that remotely interested her, and Gee, trying to be sensitive to her needs and pleasures; gave it a perfunctory glance; trying to memorize things that would interest him in the both near and distant future. With that taken care of, the two left the place; relocking everything securely and then moved down to the final set of doors.

The pair went to the last apartment on this level. Gee again unlocked the doors with his mind and the two walked in. The floor plan was the same as the other two; again, the furnishings were different as were a number of other things. Up against the wall, between where the closet and the entry way into the first bedroom, was a very nice faux electric fireplace; one that lit up beautifully once the two found the proper switch to throw. Maria, especially, had never seen such and was entranced at the fabricated flames as they bounced and danced. By this time in the history of such, these things were faked so successfully, that it was only by reaching out and trying to touch the flames that one could be sure that it wasn't a real fire. That; and the simple fact that after watching for a while, the two began to detect where the cycle began and ended, and they could easily tell that it wasn't an actual fire after all. Gee looked upward, towards where the mantle of a fireplace would usually be, and he saw some pictures arraigned neatly in a row. First was of a young couple; looking as if they were either in their very late teens or early twenties at the most. Both were nicely dressed, as if going to Church or perhaps to a party somewhere. Next to it was another picture. This was a double; one picture was of a woman holding a baby, the other side was of the man, presumably holding the same infant. Next was another double; this of somewhat older people; perhaps in their mid to later twenties. Next to that, the same couple, now perhaps in their early thirties and there were two young children with them; both were girls. Both Gee and Maria looked at this last picture and then looked at each other. "I think we'd better go look at the bedrooms;" Gee said.

For a few frantic moments Maria was not a sane girl. The bedroom was most definitely girly. The bed to their left looked to be the bed of an older girl; the bedding was most definitely feminine and the dresser directly at the foot of her bed had pictures on it of a young girl perhaps in her earliest teens. To the right was an identical dresser with a picture of a much younger girl; perhaps about Maria's age. Both were in color and were of blue-eyed, black haired girls looking out of the photographs with winning smiles on their faces. Both were very pretty; verging on beautiful. Gee's heart went out to both of them because the odds were overwhelming that neither were still alive; nor had been for more than eight years.

Maria was kinetic. Her eyes roved around the room, spotting one thing and then off to another, and then back to the first. Gee understood perfectly. She was young, female, and very human and from what little he knew of her and her history; she very likely had never seen half of the things before her; much less owned any of them. He nodded his head as his mind made the obvious connection. "Pretty girl," he began, "I'm beginning to get the feeling that pretty soon we'll be moving from our other apartment and into this one. There're just too many things in here that you're going to like and it will be easier to move us than to pack up everything else." She looked up into his eyes and burst into the most radiant smile he had ever seen; on her or on any other girl; anywhere else.

They spent quite a bit of time just looking around. The people who had lived in this apartment had evidently not been the type who planned far into the future. Unlike the first place he'd found, there were no obvious supplies built up for harder times. There was enough for the immediate future; but not for a prolonged period away from a local store. They seemed to have lived for the moment and were willing to let tomorrow take care of its self. For Gee and Maria; it hardly mattered. The top floor of the apartment building alone, along with what they could pick up at the market, would tide them well into early adulthood; and perhaps by then things would have returned more to what they once were.

The two returned to their own apartment and began sorting the things he had sent over. As they did so, Maria got a pensive look on her face as she was working. She turned to Gee. "I don't think we should move; at least not yet. We still haven't looked at the second floor; much less the first and we might find something we like even better. More than that; this is the first home I've ever had and already I've come to love it." Gee nodded his head. In truth, he felt the same, but he was trying to be sensitive to her needs as well as take care of his own. By the time the two had everything sorted to their likes and needs and had gotten some food inside of them - as well as the kittens - the sun had drifted down, first to the horizon and then ultimately, below it. By this time he was at least as interested in the giant TV screen mounted on the eastern wall as she was. The two carefully went through several hundred movies on Blue Ray and ultimately decided to try some titled 'Ice Age.' There were several of them to choose from. Maria, who could read better than Gee, read the covers and discovered that there was a sequence to them. They also discovered something called 'popcorn' a thing Gee had never even heard of, much less tasted. Maria read the instructions, stuck the bag into the microwave oven and in due process of time, got the very first popped corn that either had ever eaten. Between that and the movie, the two were very contented young people.

By the time two of the movies were over and the popcorn only a faint belch within, they and the kittens were ready for bed. They each took separate showers, got into what they thought of a 'bed clothing' and cuddled up in each other's arms, because by now, Maria was at least as enchanted by Gee as he was of her and while both were too young to feel the physical attractions that older humans have for each other; both were happiest when they were together. But tonight was slightly different. This time, as the two started to settle down, first one little fur ball after another climbed up into bed with them; and for the first time ever, all three of them were not only willing to permit their humans to pet them; they insisted on it.

Chapter 8

Dawn is the beginning of a new day as yet unopened. For the two, it began with three little balls of fluff bouncing around on the bed, evidently playing 'catch your tail' or some other such kitten game. They opened sleepy eyes and reached out their hands. The kittens quit their activities for the moment to carefully sniff their fingers; then of a common mind, began to rub their cheeks and foreheads against the hands, obviously enjoying the tactile sensation of fingertips gently scratching chins; cheeks and heads. This continued on for a few moments, then the kittens, first singly and then in three-part harmony, began to meow for their food. Gee got up, still bleary eyed and took care of the little animal's needs; then aware of his own needs, headed for the bathroom. He no sooner came out than Maria shot in; she, too, had things that needed to be done. With the immediate concerns taken care of, first Gee and then Maria got together and got the kitten's quarters all taken care of; water and food bowls filled and sand box emptied: so much for the quick and easy.

Um, yes, the sand box. He had been carefully cleaning out the solid waste, cleaned and flushed, but the dirt itself was getting to the point where it desperately needed replacing. Instead of leaving the box in its normal place, he once again took the small shovel In hand and with both it and the litterbox, headed out while Maria busied herself with things she wanted to do. He walked down the stairs on his left, which was to the west, and found his digging spot. He dumped the detritus in a convenient place and then started scraping around in fresh dirt to fill the box back up. He picked up box and shovel and started to head back upstairs; he stopped. He looked to his left, towards the southeast. He had as yet to explore that section of what he now thought of as his property. He set the box and scoop down, just at the base of the stairs, and walked that way.

The first thing he noticed was that there were not three doors on the bottom level as he supposed; but only one; and that one was well to his left; the east. He continued on. As he headed towards the door he then noticed that it wasn't a sliding door as he expected, but a regular swinging door like most houses. The very next thing he saw was that the door was not closed; but somewhat ajar. As he got closer yet he saw something lying just outside of the doorway. And then he was there. He stared down; it was a human skeleton, outside a partially gapped door, but only barely. Now as much alarmed as curious; he stepped carefully past the bones lying on the cement and cautiously pushed the door wide open. A stale, unpleasant, off odor wafted out to his waiting nostrils. He put one foot in and glanced around.

The interior was by far the most opulent he had ever seen; even Mr. Coldbrick's home could not compete. He eased further inside. There was an odd, stale, and most disagreeable scent to it. He sniffed cautiously but could detect nothing that alarmed him. Poised, ready to retreat in an instant if needed, he took another step and yet another. He moved further in.

The interior stretched out before him. He now understood the reason there weren't two more doors outside was because the interior took it all up. Then he realized that wasn't quite true; perhaps it took up half of it or two thirds. On the furthest, most western wall there was a large door; much bigger than on any home he had ever seen and even over the distance the doorknob and latch did not remotely resemble anything he had ever looked at. Before his mind could think else, he heard Maria calling his name. He turned and promptly exited the building. He glanced at the bones that had been lying in that exact spot for many years now and mentally marveled how very clean they were; other than a few rags of what looked to be nightwear of some sort;

they were almost surgically scrubbed of anything remotely resembling flesh. In that moment, even before the question could arise, his mind provided an answer: ants. Of course!

"Coming:" he yelled to Maria, then bending down, picked up the box of dirt and shovel and headed back upstairs; his mind more on what he'd just seen than what he intended to do next.

He entered the door on the bounce and put the sandbox down in its proper place. Next; he looked for Maria. He found her in what was rapidly becoming 'their' bedroom; she had a brush in her hand and she was brushing her hair; a cross, irritated expression on her face. He came over to her and leaning over; kissed her cheek. "What's wrong, pretty girl, what's got you so worked up?"

"Oh; it's my hair. It's got a tangle in it and I can't get it brushed out. Sometimes I almost hate it; it can be such a bother." With a cross expression on her face she once again started trying to brush out a tangle in her hair. He took the brush out of her hand, gently turned her around and began brushing her hair, starting just at the ends and then gradually working his way towards her scalp as he got each and every tangle worked out. In short order her hair once again hung straight and beautiful as before. She gave him a grateful smile; taking the brush from his hand she gave her hair a few more swipes and then dropping the brush onto the desk top; she quit.

"Tell me, beautiful one, if you hate it so much; why don't you cut some of it off?"

"Oh: she won't let me. I have to . . ." and her voice faded off into silence.

"You don't have to worry about her anymore; beautiful one. For one; you don't live with her and them anymore; you live with me. And I say that it's your hair and that you have a right to do with as you wish. I do admit you have the most beautiful hair I've ever seen.

But your hair would still be as beautiful if it was much shorter. That woman the other day; she didn't mean you any favors. But in one thing she was right; it do . . . I mean; it does give you headaches. Maybe not actual, but it does fuss you, and that's something I can see for myself. I'm thinking . . . maybe you need to talk to the police officer; Carol Donovan, the one who said that she was a licensed beautician before she became a police officer. Perhaps she could advise you on something shorter; something that wouldn't fuss you so much when you brush it. You might want to think it over. Alsos too . . . I mean, another thing is; you can keep the hair, and if you change your mind, you could have it made up into a wig."

"You won't mind?" she demanded anxiously.

"What I mind, mostly, is anything that upsets you; and this is one. One thing to remember is; it grew out in the first place. If you cut it off, it will grow back some day. Then, you'll be older and maybe have a different look on things. Alsos, too, you mights just like . . . I mean; you also might just like the 'new, shorter' so much that you'll never want to go back to the 'old, long'. All of these things are part of growing up; 'learning by trial and error' as my Da useta say."

Maria was kinetic. In a blink she was up and hugging Gee as if her life depended upon it and she covered his face and lips with passionate kisses; eight-year old style. He returned kiss for kiss and both were the happier for it.

It doesn't take long for the average child to get over things and Maria was no exception. Before many minutes passed, she was back to her usual sunny self. Gee watched her, timed her actions to what he imagined was going on inside her head, and once she was fully returned to her normal state of mind; he changed the subject.

"As you no doubt know; I just went outside to fill the cat box with fresh diggin's. What you don't know yet is; I found something that interests me. And maybe you for all I know; part of its pretty sad; the rest, quite interesting. If you've nothing else to do right now I'll take you down and show it to you. Some of its kind of bad; but it's not recent-bad so that might make a difference. One thing's important; we both gotta remember to keep it to ourselves; at least for the most part. Some of it I may have to tell Captain Taylor or maybe somebody else. But you must remember not to tell others; at least for right now." She nodded her head and looked very interested. In the next few minutes the two got ready, and then they headed out the door and down the steps, down to the ground where Maria had not yet been. He let her look around to see what there was to look at and then he took her over to where the skeleton lay.

"What's that?" she demanded. He understood that as young as she was; she very likely did not understand that around all of that bone laying on the ground, there was once a living, breathing, human being. Either male or female: which, he did not know, but being male himself he rather thought of it as being that of a man.

"That, dearest, is a human skeleton. That was once a human being; a human who walked and talked and did things much as we do. And some day in the far future; we both will no doubt also be a set of bones. Only I hope that ours are buried under the ground; which is very likely where we should put these just as soon as we get a chance. But until then; let's go inside: I just got that far when I heard you call my name and I came as fast as I could to see what it was you wanted. One thing . . . no; I won't say it. Come with me and I'll show you instead." She, more than interested, quickly followed.

The two walked in. He sniffed the air cautiously. Either he had gotten used to it, or the short time the door had been left wide open was enough for much of the stale odors to waft out the door and into the open air. Maria, her elbows akimbo, moved in almost jerky motions as she vainly tried to get it all into her eyes and head in one single glance. The pair continued on in.

It was much as he remembered; only more. Everything within the room spoke of wealth; not the marginal wealth that many people who thought themselves rich had, but absolute, "money is no object" wealth and the furniture, the tapestries and even the rugs on the floor spoke mute testimony to these truths being so. The odor he had first detected, returned, but to a lesser amount. He went over to the eastern wall and opened several windows that led to a very small outer space, a kind of private yard, that ended in a great block wall that stretched upward as far as he could see from the inside. The great door on the other wall interested him for reasons he couldn't quite grasp. His 'meller should have been working at critical mass but for reasons he couldn't imagine; it was quiet. Perhaps it, too, was overwhelmed by all the surroundings. The pair, having gotten their fill of this part of the place for the moment, went westward to the furthest wall when the mysterious door stood.

He eyed the door. It had a sort of combination lock on it, but not one he had ever seen. Instead of a knob to twist and turn, there was a lever and a keypad of sorts, with a total of ten buttons on it. Clearly, one had to punch the proper buttons in the proper order to get the door to open. He tried to turn the lever in the off-chance it had been left in the open position but it was not to be. It was, In its own way, more perplexing than even a safe. He stared thoughtfully into the insides of the devise and could make no sense out of them. There did seem to be a reset button on the bottom. While peering deep into the devise he pushed the button down. An inner plate moved forward, evidently to press any wrong button back; along with all of the right buttons; of course.

It took him considerably longer than it had ever taken him to crack a standard safe. The first correct number he found was 5. That one seemed to be solid. He pressed other numbers in the proper sequence, having to reset at each failure. In time he found that 5 and 4 stayed in place; until he pressed yet another wrong number. Then he had to start over. The next number was a zero. Now he had 540 before he was again rerouted to start all over. The next number he found was a 3. And finally, he managed to locate a 1. That turned out to be the magic number. Pushing 54031 would get him in the door, and it had to be those exact numbers and in that exact sequence or it was no-go. By the time he was done; he decided that this crazy door was far harder to crack than any safe he'd ever come across.

But in time, he made all of the right choices, and in the right sequence, and seeming to almost be magic, he was able to at last twist the lever on the door and walk in.

He was, of course, far too young to have ever walked into a modern store, but if he had ever done so, he would have recognized many things. There were shelves along the four walls that lined the room as well as free-standing shelves lined up along what would have been thought of as middle aisles. And each and every such had something on it. Boxes of canned goods of one sort or other, from soup to nuts, more boxes of yet other boxed items like breakfast cereal; both canned meats as well as every kind of canned vegetable one could imagine as well as other food stuffs. One whole end wall was lined with glass fronted containers that held guns and other weapons including, but not limited to: rifles; shotguns; hand guns; as well as ammo from the lowly .22 rim fire on up to the biggest shotgun shells. As well as archery equipment both in standard bows as well as cross bows and the like; and even what might be thought of as pygmy blowguns. Knives and swords and great swords lined yet another end wall. If it was a weapon that could be used against an enemy or something that could be both stored for a long time and be eaten: it was there.

One entire corner was dedicated to medicines; from basic bandages to surgical equipment. Another area nearby was dedicated to supplements in the way of vitamins, minerals and other such. And salt. That caught his eye. From what everyone had said, salt was unobtainable, but here before him was salt in every form; from small salt shakers one might find on a picnic table to entire salt licks that farmers would have out for their livestock. It was all there; and more besides; he couldn't even begin to take in. Maria stood beside him, and perhaps the greatest miracle of all, since the two had stepped into the room; she hadn't said a word. Neither had he; now he considered it. He walked over and picked up a medium-sized salt shaker; the kind that has a flipable cap that both permits salt to flow out as well as seal it up to prevent leakage. He turned and taking Maria by the hand he moved both outside and closed the door. Just as an afterthought, he tried to reopen the door but it wouldn't consider it. An instant later he recalled the door knob on the other side. He mentally tried turning the knob and in the next moment the door swung open. He turned to Maria; "Y'know, sweets, sometimes I'm just too smart for my own good."

The two returned to their upper apartment and when Maria had done all the things she thought she needed to do, the pair of them clasped hands, and in the next instant both were standing in their usual spot. He mentally checked for people nearby; finding no one, they moved out and started heading towards Forrester's Groceries.

They walked through the door. The place was busy, almost crowded compared to what it often was, and both Mr. Forrester and William looked to be both pressured as well as frustrated. Both saw him almost the same instant. The two, waving off a number of persistent folks, headed their way.

"Gee; I gotta tell ya;" Mr. Forrester began, "It's turning into a nightmare. They want salt; they demand salt; and if I don't give them some salt they're going to tear my building down." Another man, overhearing the grocer, began to yell that he wanted some salt and somebody better give it to him right now or he was going to . . . Gee gave vent to a primal scream that stopped everyone in their tracks.

"*You is about the stupidest bunch of apes I ever see,*" he yelled at the people milling before him. "*You got the mentality of a turnip. Don't you knows anything? Mr. Forrester buys his produce from farmers. Not always the same farmers; dependin' on who's got what. The food grows in the ground. And not the same ground; dependin' upon which farmer is selling. You gots that much? Good. Next thing is; not all ground is the same. Some ground is dirt that's been dirt for thousands of years; some from dirt only a few hundred years. But at one time, all dirt was under water. And the oceans of the world have salt. If one piece of ground has more salt innit, the foods gonna have more salt innit. An' if the groun' has less salt, the foods gunna have less salt. Mr. Forrester gots nothing to do with which farmer grows what food on where piece of ground; he just buys what they brings and then tries to sells to you stupid apes what don't know from up. And then you not only blames him for suthin' he can't control, you threaten to tear his place up. Then! Where you gunna buy you foods tomorra? What then? Stupid bunch of apes! An' I knows this is true, 'coz my father was P'fesser Evansen at the college before it was destroy; and he tol' me so."* He glared freely around the place at everyone with no regard for sex, race or age. The people began to look at each other and mutter under their breaths. "I remember Professor Evansen; I took some of his classes." "He was a smart man; Professor Evansen." Others began to hang their heads in shame.

"You better hang you head. You; you just turn that fruit stand over; bend you back and pick them apples back up and puts 'em where's they belongs. You two; gets youselfs over there and gets those other boxes back where they 'pos'tbe; and then goes over to Mr. Forester and 'pologize for bein's such stupid asses. I MEANS NOW; FOOLS!" he bellowed at the top of his voice.

At first slowly and then with increasing speed people began to put the shop back to where it was before they began their riot. Then, with heads hung in shame, they apologized to Mr. Forrest, to William and finally to Gee before they slunk off; were they dogs, every single one of them would have had a tail tucked between their legs. In a short period of time it was only the four of them in the shop; the two who worked there; Gee and Maria.

"I'm awful sorry, Mr. Forrester," Gee began; but Mr. Forrester shook his head and waved his apology down. "Please don't; Gee. And I don't actually blame them. Partially, it was my own fault. I wanted to help them so I put more salt into the food that I actually should have. I should have known better, but . . ." and Gee waved him down. "Tell you what; instead of blaming ourselves or even each other, let's blame the one who is actually responsible. The Devil. He brought about this war, he deliberately put people in trouble, killed off many millions of people, turned cannibals loose upon many cities and has done everything else to cause trouble. Let's do what the angels do and just put the entire mess into God's hands and let Him take care of it. M'da tol' me 'bout th' devil and the terrible things he's done. All we can do is our best and let God sort out the rest." "Amen" Mr. Forrester said. Gee turned to Maria and with a polite wave over his right shoulder he headed out the door and towards the police station and Captain Taylor. He only had a few minutes before he would stand before that man and he had absolutely no idea how he was going to start this specific conversation; much less end it.

The pair walked towards the main building that housed the police station as well as the Courthouse and a number of other allied groups. The two of them walked in through the front door and turned right, headed towards the police station. They walked through the door; the first person they saw was patrolwoman Carol Donovan. She, spying them waved and called their names. In a blink at least half of the people in the room turned to look at them and several promptly headed their way. They, in turn, headed towards Carol. The two females met somewhere in the middle and both hugged each other. Gee stood back and smiled. A moment later it seemed that half the people in the room descended upon them; and Captain Taylor was not the last one in the group. "We've been wondering what you two have been doing," the Captain boomed jovially.

"Tryin' to stay out of trouble," Gee admitted; "only problem is; trouble won't stay out of us. We no sooner turn a corner and there it is again."

"So I just heard. I just got off the phone with Mr. Forrester. He gave me an earful of what you did and said over at his place. I have to admit; I'm most impressed. He said by the time you finished yelling those idiots down; they all slunk out of his place with their tails tucked between their legs. You must tell me your side of the story."

"Can do;" he admitted. But before we can do that, we have a minor problem we're hoping you can help us with. Or more specifically; that Carol can help with." And he nodded at the policewoman and smiled. She, looking startled, stared at him. "It kind of started with the other day, when that woman came at Maria with the scissors, wanting to cut all of her hair off. Only thing is; she was holding them like she was going to stab with them. In any case; she was yellin' about headaches, and as it turns out, she was almost right. It doesn't actual give Maria a headache though; more like a pain in the butt. I came up on her this morning; trying to brush out a snarl in her hair; she wasn't at all happy. It turns out that she doesn't specifically want her hair all that long; it was that woman who wanted it. And Maria thought I did too. But what I want most; is she's happy. We talked it over and decided that she should talk to Patrolwoman Donovan and get her slant on things; see what would be best for her face and everything; that sort of stuff. Are you willing to do that?" he asked her, turning her direction as he spoke.

"I would love to do that for her," Carol admitted. "She really does have the most gorgeous hair I've ever seen; it would be an honor and a privilege to cut her hair."

"Then why don't you take her in hand and do what the two of you think is best. No matter what you do with her hair, she will still be Maria; and that's the part I love most. One other thing though; I don't want her hair left lying around; I want all of it back. Partly because it's part of her and mostly because I don't want to see some other woman walking down the street with Maria's hair on her head."

As it turned out, once the main troublemaker had been taken from that specific salon, they were a stylist short. Carol had done such a fine job on the one woman she finished up that she was offered a job. Since police work wasn't full-time for her; that worked out to be a win-win solution for everyone involved. And it wasn't that far of a walk and the weather was nice and best of all, Carol had a few hours in-between she could use. The two walked out, hand in hand, headed south towards where the salon was. Gee watched the two go and it was almost like a part of him was leaving with her. How could one small girl get so totally intertwined in his mind that even watching her leave for an hour or so was almost more than he could bear? He did not understand. He turned to Captain Taylor; maybe if he got busy doing something else; time would pass more quickly.

Captain Taylor looked down at Gee and nodded his head. "If you've some time, I've got some things I want to talk to you about; some things I really *need* to talk to you about." Gee nodded; this might be the exact thing he needed to turn the conversation into the direction he wanted. Captain Taylor turned and headed back into his office, closely followed by Gee. Captain Taylor closed the door behind Gee, then walked over and sat down at his desk and stared. And realized he had no way of knowing how to ask the questions so important to him at the moment; he didn't even have a clue where to start. Gee stared at the Captain and he stared back. The few moments seemed to stretch into millennia.

"You ever heared about a man named 'Ed-grr Ca-see?" Gee asked, trying to start the conversation out in the direction he wanted to pursue.

"Oh; absolutely," Captain Taylor said joyfully, grateful for someplace to at least start talking. "Edger Cayce was a brilliant man; known as 'the sleeping prophet'; why, many of the things he came up with and did have never been explained." He started to say more; but Gee held his hand up.

"You knowed him; met him, talked to him sometimes," he asked quickly.

"Absolutely not; I'm not that old, young man, he was dead long before I was ever born."

Gee stared at the Captain, confusion in his mind, then a thought came to him. On the Captain's desk lay a truly ancient piece of blackboard and several pieces of chalk. With paper becoming scarce; he had gone to these things to write messages. This way, with a single swipe of a cloth the words were gone, and there was no paper waste. Gee reached out, picked up the slate and chalk and carefully lettered the word 'Case.' He turned the slate around so Captain Taylor could easily read it.

"Case"; Captain Taylor read, a blank expression on his face for just a moment. Then, like sunlight coming out from behind a cloud, he broke into a broad smile. "Eddy Case! That's who you mean. Yeah; I knew him; virtually everybody knew him. He was the richest old boy I've ever met, but talking to him, you'd never know it. He never talked over anyone's head; was always down to earth about everything. One thing about him though; he was a mono-conversationalist when it came to "end of the world" kind of thing; all he could do was go on about that someday, someone, was going to push the button and we were all going to be blown to hell. He was one of the original 'preppers;' always blithering about how we needed to stock up and get ready because . . ." and he stopped and stared Gee in the face. "Is there any particular reason we're discussing this right now?"

"Maybe;" he admitted. "I thinks I met Mr. Case this mornin'; din't have much to say, tho. Just some bones lying peaceful. And I hope you understand most carefully; you most definitely must not mention this to anyone. Anyway's; I thinks he sent you this." He handed Captain Taylor the item he had picked up earlier when he was in the second room. The bottle was labeled; "HIMALAYAN PINK SALT; FINE" and below that it said, "net wt 17.6 OZ". Captain Taylor looked at the bottle in his hand, read the label and tears began to run down his face.

"Son; you've just saved my life. My wife of many years suffers from a weak heart and is not expected to live much longer. Her main problem, according to every Doctor I've spoken to, is; the heart is a potassium/ sodium pump and it cannot function without those two things; along with a bunch of others; of course. And with salt in such short supply her heart is slowly weakening, to the point where at some time in the future, it will stop altogether."

"This goes no further than betwixt the two of us," Gee said, "but I know where a considerable amount of salt is. Not near enough to provide every man, woman and child in the city with enough to last their lifetimes; obviously. But enough for some; and for the near future, what lies beyond that, is in the hands of God. Or whatever; I'm not sure what I believe when it comes to God. Then again; I'm only about 10; what do I know about anything? What I suggest is; stick that someplace where folks can't see it and go home for a short while to check on you wife; people will understand that. Take a generous sprinkle on the palm of her hand and let her lick it up; then give her a glass of water to drink. Wait awhile and do it again; but not too soon, 'cause it might make her sick. I doesn't know what that other word you said is; maybes if you spells it out for me. One thing I can say is; Mr. Case most definite practice what he preach; I be a finder, and I finded the mother lode that I think maybe-so he left behind. May be right; may be wrong; I just play it by ear and see what falls out of the pockets."

Captain Taylor nodded his head. He grabbed his coat, stuffed the salt into an inside pocket and instead of putting the coat on, he folded it over his left forearm and headed for the door. Gee followed him out of his office. "I'll be back when I return," Captain Taylor called out over his right shoulder as he exited the office and headed down the hall. Gee looked around, found an old magazine of sorts and sat down and started reading. Ever since meeting up with Maria, he was wanting more and more to learn how to read. And it often didn't matter what; he was very slow in his reading but it was getting easier for him; almost every day now, and he was beginning to understand words he had never heard before just because of how they were used within the sentence. He progressed. Slowly, it is so, but progressed none the less.

He was perhaps half-way through his second page or maybe on his third when Patrolwoman Donovan came through the door; and with her was a young girl, absolutely the most beautiful girl he had ever seen. Somehow; she looked familiar but he couldn't quite put his finger on it. Then, in a blink, it came into focus. "Maria?" he asked in astonishment as he slowly got to his feet. He didn't know if the cut was considered a 'pixie' or 'elfin' or what; but it was quite short, came up, covered part of her ears from the front and then swooped down, backwards and then up. Between the hair and the face; she looked like a very young angel God had sent down to live among men, that they could admire her and understand exactly what awaited them on the other side, if they would only just behave and do what they were supposed to and not what they thought they wished. He dropped the magazine to lie on the floor, unloved and unwanted, and moved towards Maria.

Carol Donovan was watching Gee's face carefully. As different emotions played freely across his face; she began to clap her hands softly while laughing aloud; "Oh Gee," she said in absolute delight, "the expression on your face is worth everything!" She laughed and again clapped her hands. Gee paid the woman no attention; his mind and eyes were on Maria; that was the only thing he was interested in because she was the only one that mattered. A moment later the two met in the middle and hugged each other as if there would be no tomorrow.

In time the two got their emotions under control. Gee walked around Maria repeatedly, staring at each and every hair and line on her head and face. "I just loves it; Maria," he admitted. I gots to admit, did you comes back with no hair at all; not even you eyebrows and eyelashes, I would have still loved you because you is the girl I adores. But this; this is so much better than I could have dreamed." He again took her in his arms and, giving her a quick kiss on the lips, again began to cuddle her as if his life depended upon it. As for her; she was a very happy little lady. Females are often unsure if what they do will be well with the males in their lives and for a male to react as positively as Gee did was confirmation to her mind that she had done right; and at the moment that was what she needed most.

Carol brought a plastic bag over and handed it to him; he looked inside. He saw three smallish braids almost the full length of Maria's hair, each braided up in threes. "I did it this way because it's the most efficient way of doing it, and should you ever change your mind, they can each be turned into a wig. I know of many women who would almost kill to have hair as beautiful as this; but I also understand how you feel about her. You wouldn't believe all the wails and screams that were sounded when people learned that they couldn't have them or even buy them at any price." Gee nodded to the police woman and thanked her, then turning, curled his arm around Maria's trim waist and almost head to head the pair walked out of the precinct and headed back to their own home.

They swung by Forrester's. On the way in they had averted a riot at the grocer's store; now they both wanted to see how things were going as well as picking up some groceries for their own use. They stepped into the store; within moments first William and then Mr. Forrester spotted them. The store was almost empty at the time and both men came over to the pair. Both men looked at Maria and marveled at how nice her hair now looked. As almost waist-length hair; it was beautiful, but as it was now, it was far more fitting a young girl and Maria actually looked older than she was; which pleased her; thank you very much. The two did their shopping and Maria made her usual raid on his apples. Again, Gee tried to pay for their purchases and again the grocer turned them down. "I'll keep trying to pay you because I don't know how long that salt will last;" he admitted to Mr. Forrester. He, in turn, nodded his head.

"Considering what you did for me this morning; you may never have to pay for anything in here again. And that doesn't begin to take in account the time you saved those three from stealing my cash. Speaking of which . . . have you heard the latest on them?" Gee looked up at the grocer and shook his head. "From what I've heard, the three of them had one heck of a fight and Arvin took off and hasn't been seen since. And that's not all. Believe it or not, the other two showed up at the work center and asked for jobs. It turned out that they desperately needed some new help and despite the Brandon's bad record; they gave them a chance and put them to work. And here's the most amazing part of all. They turned out to be top workers and they've already moved out of being just laborers and are being trained in techniques that will enable them to oversee others. Who'd of thought it; the Brandon's being that ambitious! I wonder what got into them; wonder why they changed so."

"Arvin always was the bad apple of the bunch," Gee said. "I expect the other two finally figured it out for themselves and just kicked him out. And I'm glad that they're making something of themselves. I don't think the two of them were actually all that bad; it was just that Arvin was rotten to the core and as long as they kept listening to him; they couldn't be what they should have been all long."

The pair, their arms filled with their purchases, headed towards home. The moment they cleared the next corner, Gee triggered the impulse within him and in that same blink, they were inside their own apartment. A moment later a tiny voice began to meow, quickly followed by a second and then a third. They were home.

The two moved over into the kitchen area, nearly tripping over a different frantic kitten with every step. The three animals had, almost in a single day, gone from skittish kitties to little furry animals that so wanted to be underfoot and paid attention to, that from the moment the humans came in, they were almost a danger. That, too, was just part of being a pet owner. Or being owned by a pet. Sometimes; Gee wasn't sure of which was what.

Gee got his arms empty and everything put where it belonged. Then; he cleaned the cat box of flushable objects and got their food and water dishes taken care. Next, because he was nearly as hungry as his furry little friends thought they were, he got busy stuffing food in his own face.

Then; he got busy with Eddie. He walked down to ground level and went over to where his bones still lay; in the same spot and position they had laid for more than eight years; since the bombs had fallen. He still didn't know for sure what actually happened, but he had since learned that all of the apartments were heated by electricity while others also had natural gas as a supplemental heating supply. Natural gas was considerably cheaper to heat with, but it had the distinct disadvantage that if any of the gas lines were ruptured, it would flood the home, or the immediate area with gas. Gee didn't know if natural gas was poisonous or would simply displace oxygen; in either case the result would be death. And from the position of the bones and since the door was partially open, it seemed that asphyxiation from one direction or another was the most likely cause. It might well also explain the distinctly unpleasant scent he had detected earlier. The one thing that he did know for sure; all natural gas lines had long since been shut off because so many lines had been ruptured there was no practical way of plugging just some of them so others could again be used.

He went off into the small private lawn that lay just to the east of the building and after an hour or so of digging and plying a pick to loosen thing up, he dug a respectable hole. He then went and picked up all of the bones. Rather than trying to lay them out in any semblance of order, he packed them all into a large pillow case. Once all had been stuffed therein and the case carefully tied off with some twine, he gently and as reverently as he could, laid them into the bottom of the hole and filled it back in. He poked around in the house a bit. He found a very large ceramic plate that was once used to bake turkey on. He placed it on end and used that as a tombstone for Eddy. He often talked to God about one thing or another but didn't actually know how to pray; so he just quietly bowed his head awhile and then softly left.

Chapter 9

The next few days passed quietly by. He and Maria made several visits to Eddie's place. After getting more used to the scent that seemed to linger on, they found increasing reason to stay down there. For one; it was far better supplied with foodstuff and other things necessary for life. And that didn't begin to match the simple fact that not only was it more than twice the size of the upper apartment; it was far more luxurious in every way. And, yes, it also had electric heat as well as the gas that no longer worked and also stoves and a big-screen TV that the two were becoming increasingly enchanted with as well as even more DVDs; there were many reasons to make the trip. The old man had not only been exceedingly wealthy; he was also very intelligent, and had laid up for his future, everything he could possibly imagine.

The three kittens had never been below the third level. Evidently; they had been born up there, and then for unknown reasons their mother had either abandoned them before they were actually old enough, or more likely, had been nabbed by one of the hawks or owls that flew through the area every now and then. After the humans had made several trips back and forth and had started staying down there longer; the three little animals, of their own volition, chanced it and with a few cautious starts, finally made it all the way down to the ground floor; and promptly went berserk. There were more bugs, birds and other crawly things than they'd ever imagined; every one of which required their undivided attention. The one thing Eddy had not stocked up on was animal food; for either cats or dogs. The upper apartment held more than enough cat food to get the three animals out of kitten hood and into adult. After that; Gee wasn't sure. One thing they had noticed was that the little animals were true omnivores; they would eat almost anything; be it living or dead; vegetable, animal and perhaps even mineral. The last they weren't sure of, but from the way the little animals would eat; they weren't about to bet against it.

Once again their supply of fresh food was running low. And that meant especially apples; a thing Maria was not pleased with. Early one morning, after they'd gotten all of their needed things done, Gee slipped several more Sacagawea rolls into his pouch as well as a roll each of dimes and quarters and then with a quick glance around, they jumped over into their usual spot; turning right, to the west, they headed out towards Forrester's groceries.

They walked down the length of the block, turned towards their right and took several steps. Several street punks spotted them. Nudging each other with their hands and elbows, they walked up. "You got salt. We want salt. Give us some salt. Now;" the leader of the group demanded, a mean, threatening expression on his face.

"I has no salt," he said truthfully. "The onlyest things I gots is what I finds. I goes inter different buildings and looks around. Sometimes I finds stuff. Sometimes it be somethin' to eat; sometimes it be somethin' I can trades. But it be just what I finds; like in that building over there;" and he nodded at a partial building not far away. Before the punks could think, he looked at the building again. "Say; I've never looked in that one afore! I wonders what's inside it; maybe something I can sells." He started to walk that way but the leader of the group stopped him.

"You ain't goin' anywhere's" he growled. "See to it he don't leave; I'll take a look." He headed out that direction with determined step. Gee thought of the room back where he now lived; thought of the blocks of salt that farmer's and rancher's used for their livestock. In a blink he put one of the saltlicks just inside the front door; in open sight where the punk was sure to see it. He waited. The boy cleared the front door and went in. For a few seconds there was total silence and then the boy yelled ecstatically; "Salt! I's found some *salt!*" He came out the door, the salt block in his hand and he waved it around; all but insane with his find.

"Hey; some of that is mine, it was my idea after all," Gee yelled. In that instant, everyone within hearing locked onto what was happening and without exception, all of them headed that way; yelling at the top of their lungs. The boy took one horrified look around him and did perhaps the only smart thing he had done all day; if not in his entire life. He lifted the block of salt up and slammed it against a rock right in front of him. The salt block shattered. In the next instant, he snatched up all the biggest chunks he could grab and turning on his heels, took flight. The rest of the boys pounced on the fragments that were left lying on the ground, and in a moment or two, another half-dozen or so youth were scrambling manically about, snatching up everything they could possibly grab, from the ground as well as from each other; all the while screeching at the other to go away and that it was theirs. For a few brief moments, pandemonium reigned supreme; and in those few moments Gee took Maria's arm and both slipped away while yet others came running, trying to grab up even a few shards of the precious stuff.

The two slipped off quietly while behind them bedlam was being enacted; along with all the noise and violence that often occurs at times like these. They cleared the end of the block and Forrester's was directly ahead of them. They walked in.

The store was basically empty; only Mr. Forrester and William were in there and both were busily restocking the bins and shelves to get ready for their next onslaught of customers. One of them lifted his head, spotted the two and nudged the other. In the next moment they both quit what they were doing and came on over; broad grins on their faces. "We sure are glad to see you two;" Mr. Forrester said; "It's been several days now; where have you two been keeping yourselves?"

"Ah; you know how it is with newlyweds," Gee said with a smile; "just taking out a little time to get to know each other; our likes and dislikes: that sort of thing. How're things going with you two?"

"Not bad; not bad at all. We, ah, are having a bit of a problem with those coins. Ever since people have learned that we have even a few of them they've been after us non-stop for more. I don't suppose . . ." the two men looked at Gee with hopeful expressions on their faces. He reached into his pouch and pulled out not only two more rolls of the golden dollars but also a roll each of dimes and quarters. Both men broke into broad, relieved smiles. "Still a step ahead of us; as always," William admitted. Mr. Forrester got into his till and brought out the proper amount in paper bills and handed them to Gee. He took the money and stuck it into his pouch. Even as he did so, his hand appeared right next to a photograph of someone's parents and a moment later blinked back out, leaving yet more paper money lying next to the picture.

"I really don't know how to start this, Mr. Forrester and William, but at time I can see things, know things that are impossible for me to see or know. For example; were either of you carrying a gun, for example, under your clothes; I'd be able to see it; as clearly as if you had it outside your clothes. And sometimes I just know things; again, something I shouldn't be able to know. Also; at times I can do things that I'm quite sure other people cannot. And I don't know why. I also remember things that seem to be impossible, in hindsight, yet I'm sure that the memory is true." He was about to add more, but at that exact moment, several customers came in through the door. From their actions and the words they spoke between them, they were in a hurry and not willing to wait for a small, ten-year old boy to relate whatever it was he wanted to say. Gee sighed, nodded to the two men and then turning, walked out the door holding hands with Maria.

It was still fairly early in the day. The two of them, almost independent of each other, decided to go over to the police station. Gee was quite interested in Chief Taylor's wife and how she was doing and Maria definitely wanted to talk to Carol Donovan; perhaps something to do with her hair, but more likely, just girl talk. The weather was nice and Instead of jumping like he often did, the two just walked hand in hand and soon enough the pair walked up the steps; tuned to their right and paced down the hallway and into the police department. A number of heads turned at the movement of the door; next a voice called out for Captain Taylor. Again; they were once more among friends and it is a fact of life that one cannot have too many friends.

Carol Donovan, Maria and several other female officers got themselves into a small group and within moments, were animatedly discussing things interesting to the female mind. Gee, quickly lost amid the multiple voices, took one look at Captain Taylor, who stood watching him, an amused expression on his face. "Need rescuing?" the Captain asked, laughing softly.

"Yes;" Gee said, in quiet desperation, "please; and the sooner the quicker." Captain Taylor nodded his head, knowingly, and gestured Gee towards his office. Gee glanced quickly at Maria; she was now surrounded by female officers and off to one side, several more were headed her way. She would be more than pleased to be able to spend time among others of her sex; Gee nodded his head and started out in the direction indicated. In the next moment, Captain Taylor slipped in behind him and the two escaped into the safe, and sane quietness of his office. Captain Taylor closed the door behind him and in that instant the babble of female voices abated considerably.

The two turned and looked at each other. Captain Taylor stared at Gee for a moment, took a deep breath of air and released it. "I'm not sure I can actually explain this, Gee, but I'm going to give it my best shot. My wife has what is called 'arrhythmia'. This is a very irregular beating of the heart. Where a normal heart does what is often called 'lub-dub, lub-dub, lub-dub', her heart was skipping beats; kind of a 'lub-dub, lub. . . dub, lub-dub, . . . dub.' I know that's not much help but that's the best I can explain. What this means is that her heart was failing; because of lack of salt more than anything else. Almost from the exact moment I sprinkled salt on her hand like you told me, and she had licked it up, her heart has returned to a more normal rhythm. Now it is no longer skipping like it used to and she has far more energy; she can get up and do things that she couldn't a week ago. And I can't begin to thank you enough. I'm almost ashamed to say this next, but while the salt you gave me is going to last her awhile, I don't know what I'll do when it runs out. And I'm scared to ask more of you than you've already given."

Gee nodded his head; "I understands," he admitted. Then he told the Captain exactly what had happened on his way to Forrester's; from the moment the street punks stepped out and threatened them, to the point where the one threw the salt down in a blind panic and grabbed up what he could and ran. "The thing is, Captain, people are desperate for salt and I'm not sure what's best to do. I now actual have a lot of salt I know where is. But my problem is; how do I get it into folk's hands without getting in the middle of it? For a while, I thought of slipping Mr. Forrester some that he could sell a little at a time; also, thought of fixing you up so you could give it out to folks. Being police, they wouldn't be likely to try and mob you. Now; since this latest thing happened, I think maybe I'll just start leaving some salt out in the ruins; a little here, a bit over there; and so on. This way; people will get the idea that maybe they'll be able to find it instead of rioting and causing problems for others. But the one thing I have no control over is; sooner or later it will be all used up. And I'd be the biggest fool on Earth, did I give out every bit of salt I have and not save back enough for myself and Maria. And you and your wife; of course."

"Thank you for that last; Gee" Captain Taylor said softly. "And I wasn't aware that there was that much salt around anywhere; at least not locally. If we could get the idea across to people that there might be salt in some of the abandoned and damaged buildings, that might well take a great deal pressure off of many things around here;" he admitted.

"What we might be able to do," Gee said, "Is have two patrol officers talking about it; one explain it to the other that somebody found an entire salt lick in one of the buildings. The other officer can pretend they've never heard about it and start asking questions. They can talk back and forth about different places to look; also talk about being careful: some of these buildings are not the safest places to go. Which is yet another problem; sooner or later, someone is going to go where they shouldn't. Some floor is gonna collapse; or a wall or some other such and someone's going to get hurt and maybe even killed. People will have to take every care. I've been doing this for at least three or four years and they's been time I've actual scared the water out of myself. But I always kept from panicking and managed to think myself out of the problem; whatever it was. And from my place; I need to make sure I don't leave salt anywhere that would be dangerous for someone to try and get. The salt lick I left for that first jerk was right in the middle of the floor; almost as soon as he opened the door. If he hadn't been such a schmuck, he would have been suspicious, it was so obvious. But he went crazy and came ripping out the door, waving it about, yelling at the top of his voice. He still got away with the most of it; I bet."

"I'll bet he did too;" Captain Taylor admitted. "Gee, there's some things I've wanted to ask you for quite a while; wanting to, but almost afraid to because I don't ever want to make you mad at me or do or say anything that would offend you. You've done so very much for me in particular and the entire department that I'm afraid of making you angry."

"Wull; in the first; I don't believe there is anything you can do or say to make me mad. For one, I don't get mad at people very often. I understand that people are human and that means that whiles we are mostly alike; we're also different. That means that none of us are the same, which also means that what's good for one, may not be good for another. So what we need mostly to do, is find a place where we all can meet in the middle and can win in some ways and maybe-so lose in yet other ways; but in ways that both sides feel that their gains are better than their losses. Once we can agree on a few things, then try and make the rest work at least part of the time; then mostly, we both sides win."

"I'm not sure if I followed all of that, Gee, but for the most part, I agree;" Captain Taylor admitted, a slightly puzzled expression on his face as he tried to figure out exactly what Gee had just said. "The thing is . . . and I'm a bit nervous even asking you this . . . exactly what happened back at that house? You told me you can see things that other people cannot. Then you found that hidden room; which, by the way, is still unknown as far as I know. I put Officer Trent and his wife in that house. The place they lived in was marginal, at best, and the rent they were being charged was a shame. If so many buildings hadn't been lost in the bombing the owners of that flop would be tossed in jail for putting such up for rent; and especially at those prices. To put a point on it; I'm convinced that neither of them are remotely aware of that hidden room; I'm sure one of them would have mentioned it otherwise.

"We were down in that room, looking at everything. I started to say something about that safe we saw, sort of tongue-in-cheek, about 'Gee; if we only had some way of opening this', that sort of thing. The next thing I knew; you grabbed my arm, the door closed, the lights went out and we were both standing there in the middle of the floor. Then Maria and the other's came down and Officer Trent was cursing up a storm and we never did go back down there. Or did I just dream the whole thing? The more I try to understand it; the more confused I get."

"I think the best way to explain this is to pretend it's all something I once dreamed;" Gee began. "I tried to tell you this earlier, but something came up and we never got back to it. In any case, I 'dreamed' I was just a baby; only about a year and a half old. I was in bed, in my crib, and it was late. Mommy and Daddy and Sissy were already in bed and asleep. For some reason, I wasn't sleepy. Perhaps the best way of thinking it; I was aware on some level that something was going to happen, and I knew it, and was waiting for it. There was a smallish night light in my room and I was standing up in my crib, hanging onto the railing. I saw a small sliver of white floating through the wall of my room. Keep in mind, at that age I was not aware of the names of anything; I only have names for things now that I can apply to what I remember. Or think I remember. I'm not actually sure of which. And this all could easily be no more than just a dream.

"But in my dream - or whatever - I saw a sliver of white moving through the walls of my bedroom, up close to the ceiling, even though the ceiling. It came up to my door and the door opened. A man in white was standing there; smiling at me. He was very tall and very beautiful; his head touched the ceiling and his feet and knees were below the floor; almost like he was wading in water. He had wings; giant wings, the single sliver of light I had been watching earlier was the tip of one of his wings floating through the wall. He had four; two above and two below. He held out his arms to me; I floated out of my crib and came to him; he caught me and held me close. He talked to me but somehow I don't remember that his lips moved; but I understood him anyway. He said something bad was about to happen but he had been sent to keep me safe. Why; I don't know.

"We turned and went out of the bedroom, went to what would be my right, and headed out in to the living room. He found a place he liked and moved down onto his knees; his wings spread out and covered us up. A moment later I heard a noise. Somehow, now, I know that it was very loud; but then it was just a prolonged 'pop' and I now know that the roof and walls and other things were falling all around us. But I was with him and I wasn't afraid and I wasn't hurt. I just laid there in his arms and looked up at him and tried my best to talk to him. Somehow he seemed to understand me and talked back to me. About what; I don't remember. Baby stuff; I suppose. I don't think I ever fell asleep; at the same time, it didn't seem all that long when he said that he had to go and that it would be alright and someone was coming and that they would find me and keep me safe. Then he was gone; in a blink of an eye he was gone. And I started screaming for him; I loved him so and I wanted so desperately to be with him. Then a young girl climbed in through the wreckage of my home, found me and pulled me out. After that I don't remember much. And I still don't know if it was a dream or not. But he told me his name; it was . . . "

"Grey Bill."

Gee and Captain Taylor turned; each had been so engrossed in his story and memories that neither were aware of anything else around them. Now, it seemed almost everyone in the precinct was crowded into Captain Taylor's room and everyone was looking at Gee; it was Molly Trent who had spoken to him. "Yes;" he admitted; "but somehow that's not quite right. It sounded different and they was more to it. But how . . . thass it! I knowed you looked familiar firstest time I ever seed you; you was the girl what pulled me outta my house!"

Molly Trent nodded her head and dropped it; tears began to run down her face to fall one by one onto the wooden floor at her feet. Gee; without hesitation or thought, charged forward and wrapping his arms around her, buried his face up against her chest; the top of his head came just to below her chin. She hugged him in return and it was a toss-up as to whose hugs were the more emotional. While it seemed like forever for the two, it was a few short moments when she pushed Gee back a bit and looked down into his emerald green eyes. She stared for a few moments and then looked up into the sea of faces watching her.

"It was about noon the next day," she began; "I was out with a group of others, looking to see if we could find any survivors, as well as flagging any dead that we could find so emergency vehicles could find them and carry them off to be properly entombed. We were walking down this one street; in a residential district. Somehow, several of the bomb clusters must have gotten stuck together, or just happened to randomly hit next to each other, but the entire grouping of perhaps four city blocks were basically leveled. We were no more than half-way down this one section of street when all of a sudden a little baby began to squall. My God! What a set of lungs that little tyke had; we could have heard him a half-mile off; I'm sure of it. He was screaming for his Grey Bill.

"I've always been petite; small of body and frame and I was the only one tiny enough to squeeze between the fallen timbers to reach him. I found him in the middle of what had once been the living room; sitting upright in the center of the floor, with tears running down his little face. He looked right at me and once again squalled; 'Grey . . . Bill.' My God! He was loud! All around him were the ruins of what had once been the home he lived in; broken timbers, shattered glass, roofing tiles: you name it; all around him. Up to about five feet from him; then closer in was a circle you could have eaten off of; surgically clean; not shard of glass, not a piece of tile; nothing. And him! There wasn't a speck of dust *on* him! It was like he'd just been lifted out of his bath, dried and put into clean clothes; even his diaper was perfectly clean. And, people, this was the next day; about 14 hours after the bombs had fallen. I couldn't explain it then and I can't explain it now and for sure I'm not about to try. But that is what I saw and what I remember."

"But 'im name not Grey Bill;" Gee insisted passionately.

"No, dear, his name isn't Grey Bill. That's only what I thought you were trying to say. You were only a very small boy at the time and you couldn't actually talk very much. The name I think you were trying to say is 'Gabriel.' Does that sound more right?" Gee looked up into her face and nodded. "Thass it;" he agreed.

People began to look at each other and stir about. "Gabriel?" one voice asked softly; "the archangel Gabriel? No wonder he wasn't hurt."

"So; what happened next?" an interested voice asked Gee, specifically, and the room at large.

"Not actual sure;" he admitted. "I 'members bein' handed from one to another; eventual a siren comed up and someone else taken me. Ater that; it becomes a blur and then Momma and Poppa Evansen comed and 'dopted me and I was move into my new home; which is where I was 'til folk started disappearin' and things just went into the toilet there for a while. And now I'm here and I suppose we're trying to figger sum'thin out but I'm not sure I knows what. . . I mean, I'm not sure I know what;" and he gave a side-glance at Maria. She just grinned and whacked him on his shoulder with the tips of her fingers; he pretended to be injured.

"So; now what?" a voice off to one side asked rhetorically.

"Lendl Holmes," he replied. Numerous people stared at him, but for a moment, no one spoke.

"What about Lendl?" Captain Taylor asked cautiously.

"Not actual sure," he admitted. "Somebodies . . . I mean, someone asked a question and that was the first thing that popped into my head. Why; I don't know: but it did."

"In which case; somebody better go get him: you, you're it," and he gestured towards Patrolman Trent.

"Well; it's been nice knowing you," Patrolman Trent said; turning on his heel, he left. Gee; startled by the departing patrolman's words and expression, watched him as he walked out the door. People moved about; a number of them quietly eased out the door and returned to whatever they were supposed to be doing all along and before long; only he, the Chief, Maria and Molly Trent were still in the room. Time stretched out oddly as it has a habit of doing on occasions. Then the door was pushed open; Patrolman Trent walked in and before he even started to clear the doorway a second person loomed into view. The second one looked over the top of the first one's head and was clearly visible on either side and before Gee could fully adjust; patrolman Trent moved to one side and he was looking up at the largest man he had ever seen. He was so massive he looked as though he could challenge a gorilla to an arm-wrestling match . . . with every chance of winning. He was big. He looked at Chief Taylor; he in turn pointed at Gee. Lendl turned and looked at Gee; "Yes?" he said.

"You are Lendl Holmes; the same Lendl Holmes who called to find out about the noise a few days ago; noise that came from your southeast; as best as I recall." The big man nodded his head cautiously. "Did you ever find out what happened; what that noise was all about?"

"No I did not;" he exclaimed in indignation; "I asked about it later and they wouldn't tell me." Everything about him screamed resentment; Gee nodded his head.

"I might understand your feelings better than you know;" he admitted, "a lot of time, people won't tell me everything either.

"That's why I'm here now; I want to tell you about it; not only tell you but to ask your opinion; what you think. Are you interested?" The big man nodded his massive head, then turning, took two wooden chairs and placed them as close together as he could, turned and sat down in both of them. "They just don't build wooden chairs as good as they used to; do they?" he asked Lendl. The big man broke out into a massive grin and shook his head. "And they're building doorways smaller now; and desks and everything else you come across."

At this; Lendl began to laugh. "That's God's own truth;" Lendl said with a big grin; "and everything else has shrunk as well; especially other people." Gee nodded his head, and then turning to Captain Taylor, said, "We need to get some people on this, Captain, see if we can figure out why everything is shrinking around here." He, laughing, nodded his head.

Gee turned back to Lendl and without further ado, told the man almost everything; from when he awoke with the odd feeling that something had to be done but he didn't know what, until after the wall had fallen and killed Coldbrick. Lendl sat on the two chairs, his left elbow on one knee and his jaw against his knuckles as he did his imitation of Rodin's 'The Thinker.' Gee clearly explained about Coldbrick's obsession without mentioning the why. Again, because the man had been so erratic about his obsessions, no one paid any attention to that small omission. In the end, Lendl understood the whole nearly as well as if he had seen the entire thing with his own eyes. "You do give good reports, Gee, I've heard Capt. Taylor say that more'n once and I must agree. But how did you know that wall was going to fall? You pulled those two men back because you knew in advance;" his attitude was somewhat aggressive.

"There's a huge difference between 'knowing' and 'suspecting'. The wall looked faulty to begin with; I could clearly hear Mr. Coldbrick throwing bricks around. Or at least it sounded like brick hitting brick and he was the only one on the other side. Even more; a very large storm was coming from the southeast, as many storms around here do; and strong winds often come from that direction during a storm. Beyond that, there was a sort of niggle inside of my head that made me believe it was so. I don't know about anyone else, but in my case, a 'niggle' in my head is something I pay attention to; for one, it just won't leave me alone; and for two, I won't like what might happen if I don't pay attention. They's yet one more thing we needs to talk about, and that is you. I'm getting an overpowering niggle that you know something that we need terrible-bad and it's something you don't know you know yet, and something we don't know yet, but we need to get our thinkers together and work it out because they's some innocent lives at stake. How many's I dusn't know; but mor'n just one or two." He stared Lendl straight in the eyes and the man, so very much larger than he, backed down.

"Gee;" Lendl began; "I've no idea what you just said, but if there's anything I can do to help, it's already done."

Gee nodded his head. "Thing is, Lendl, there's nosy Parkers; and then there are Parkers who are nosy. I know that sounds like the same thing; but it's not. One of 'em is nosy because they want to know for bad reasons; to frame or black mail someone; among others. The other just wants to know because they has . . . have an in-quis-it-ive mind. That one word I got from my Da; sound impress but not sure I knows what it means. Bottom line; one is being nosy to cause trouble somehow; the other wants to know because they gots to know; like there's something inside them that is curious about just everythin' 'round 'em. I knows about the latter 'cause that's what I am; just gotta understand 'bout everythin'. An' I thinks you are one of the latter; same as me. What this means, if I'm not wrong, you know something you learned in the past; maybe even has notes on somthin' you doesn't even know you has. And what we gots to do is find out what it is and where it is and get it out to the place where we can use it because, people, we runnin' outa time and if we doesn't want everything blowin' up in our faces we gots to get off the ball. Or is that 'on the ball'? I'm not actual sure 'bout that."

"Do you have any idea exactly what that might be?" Captain Taylor asked politely.

"An idee; but not for sure. What be the thing that's the most and biggest problem 'round here right now? Salt! Nobody gots any and it's causin' all kinds a'ruckus 'cos of it. . . because of it. Sorry. Anyways; just as an aside; how long you been working for the police department; doing what you be doing right now; since after the bombs or before?"

"Actually; long before the bombs. My father was a policeman here some years ago. I used to come here with him when my mom was doing something else. I got interested in the records end of it. Despite my size; I've always been more interested in the intellectual part of it; records keeping, maintaining the ebb and flow of needed materials; that sort of thing. I really never got into the criminal end of records-keeping though; mostly it was supplies: anything from guns and ammo to uniforms to keeping track of different officers: work time tables: that sort of thing. And it's probably just as well; there for a while when I was in my early-teens I was about the size of the average police officer, but after I got my full growth, I was just too damned big to fit into the average police cruiser and many of the men didn't like riding with me; I took up too much seat-room; you see. And besides; I just always liked records more."

"Slowly; the pot comes to a boil;" Gee quoted quietly. "You were in records most of the time. And part of police records is, or probably is, records of different buildings around the city; around this specific part of the city since this department is part of this section of the city. And somewhere within your records should be the names and locations of different supply houses; houses that could contain anything from shirts to shoes to . . . wait for it . . . salt."

"Gee; you don't think . . . ?" Gee turned and stared Captain Taylor right in the eyes.

"It kinda fits;" he admitted; "there must have been large buildings built just to hold different kinds of supplies; anything from shoes to clothing to food stuffs to everything else people need to live: from apples to zucchinis: that sort of thing. But the problems is . . . are; where are the buildings and have they been destroy? Many of such buildings were built extra strong; to last many decades and not just a few years. And lots of 'em 'round here were built out of cement block and not metal walls; partially because they was a fairly large cement plant out on the edge of town what built such, and not only was the cement blocks stronger than metal walls, should something bad happen, it was in ways even cheaper in the long run. I don't know this from experience, but from what I heard my Da say, when he was talkin' to others about one thing or another."

Gee turned his attention fully on Lendl. "What we probably are looking for; would be some sort of supply house or depot: I'm not sure of the last. A place that would hold things until they were needed; a place where such things are kept. In other words; a supply point that may well be part of the information that a police station would logically know about. What is your opinion?"

Lendl sat quietly, thinking, gnawing on a knuckle of his right hand. He sat still for a few moments and then looked Gee in the eyes. "To tell the truth; I've no idea what you are talking about nor how to figure it out. But I do know that a great many storehouses were set up all over this city; most of them down in the middle of town, but also some were out in the suburbs, and even further out. And while I don't know where even half of them are . . . or were; I do know how to find out. Captain; is your monitor connected to our mainframe? If the information exists anywhere, it would be on our mainframe. Which I am proud to announce, is not only up and running, but I was in it and rummaging around when Officer Trent came and got me."

Captain Taylor got up from his seat, and moving to one side, gestured to Lendl. Fortunately for both Lendl and the Captain's chair; it was on the large side; Lendl easily fit in it as he sat. For a man of his dimensions and considering the size of his hands in general and his fingers, specifically, he was remarkably adept on a standard keyboard. In a moment his fingers were flying across the keys, clicking and clacking, and before long one warehouse after another popped up on the screen. A depressing number of these had a long line drawn through the middle of them. Yet others did not. "Exactly what are we are looking for?" Lendl asked Gee as he turned his head slightly that way.

"Salt, specifically, and I presume anything else of that sort would be greatly useful to a large number of folk;" Gee admitted. Lendl typed in 'spices' and hit 'enter;' a few moments passed by as the mainframe did its job and at first a few and then a torrent of different spices; including salt, as well as sugar which was also in short supply, began to flow across the screen. Before too much time had elapsed there were a number of addresses on the screen; addresses that were not lined out, and therefore, presumably still available. Gee turned and looked at Captain Taylor: "What about these; will these be of any help?" he asked politely.

"My God; Gee. I had no idea there were that many places, that close, that carried salt; much less all the rest of those things. Everything on the screen is either in short supply or can't be found anywhere. And yet you, and Lendl, in a few minutes; trot out an entire list of places. Even if half of these places no longer exist, and half of those which do still exist don't have anything left, that still leaves almost a dozen places to look. My hat's off to you, young man, to you and to Lendl. And a special thanks to you; Sir," and he gave a quick, shallow bow towards the big man sitting at his desk. He, in turned, nodded gracefully to his superior.

As petroleum gradually became harder to find and as science progressed, the internal working of rechargeable power supplies as well as the motors they propelled also increased. By this point in history, most people's cars and all of the government vehicles included, and specifically those of police stations everywhere; went electric. Where once such a vehicle needed to be charged often; sometimes more than once in a day, now they could run nearly a week on a single charge. And because of the batteries, or rather mega-capacitors, that now existed; a standard charge was good far longer than an old-fashioned gas tank would carry the driver and passengers. Lendl bowed out. In the first; because of his size, he scarcely fit inside of the newer cars, which were also smaller than their older counterparts. But more than that, this was moving over into police work, where his mind and desires lay purely in the academic.

The first place on the list wasn't far off. They got there in a very short period of time, but even before the five got out of the car, they could easily see that the place had already been ransacked. The door hung off of one hinge and had a battered look to it. One quick glance inside proved their first thought to be correct; other than a few scattered items and a great many overturned shelves, there wasn't anything there that required a second look. The next place on the map was just more of the same.

The third one on the list turned out to be a problem. They drove to the place listed; but could not find it. There was a battered old barn on the premises as well as the remains of what was once a farm house. And off a bit, what looked to be a rock wall. A wall that was somewhat secluded, and that requited a more round-about approach to what was ultimately a door that looked like it belonged in a bank, rather than out in the boondocks. The door hasp was the clincher; it was a lever, rather than a knob, and below the lever was a key pad with ten numbers on it. "Forget it," Officer Trent declared, "I've seen those before. No one can crack that code, and we'll need at least a diamond saw or drill and nitro to . . . ." He watched with disbelieving eyes.

Gee walked up to the door. Making no effort to hide what he was doing, he punched in 54031 into the keypad below and with a single press of the lever, the door easily swung wide open. "Well shut my mouth," Officer Trent sighed softly; "how in thunder did you do that?"

"I've seen one of these before;" he admitted. He pulled the door to him and they all walked in. The supply was intact. It was very much like the supply that lay in his place, but at minimum, ten times more, if not twenty. There looked to be everything that his own private supply held and yet so much more. The salt supply stacked up in one spot alone looked like it would supply the whole city, or what remained of it, for at least a few years to come. Perhaps by then the world would have become more normalized and the salt supplies of years before would once again be able to provide people with this most basic of all needs. The four of them began to look around and take stock of what they could. Chief Taylor and Patrolman Trent carried out as many cases of salt and other things they could stuff into the car's interior; including trunk and passenger compartment; and still leave room for people. Once they got the car packed with salt and other supplies, they all exited the room, and Gee carefully shut the door. As he had in his own place; he tried once again to open it but it wouldn't budge. Evidently; it had been designed to be used only once and then had to be re-entered in order to be opened again. Only; this door had no handle on the other side. They drove back to the precinct; some on-duty officers were radioed ahead so there were many willing hands there to help unload the boxes; all but two of them. These he set aside to be taken to Forrester's; he in turn could start selling the smaller-sized salt containers to everyone who wanted them . . . but only one to a customer. The rest of the boxes were to be broken up and left with yet other stores in the area that could sell such. It wouldn't be enough to entirely end the salt deprivation and panic among the people, but it would be a start, and in time people would begin to get used to the idea that salt was once more available for sale.

175

Chapter 10

Gee, Maria and several of the Patrolmen including Trent and his wife, got two of the smaller boxes of salt; and stuffing them into several of the patrol cars they headed towards Forrester's. As they arrived, several customers were walking out of the door, their purchases in their hands. He turned to them. "You might want to go back inside for just a few moments; something has just come up you just might be very interested in." The people stared at him, the Patrol people with him, and nodded; they and the rest returned back to the store; along with two cardboard boxes carefully carried by two of the Patrolmen. They walked inside.

Inside; Mr. Forrester and William were busy with one customer or another. As the group entered, the sound and shadows of their coming, turned every eye upon them. "If we can have your attention for just a moment;" Gee began; "we have some very welcome news for you. Working with the police and their computers; we have found a source of some salt. Before any of you get too excited; they's some set-backs. One; they's not cheap. Two; you can only have one shaker for each family; does you have six people in you family you only still gets one container . . . for now. Tomorrow; there should be more; and perhaps the day after. But they's not cheap. Was a time when salt wasn't worth hardly anything. But those days are gone; as are many peoples and buildings and a lot of other things. Do try and be civil about things and each family can buy one container. Start a ruckus and you'll get yourselves tossed out on your butts; if not arrested and thrown into jail. Mr. Forrester; if you will." And he backed up; showing the boxes that had just been carried in.

What followed next might be best described as a controlled chaos. People rushed forward, mouths going full, screaming that only one container wasn't enough and they had (however many) in their family and they needed (however much) more. Gee yelled even louder. "Peoples; this is all we gots . . . for now. Tomorrow's we'll have more. And prolly even more the next day. We has . . . have found a source of some salt. Nothing like it used to be, but enough to get us over this hump we are in. But we have to work together on it and not one person try to hog it all. After all; did we want anybody being pigs; we would have been the first pigs of all and just not told you anything. You, there, start a line right here; the price is two dollars for each package: pay Mr. Forrester for it. And, no, you can't buy two because you got a big family; or because you're just greedy. That, people, is why we have the cops with us."

Considering how badly people needed the salt and craved it, they were fairly civilized about it; a few tried cheating, getting a family member to break off and buy it separately, but Mr. Forrester knew his customers quite well and it quickly became obvious to even the dullest of them that wasn't going to work either. Before long; the two boxes were empty and those who came late were informed to try tomorrow. It wasn't much; but it was a start and slowly and then with increasing speed people in the area came to understand, that while the salt crisis hadn't entirely passed, it wasn't the crunch it had been either.

The next day Gee got some people and a moving van of sorts and went to the first place they had gone to the previous day. With a minimum of confusion and a bit of patience, they got most of the overturned shelving moved out to the barn found on the third place they had gone to. Gee, thinking it over, decided that if they were smart enough to look things up on the computer; others would as well. This way, should anyone come out to the third place, looking for stashed items; they would look inside the dilapidated barn and presume that this was yet another storage place that had been hit before they got there.

By the time a week was up; much of the crises had, if not exactly vanished, at least had calmed down to a quiet rumble. Now, most people in the area had at least some salt, and many had several containers; enough to last them at least a month. And that was far more than they had just a few days earlier. With this taken care of; Gee turned his attention to yet another of his problems. The place where he lived was more than just nice; but so far, the only way anyone could get into the place was how he did it, and there were now at least six very nice apartments that could be rented out. Mainly to the Police; Gee thought. The comment Captain Taylor had made the previous week, about the rental Patrolman Trent and his wife had to endure, triggered an entire thought sequence in his brain. If he could get the front part of his building cleared away, that would open up the apartments. And having police for next-door neighbors seemed to him like an idea whose time had come. He talked with Maria to get her thoughts on it. The thought that she might soon have some female-type neighbors, not to mention female-type that were closer to her age, rang a bell; she was more than interested.

The next morning the pair, once kittens were properly fed and catered to, again joined hands and in the next eye-blink were again standing in their favorite spot. As of one mind, the two headed off towards Forrester's produce. It was yet fairly early, the sun was out and shining brightly, early spring was upon the land and everywhere birds and yet other creatures were getting ready to begin their 'spring fling' that would in time bring yet another generation of creatures out to continue the ongoing march of life.

The pair walked into Forrester's groceries and looked around; there were the usual number of people who were checking out the produce, putting their choices into a basket or headed towards the checkout station to buy what they wanted. Off, more to one side, one person was arguing with William and his voice was neither quiet nor polite. "You do so have some salt; you have some in the back room and I want some right now. Or you're going to be on the floor looking for your teeth!"

"Citizen; they don't have any salt;" he told the man as he walked up; "yesterday and the day before they had some salt, but they sold it all; every single container. I don't know did they keep any back for themselves, but if they did, it is theirs; not yours. My name is Gee, and for whatever its worth to you, the last four men who started in with me were carted off in meat wagons; dead. Does you want to start up again and I'll see you get carried off the same way." He stared up at the much larger man and his emerald green eyes held no questions but what he meant what he said. The man, much larger than he, had heard the story about what he had done to the cannibals. Recognized who he was, and everything he'd heard discussed, led him to believe that the child not only didn't lie; he was capable of doing exactly what he said: could do and would do. He promptly backed down.

"Thass better;" Gee admitted; "now then; why didn't you get some salt yesterday? And if you did; why do you think you need more now? I'm a finder; almost everyone knows that. I hunt and look and seek and from time to time I finds things; or sometimes, just find clues where something might be found. That's what happened with the salt; I, and others, found clues where salt might be; along with some other things. Now; what we could have done; is just keep it all to ourselves and not shared it with anyone. But, no, we knew that people were hurting so we brought it to Mr. Forrester's, among others, so that others could also share. I didn't make a penny off of it; I gave it all to the Police and they gave it to Mr. Forrest and Mr. Forrest and the Police split the monies betwixt them. They didn't give me any moneys because I didn't want any. The Police can only barely get by on what the State can gives them and Mr. Forrester only barely gets by; mainly because so many peoples who come in here steals things when they thinks nobody is lookin'."

As he spoke he picked up a fairly large potato, swiveled about and launched the spud at the head of a citizen who was at that very moment trying to slip some carrots and celery under his coat. The tuber spun through the air and smashed into the head of the man, causing him to drop everything he had managed to slip under his jacket. For a few frantic moments things got very loud and then an off-duty police officer, who was there, trying to get some food for his own family; pounced on the perp and cuffed him on the spot. Gee walked up to the pair and glared at the handcuffed man. "You a mess; you know that? Mr. Forrester keep his prices down as best he can 'cause he know many of you's don't have much monies and he don likes t'see folk goin' hungry. So what doos you doos? Tries t'steal from him. Was I him; I'd kick you outta here and lets you tries going to somewhere else to get your food. And I knows for a fact that Mr. Forrester's prices be the lowest of all around here." He turned around and walked back to where Mr. Forrester, William and Maria all stood; staring at him. They talked for a few moments more, and then taking Maria's hand in his, they headed for the door.

They walked to the Police Station instead of 'jumping;' it wasn't far and spring was in the air; birds were flitting about, building nests and yet other animals, some not so small, were all getting ready for whatever the day might bring them. In time, they entered the great building that held both the court house as well as the police station, walked in and turned right. And soon were once again among people they knew and loved.

The moment the two walked in several heads turned in their direction; looking to see who had just entered. "Gee" one voice exclaimed and within seconds everyone in the room at least turned their heads with many coming over to see what the two were up to now. In a few moments they were surrounded by many women, all of whom were calling to Maria. In the next moment, Captain Taylor's office door swung open and he stuck his head out to see what all the noise was about. Gee locked eyes with him and waved; in the next instant he abandoned Maria to the women who surrounded her and wading through a crowd of mixed sexes, he headed toward the Captain.

Captain Taylor met him at the door; a broad smile on his face. "It's always good to see you, Gee, but today is especially so. I've got some puzzles I just can't figure out and since those puzzles are mostly about you; maybe you can help me understand." Gee nodded, a smile on his face, and he entered the room. Captain Taylor shut the door; but not all the way. This way, they had a measure of privacy, but if someone had a serious question to ask they wouldn't feel like they couldn't come in and take care of their needs. Each chose their chair and both sat down, facing each other, and for a few moments; just stared.

"Ya know;" Gee began with a soft chuckle. "it be a puzzle to me how any two perlite peoples get anything decide betwixt 'em." Captain Taylor immediately nodded his head and began to laugh softly. "So I guess I be the rude one and just start talking. As you already knows; m'mamma was a woman of few words. I believes she was limited in her smarts and just din't know many words . . . or maybe just lazy that way; not sure which. But as you also know; I'm tryin' to learn more words; and more important to me, learn how to use them right. If I stop and think ahead, I do fairly well. When I get excited, or mad, or confuse I go back to what seems more familiar to me and just rattle on. Not long ago, I heard someone say they were their father's 'air' and they got some things after he died. I also know that we breathe 'air'; and I've heard someone say 'air long and spring will be here.' I honest does not understand."

Chief Taylor broke into a broad smile and nodded. "I understand your confusion, Gee, especially so because of your upbringing. You had two parents; one with a very limited vocabulary, and one who was a college professor; and a very intelligent and highly educated person at that. Caught between the two, a child could easily get confused. There are, what I believe are called, 'homophones'. These are words that sound alike to the human ear; yet have different meanings." He reached for the scrap of blackboard on his desk, picked up a chunk of chalk and began to write: 'air' 'heir' 'ere' and 'err' among others. He turned the slate around so Gee could see the words more easily. "Each of these words sounds either exactly alike or very similar; yet each has a different meaning. When people are talking, as we are now, we can easily stop the other and ask what is meant or ask the speaker to say it yet a different way. When it is written down; we can't do that. Therefore; I suspect that different people over a prolonged period of time; began spelling each word somewhat differently so the person reading what was written down would understand what the writer actually meant."

"Thank you," Gee said softly, "everything you said makes sense to me. Sometimes I gets so frustrate; I just feels so stupid at times."

"Gee; the one thing I can say with complete conviction; you are not stupid. Just the opposite; you are, perhaps, the smartest kid I've ever met. What you are; is ignorant. All that means is; you don't know right now, but you can learn. 'Stupid' means that not only do you not know; you can't be taught: not even if you're beaten on the head with a hammer. If you want an example of 'stupid', I would submit Arvin Brandon. Now *there* was a stupid boy. You couldn't teach him anything: arrest him; throw him in jail; fine him; and he'd just go out and do it all over again. Even if you shot his earlobe off; he wouldn't learn."

With those words Gee clapped both hand over his mouth to stifle the giggles that erupted out of him like Vesuvius popping its cork. For a few moments; laugh was all that either of them did. "An' that wasn't the worser part;" Gee exclaimed. "I tol' 'im I wuz gunna shoot 'im in the head with the nextus shot; only him thought I meant the head on him neck. Then I pointed the gun down betwixt 'im legs and I thought him wus gunna break down and cry on the spot."

By now; Captain Taylor was howling. He lay sprawled over the top of his desk; his face buried in the crook of his left arm and he was weakly trying to pound on his desk with the base of his right fist. He made so much noise that others from different rooms - some not all that close - poked cautious heads inside to see exactly what the commotion was about. They, not even knowing what had been said nor done, began to also laugh because it is a fact of life that nothing in the Universe is as contagious as laughter; a head-cold is a sluggard by comparison. In time, that too faded into the past, and people went back to what they were doing before.

Eventually, Captain Taylor got his mirth under control. He took a handkerchief out of his pocket and gently wiped the tears from around his eyes and off his cheeks. He carefully folded it back up and replaced it back where he'd gotten it from. He looked back up at Gee. "I've said this before and will no doubt be saying it again, but young man; you have an absolutely wicked sense of humor. I can both see with my mind's eye and identify with Brandon. The thought of being shot in that specific 'head' would put any male into a blind panic. And if you will permit; this specific event leads me exactly to what I want to talk to you about.

"The two officers present at that time told me very much the same story you just told me. But you tell it better because not only do you repeat the exact words, you enact the expressions and actions of Arvin Brandon: it's almost like I'm there and actually watching. As a brief aside; I also know that you were the one who told the Brandon's to go and ask for jobs; and I also know that both boys have proved themselves and are now on the fast track towards making something worthwhile out of themselves. But the thing I cannot get my head around is the simple fact that two officers swear - under oath - that you had a gun in your possession when you walked up; had one; they saw it, handled it, and gave it back to you. Only to have you stick it back into that pouch of yours. And then they couldn't find it. Anywhere! And this is impossible! As are half of the things I've seen you do since. If you can explain that to me I would be most grateful as it's driving me nuts; because it just can't be."

"Actual, I think this is good 'cause it leads me to the exact reason I've come here to see you today. Not about the gun, specific, but other things that kind of blend into the whole." He stood up and stepped slightly to the right side of the desk; he held both of his hands up; as if he were surrendering to the Law. "If you will be so kind; please frisk me; does the best job you can and don't miss anythings. And don't be afraid of 'rackin' me out' as I'm still too young for that as nothin's dro'ped on me yet that I has to be concern."

Chief Taylor nodded his head. It had been some years since he'd been a duty officer and even longer since he'd had to frisk a perp; but there are some things, that once learned, actually never goes away. He did a full, complete, 'frisk' and missed absolutely nothing; not even in his pouch. The boy had nothing on him; not even some loose pocket change. Not even in his shoes; he knew because he looked. Finally convinced; he backed up and stared at Gee.

For a moment Gee stood as still as a statue, then with a slow, deliberate move, he slipped his right hand inside his pouch; Captain Taylor didn't take his eyes of the hand for a moment; he might have not even blinked. Then he saw the shape of Gee's hand somehow change beneath the cloth as in the same instant something else took form. Gee pulled his hand out and he was holding a gun; something that couldn't possibly be, but undeniably was. Captain Taylor wobbled as far as his chair and more collapsed than sat down in it . . . and stared.

Gee, being as professional as he could, carefully pulled the release on the side of the weapon, swung the cylinder out, and turning it around; handed it to the Captain. He, with only a slight hesitation, reached out and took the gun. Then, and only then, he took his eyes off of Gee and gazed at the weapon in his hand. And stared some more. He turned the gun around, looking at it from every point of view and then looked at it over again. Finally; he gently aligned the shells so that the next one under the hammer would be a live round; in case of need. He closed it up and handed it back to Gee. "Gee; that gun is more than 90% original. That means that it is not only a collector's item; but one worth a great deal of money. If you want a gun to carry around I'll get you one; but that should be put under glass and kept as pristine as possible: it just might be the best sample of that model left on Earth for all I know."

"I thinks about it, but I gotta admit, I've also got some others I knows about; quite a few others; matter of fact. And that doesn't count the ones that are still down under that house that the Trent's be livin' in now. But I gotta admit; I does like this one because of its size. Also-too, it's the one I shoot's Arvin's ear off with and I kinda likes that part as well." Which kind of brings up why I wanted to talk to you today; you remember us talking about 'air?" Captain Taylor nodded his head; cautiously. And you remembers, I mean, 'remember' us talking about Eddy Case?" Again, Captain Taylor cautiously nodded his head. "Wull; I . . . well, I think I may be Eddy Case's heir. If that be the correct spell of it and if that is what it means. What I'm trying to say is . . . if you have the time, I've got something to show you. It has to do with Eddy Case and it has to do with Patrolman Trent and his wife and maybe other police as well. I'm not sure exactly how long it will take, but I think I can show you a lot faster and better than I could possibly tell you. Then once you understand all the bits and pieces of it, maybe then you can tell me the beginning and the end of it. It might take half an hour or maybe longer. If you don't have the time now, maybe you can 'pencil it in' some other time. Provide I'm saying that last part right."

The two talked it over briefly and once they had everything down to their mutual satisfaction, Captain Taylor picked up the two-way radio and the snub-nosed revolver he felt naked without, the pair said goodbye to Maria, who wanted to be with the girls a while longer, and both walked out of the building and headed towards the corner of a building just north-east of them. As they came upon the corner; he turned slightly towards the Captain. "You know what be just on the other side of this corner; don't you?" he asked courteously.

"Yes, obviously, it's a parking lot;" the Captain said.

"You won't be disappoint if it's the insides of an apartment; will you?" he asked politely. As he spoke he reached out and took the Captains left hand in his right and in the next blink, they were inside a building. The Captain froze and stared around, almost panicked. "My apologies, Captain, but this is something you'll eventually get used to.

That; or start staying away from me most of the time. But this is the apartment Maria and I've been stayin' in for the last while; I've been here ever since just before me and Clarence had that little set-to."

He took the Captain gently by the arm and opened the door and showed him both the rubble filled atria as well as the door to the outside; all the while filling him in on what had happened with the Brandon's and how he had evaded them. He had never entered any of the apartments except by the back doors, but since they were there, he unlocked each door with his mind and let the astounded officer look at first one and then another. Next they went to the second floor by way of the back stairs because the rubble that filled the front area up had also eliminated access to the front stairwells entirely.

Ultimately, he led the bemused man down to the bottom floor and showed him both the weed-infested area that used to be a great lawn, as well as the partially filled-in remains of what had been the swimming pool. Ultimately they ended up at Eddy's place. Gee led the bemused Captain over to where Eddy's skeleton had laid for so very many years; there was a stain of sort in the exact place so it wasn't hard for them to find. He opened the door and let the Captain enter. "The first time I came in here, the smell was almost more than I could bear. I'm of the mind that the gas main was somehow ruptured when the bombs fell and that the place was full of natural gas or whatever they were using. Since we found it and since we have been leaving the door open full, the smell has most gone away, but there's still some that lingers on afterwards. I also think that's what killed Eddy Case."

Captain Taylor nodded his head, then on a whim, dropped down onto his knees and put his face to the floor; he sniffed cautiously. He immediately stood up and moved a step or two away. "I believe you are right. Both propane and natural gas are actually heavier than air. This being so, they would tend to settle; and that means the rugs were left in contact with the gasses for a prolonged time. The years have no doubt helped reduce the scent, but from what I know of Eddy and remember of him, I'd bet almost anything . . . He moved off away, toward a door that looked very much like a closet. He opened it, looked around briefly and then closed the door. He went over to a second one and repeated. It was his third effort that turned out to be the one he wanted; he pulled out what looked to Gee to be a very large; oversized vacuum.

"This, my young friend, is known as a rug shampooer;" he announced. He rummaged a bit more in the closet and pulled out several bottles of liquid soap. Between the two and with only a minimum of head scratching, they got the shampooer filled with water and soap, all according to the directions on the machine. They plugged it in, turned it on, and within a matter of a very few minutes had started shampooing the nearest patch of rug. They worked for some minutes and then Gee bent over and smelled the area they had just done. The difference was night and day. Where the un-shampooed area just plain stunk; the area they had just done smelled fresh and clean and even had a light floral scent to it. He turned to Captain Taylor and smiled. "I don't know how much the department pays you, but I'll double it if you come over here and finish this," he said. Both laughed and then of a common mind, continued on until the shampooer was out of water, and needed to be drained and refilled. Already; the smell within the room had improved. Captain Taylor showed Gee how to drain the machine; both were amazed at the amount of dirty water that was extracted by just the first pass. Gee put the machine off to one side. Now that he knew what to do, he could finish this some other time.

He led Captain Taylor over to where the far western door was. As they walked up; he gestured at the door. "This is where I learned that combination that let us in to that other supply point we found. Because the doors are the same and the numbers are the same, I'm guessing that the third place is yet another of one of Eddy's supplies." He moved up to the door, entered the code in and opened the door. He turned to Captain Taylor. "I have to tell you; this door lock is the hardest combination lock I've ever broken; a safe is a snap by comparison. He led Captain Taylor in and let him see what there was to look at. And there was a lot to see; Captain Taylor all but drooled all over himself when he came up to where the guns and ammo were. He stared, looked around, and then turned to Gee: "I don't suppose . . . ." he began.

Gee nodded his head. "I'm aware of the problems the police have in securing ammo and weapons for their use. I'm also aware that there are a number of light-fingered people within different departments; who are stealing from the police. And then, when they get some ammo or a gun or else, they either keep it for themselves or go and sell it at a hock shop or whatever they are called; and just pocket the money. This is wrong on many levels and just gotta stop. But until then; I'll be glad to help out the Police. Your precinct first, and then what I feel like sparing for some of the other precincts. But I got no intent of putting money into some jerks pocket just because he wants it. Like that moron who tried to steal that five dollar bill from me. And I know you feel exactly the same way; if not more."

The two looked through the handguns there. Gee was aware that the gun that he favored so much was valuable in its own right and that there were those who would love to have it . . . just because. With the Captain's help he found a fairly lightweight .38 revolver in a stainless five-shot that was very nearly the same size and weight of his favorite gun. He picked it up, made sure it was unloaded and played with for a while; it looked like it would do. Plus; it had the advantage of the mere fact that there were far more .38s around than .32 longs.

The pair looked around inside the room. Gee found an even larger package of the pink salt and handed it to Captain Taylor. "Here; I know now that some salt is getting more available; the crunch isn't so bad. But to tell you the truth, I've kinda gotten to like the pink stuff more than the rest, so I'll share some more of it with you. It's not like I'm out or anything," and he pointed at an unopened box that had words written on it stating that it was more of the same.

"I guess the main reason I wanted to get you down here was both to show you the guns and other things, but also to show you the apartments. I remember you sayin' how Officer Trent was stayin' in a terrible flop and paying such an awful price for it; mainly because there just isn't any apartment's to let; which is why we are here. I am the only one who can get in or out of here; you wouldn't be here if I hadn't brought you and even though you now know about it, should you be outside of here, it would be impossible, or exceedingly difficult for you to get back inside unless I brought you. You've seen the pile outside the front. I'm no expert on such, but it looks to me, did I get all of the bricks and stuff dug out, people could come and go out the front like they used to. Maybe even so; if there's folks who still know how to 'lay brick', if that's the right words, maybe betwixt the fallen brick outside that's still intact and combined with other bricks laying around, in time, maybe I could get it all built up to what it used to be. And because Mr. Case didn't have any living relatives, from what you said, and because I'm the one who found it; it seems logical that it now belongs to me.

"Another thing is . . . I've been in each of these apartments. Most of the folks who lived here had small safes where they kept things; matter of fact, that's where I found that revolver I shot Arvin's earlobe off with. But more important, most of the folk's had saved up some monies; maybe because of Eddy and because he owned this. And that doesn't include the monies I finded in his safe. 'To put a point on it' as my Da used to say, I now got a lot of monies; what between one safe and another; and after eight years or so, they's a dim chance that any of the folks who used to own these monies is still alive; 'Finders keepers' and all that sort of things. There's two things I actually wanted by bringing you here. First; I've already done; I've shown you that it is and that I've got it. I also need to know exactly how to get it over into my name; legally in my name. And if I'm going to put people in here with me and Maria; I'd rather it be Police than folks I know nothing about. I also need to know how to get all of that rubble out from the front of my place and find people who know how to 'lay brick' if that's the right word for it. Somebodies who can rebuild the place more back to what it used to be." He finished his short spiel and looked up into Captain Taylor's face and waited.

Captain Taylor stood awhile in thought; then he nodded his head. He turned slightly and stared Gee directly in the eyes. "I must agree;" he admitted. "I think we need to bring Judge Clark in on this; he would be the logical one to ask about the rights of heirs as well as any rules and regulations that might be involved. He would also be the one to ask about what paperwork that will be needed to bring everything over into your name. He would also be a good place to start asking questions about what's needed to bring the building back up to code so that it can be rented out. He also would be a good place to start in asking questions as to exactly what would constitute a fair price to charge for rent. One other thing I might warn you about; he might want to come and look the place over. That might mean having to let him in on your little secret about the things you can do. The one thing I can say in his favor without hesitation; he is a very honorable man and you can depend upon him to be discreet. That last word means that he won't tell anyone." Gee nodded his head and promptly agreed.

The two discussed matters for a few more moments and then ultimately decided upon the best way to proceed. Judge Clark was not aware of Gee's abilities, and he wasn't all that happy to let yet another person in on this particular facet of his gifts, but the Judge was a very honest and humble man; one who the Chief assured him would keep his secret. Rather than taking the long way back, the two talked it over between them and decided to just 'pop' into his office. This way, should anyone ask, they could claim that they had arrived earlier and had just gone in unnoticed because they didn't want to disturb others. Gee took Captain Taylor by the hand and began to visualize where he wanted to go.

He had only got started, when he detected a presence where no one should be, as the Captain had locked his office before leaving. He advised the Captain with a very brief explanation; the two ghosted into the office; they could see, but could not be seen. A man was poking around the Chief's desk; talking to himself. "Now then; let's just see what the nice Captain left in his desk for poor old Benny. Benny has his pride; yes he does. But he also has his bills and they don't pay poor old

Benny half of what they should." He had a very slim piece of something in his right hand; in a blink, he jimmied the latch aside and gently slid one of the drawers out and looked inside.

"No; not the gun;" Benny muttered to himself; "plenty of money there, but Chieffy be sure to notice if *that* is gone." He continued pulling out other drawers, looking for pocket change or anything else he could use or sell for a profit. Gee was still holding on to Chief Taylor when they had popped in, unseen and unseeable, and for the time; unheard. He pulled the Captain down closer to his level and began to whisper: "He can neither see nor hear us at the moment; this is what I suggest." He talked softly to Chief Taylor for a few brief moments; the grin on the Chief's face got big and bigger yet. In the end, he nodded, his face reflecting endless delight. Gee nodded and softly said; "The curtain now parts; Act 1 ready to commence."

"Benjamin Curtis; what the *HELL* do you think you're doin' poking around in my desk?" he bellowed at Benny's back; Benny twisted around; there was nothing behind him except a blank wall. At least; there wasn't supposed to be anything but a blank wall. Instead, he faced his Chief . . . at least the upper part of his Chief; the rest of him wasn't there. Instead there was part of another room and yet someone else with him. And surrounding him was an oval of strangely patterned light and the part of the Chief staring him right in the eyes was exceedingly angry. Benjamin Curtis took one horrified look, screamed well up into falsetto, turned and ran as fast as he could. He yanked the door open, and before it was well begun, shot through. At least; that was his intent. Instead; he centered himself directly into the door jamb, and it is an immutable law of physics that two solid objects cannot occupy the same space at the same time, no matter how much one of those objects might wish it otherwise: that's why it's called 'immutable.' Gee stood and stared at the mess he'd helped make of Benny and then touched Chief Taylor on his right wrist with his left hand. "Y'know; under the circumstances, perhaps we *should* take the longer way in." In the next instant the two were standing with the parking lot at their back; and with the Courthouse building just ahead and slightly to their right. Of one mind, the two began walking that way; the only sound heard was Captain Taylor's laughter which had yet to leave him. They walked slowly and by the time they'd made the right turn and actually reached headquarters; Captain Taylor had his mirth under control . . . mostly; anyway.

The pair walked up the steps and entered the building. Once clear of the doors, they turned right and walked down the hallway. They reached the door; Gee put his hand out and grasped the knob and pulled the door open and first Captain Taylor and then Gee walked into a room, which was at the moment, filled with numerous people staring about and asking each other many questions. The two glanced about and then Captain Taylor spoke; "What's the problem, why all the commotion?" For the moment; no one seemed to be sure. Gradually, different people added their impressions and slowly a few facts came to light. Everyone knew that Captain Taylor was out with Gee and that no one was in his office. Without warning, a high-pitched scream was heard and Benny Curtis, who wasn't supposed to be there in the first place, yanked the office door open; yelling hysterically. And promptly ran face first into the door jamb. No one knew further because Benny was out cold, and no amount of effort on anyone's part could bring him back around. He was 'out for the count;' as it is sometimes said.

They frisked his unconscious body, looking for both items that might not be his as well as drugs, because for the moment, no one actually knew exactly how he had gotten inside Captain Taylor's office in the first place; nor why. And there was always the chance that Benny might be on some sort of drug; either licit or illicit; no one could tell. In any case, other than loose change and a few objects that may or may not have been questionable, there was nothing. Some people packed Benny down to medical and let them do with him as they saw fit. The two turned and walked into the office; closely followed first by Maria and then Carol Donovan. Captain Taylor looked Gee in the eyes and grinned. "I've said this before and will no doubt be saying it again; but you are a most interesting young man to be around."

Chapter 11

The two got everything back into proper order; then Chief Taylor picked up his phone and dialed the Judge. He was at his desk, going through some paperwork when the phone rang; he picked it up before it rang the third time; "Judge Clark speaking; what's the problem?"

"Your Honor;" Captain Taylor began, "I have Gee here with me. Whenever it's convenient, he would like a few words with you; he has some things he would like to discuss; to get your insight on the legality of things. I'll let him explain further; whenever it's convenient for you; that is."

"Is he now? As a matter of fact, the case I was supposed to preside over got settled out of court; the two involved found a middle ground they could both agree on and they no longer need to come before me. In fact; I have several hours to while away. I can think of far worse things to do than spend it with that particular young man." Captain Taylor had put the conversation on the intercom and both Gee and the Chief could hear everything clearly. "We be right over if that's well with you;" Gee said into the intercom. Chief Taylor shook his head slightly and handed Gee the phone; "That's not exactly how an intercom works," he said softly. Gee took the phone and speaking carefully into it, as he had very little experiences with a telephone, he repeated his words to the Judge.

As it turned out; Judge Clark wanted a bit of exercise and used the call as an excuse to get out of his office and stretch his legs. He slipped off the robe he was wearing, revealing street clothes beneath, picked his hat off the rack where it awaited him, grabbed his coat and within moments of hanging up; headed towards Chief Taylor's office.

Maria and Carol Donovan watched and listened to the conversation; both knew who Gee and Captain Taylor were talking to and both heard the Judge's end of things but neither knew nor remotely guessed at what the two had to do with Benjamin's mishap with the door. The pair waited and watched, and almost before they were ready, Judge Clark walked through the door. He took a single look at Gee; his face instantly broke into a broad smile and with his right hand out, moved to greet the boy. Gee, more than willing, scooted forward and the two met somewhere in between. The two shook hands, then when that wasn't enough, each hugged the other.

Carol started to greet Judge Clark; almost before she was begun, she glanced at her wristwatch and gasped. "Omigoodness; I'm off duty now; I'm supposed to be over at the hair salon five minutes ago. Please forgive me but I've got to run;" and she did. Judge Clark watched Carol as she darted out of the door. He watched her depart, a thoughtful expression on his face. He turned to Captain Taylor. "Tell me if you may; is she married, is she seeing anyone or otherwise dating?"

"I don't know," Maria said thoughtfully, "but if you're interested in finding out; I can ask her. Without saying why I'm asking; that is." Judge Clark looked at Maria; first in surprise as she began speaking and then with interest clear in his eyes. "That might be nice;" he admitted. "My wife of some years passed away just less than a year ago. And while I admit that I still love and miss her, I also admit that I'm still young enough that I truly miss not having a woman around; especially someone as lovely as she;" and he gave a single nod in Carol's direction.

Judge Clark seemed to withdraw into himself for a few moments; obviously remembering some thoughts from before, then shaking his head to clear it, he turned his attention to Gee. "I believe you have something you want to discuss with me, young man," he said with a smile coming back into his face.

"Yes sir;" he admitted; "it has to do with Eddy Case; do you know of him, know who he was and where he lived; that sort of thing?"

"Indeed I do," Judge Clark admitted. "He was, in many ways, a man before his time. He understood human traits better than anyone I ever met; understood our foibles and strengths as well as our, how shall I say this . . . our ability to just be so 'human' in our actions. As you may already know, he was largely responsible for persuading a great many people to 'stock up' on certain things; just in case. Unfortunately; quite a few of those who listened to him were also people who were directly hit by the bomblets; and all of the prepping in the world cannot withstand something like that. Also, unfortunately, he was one of those who were hit. His building was one of the strongest-built in the entire city. He was a very wealthy man and he had his place built far stronger than specs called for, but a bomblet took out the front of his place and basically destroyed the entire structure. Should you want to see it, I could easily take you there so you could look at it, but under no circumstances can you get in: it's totally destroyed."

"Wull; maybe not totally," Gee admitted. "And that's the reason I've come to see you today. I has . . . have his property; that's where Maria and I now live. All six of the upstair apartments be in good shape; all 'cept the front part; that's all bash in and you'd be right if I had to try and go in that way. But I has a different way of getting in."

"That's not remotely possible," Judge Clark said, interrupting, "you'd have to be able to levitate to clear the rubble and the only thing you'd find on the other side, would be yet more rubble. I've walked around the building; well, as far around as I could get, and there's nothing but piles of busted brick and twisted rebar and . . ." Judge Clark stopped talking and stared at the expression on Chief Taylor's face. "Am I missing something here?" he asked quietly.

"Rath-ther!" Chief Taylor replied.

"What be lev-i-tate?" Gee asked innocently. He had never heard the word before and had no idea what it meant.

"Oh, God, here we go again!" Chief Taylor said; sadly shaking his head. "You know how birds fly; they flap their wings, pushing air around; in a way, birds 'swim' through the air. Levitate is sort of similar, only it's not done with wings but with the mind. From what I've heard, all a person does is to 'think' they're going to float up, kind of like a soap bubble, and then they can move in whichever direction they want to go."

"What's a soap bubble?" Gee asked. The expression on his face was intense; he wanted to know because he needed to know. Not some minor, surface-type curiosity, but a deeply rooted, inner need to understand. And he wanted to know NOW! Chief Taylor held up both hands. He got up and walked over to a sink that was located in the corner of his office; a sink in case someone needed to wash up. He turned on a faucet and started water flowing. Next, he took a bar of soap and rubbing rapidly, he lathered up his hands. With both hand full of soapy suds, he blew between his hands and a number of very small soap bubbles were blown off, only to move out into the air a short distance and then pop and disappear entirely.

"I'm not sure of the logistics of the thing, but there are different types of soap. Some soap is just for scrubbing hands. Other soaps are used for washing clothes as well as washing dishes. I'm not sure of the way of it, but some combinations of soap and . . . I'm not sure of what else, will make bubbles that are bigger and just float around in the air until they come in contact with something; or just pop. Levitating is similar in the sense that the one levitated "floats" through the air. As far as I know, that one does not 'pop' or disappear." He stood and stared at Gee.

Gee stood; looking at the Captain. Deep inside his mind, something was stirring and his 'meller, something that hadn't been acting up as of late; switched into high gear and was going all out. He thought. Something seemed to move within his mind and he both felt and saw the floor and the people on it getting smaller and further away; a moment later his head gently bumped against the ceiling. He glanced up at it and a brief time later he floated back down to the floor; as his feet touched the wooden surface, the stirring within his mind abated and then vanished; exactly like the soap bubble they had been discussing shortly before. He turned eyes onto the astounded Judge. "Be that what you meant?" he asked innocently.

"Yes, Gee, that's exactly what I meant;" he said as he stared at Gee helplessly.

"Your Honor," Captain Taylor started out quietly, "there are a number of things our young man here can do; not only that, there is seemingly a very logical reason as to *why* he can do it and how it came to be; not the 'why' so much, but at least the 'how.'" But before we can remotely begin on that, there are other things that he wants to talk to you about and those things are directly involved with Eddy and his property. I explained to him that you are the most logical person to handle his needs, but I warned him in advance that you might want to at least go to and do a walk-around to see what his needs and wants are. If you have the time; I suspect that we can do it in under an hour. If 'now' doesn't meet your schedule, perhaps we can postpone it until 'later'." As it turned out; Judge Clark was more interested in the 'now.'

Gee moved out to the more central part of the room and extended his hands. First Maria and then Captain Taylor and finally Judge Clark all joined hands in a loose circle and before the Judge could actually prepare himself for the unknown, the surroundings shifted, and without otherwise feeling anything different, he was in another room; a room that was somehow vaguely familiar. "I've been here before," Judge Clark thought to himself, but at the moment he had no clue exactly where "here" actually was.

Gee led the bemused Judge over to the southern door and opened it. As the four stepped out he, the Judge, could see the atria that was filled more than human-high with fallen brick and roof girders and tiles and only in that moment did he understand where he was. He looked around; all but in shock. Gee led the other three over to where the exit door was and opened it, showing the debris-strewn parking lot lying below. With an economy of words, he filled Judge Clark in on what had happened on that fateful day. By the time he was done, the Justice understood things as clearly as if he had seen the entire thing.

In time, he had led everyone through the apartment complex. Most of the apartments the Judge had never seen because the times he had been there with Eddy, people lived in those apartments and he had never actually gotten higher than the first floor. In time, the four of them were down on the ground. As they stepped on the ground, first one little grey ball of fuzz, and then an orange ball shot across the tall grass and vanished into a nearby bush. "What the heck are those?" Judge Clark gasped; "kittens? Nobody has kittens anymore; they were all killed when the bomblets fell."

"Not all of them," Gee admitted; "there are three of them around here; or there were the last time I counted noses. From what I can guess, their mother had them up on the third floor, in one nook or another, and then for unknown reasons, about the time they were weaned, she vanished. Either she abandoned them, or what is more likely, a hawk or owl or other some such got her. When Maria and I first found them, they were rapidly starving to death. Now that spring has arrived and now that the kittens have discovered the ground floor, they're gone as much as they're inside with us. No doubt that in time, they will either go feral again or end up inside some predator or other. But until then; they are reasonably tame when it's just the two of us here."

The four walked over to where the bottom entry door was and Gee permitted the two adults in and then he came in last. Judge Clark looked around the room and nodded; "Yes; this is Eddy's place all right; I recognize it immediately. The last time I was here, he was having that far off door installed. As I understand it, they were having a terrible time getting something with it done right. I doubt you'll ever get it open; short of dynamite."

Gee walked up to the door and punched in the proper numbers and pressed the handle down; the door promptly opened. He turned to the Judge. "They musta figured out the problem 'cause it works just fine now." He led the Judge and the rest inside.

It was very much the same as the supply they'd found out in the countryside, near the old abandoned farmhouse and barn, but much less. The Judge stared around inside and then turned around to Gee. "I'm going to impound all of these things for the people within the city;" he announced. Gee shook his head. Before the Judge could get his wind up, which he was preparing to do, Chief Taylor butted in.

"This is only the smaller group we found, Your Honor. As I told you the other day; Gee helped us find another lot, very similar to this, but between ten and twenty times this size. From where I stand; this belongs only to him. And to Maria; of course, as well as anyone else he might wish to share with." The Judge looked at him out of narrowed eyes; this was, perhaps, a facet of the Judge's personality that Gee was unaware of. Or perhaps not; the Judge looked first at Captain Taylor and then at Gee and then nodded his head.

"There, just for a moment, I forgot who we were dealing with. Young man; you've done so very much for the city, or rather, what remains of this city, that I'm more than willing just to cede this building to you, with only a minimal amount due to pay for my time and effort. Just off the top of my head; the value of this place was once several million dollars. But that was before the bomblets went off. In its current state, I think it's not worth much over perhaps five thousand. Once the debris and other gets cleared off, the intrinsic value would be more; but I've no idea how much more until that time comes. If you can come up with five hundred dollars, I'd consider that more than fair for the time and effort I'll have to put into getting the title changed over; even then, that amount reflects the current value of money and not what it might have been before the bombs fell. What do you think?" he asked Gee.

Gee stared at the Judge and then nodded his head. He moved his right hand carefully into the pouch that still hung just under his belly; he groped around a bit. The Judge watched his actions out of astonished eyes; Captain Taylor covered his mouth with his left hand; trying to stifle the giggles that threatened to erupt any moment. A blink later the hand came out, holding a bundle of money; they were $50 bills and there were ten in the slim packet; he handed it to the astonished jurist. He looked at the bills, fanned them with his thumb and then stared Gee in the eyes. "How in thunder did you do that?" he demanded.

"I thinks you both deserve a tip; for your time and for the help you've given me and Maria." Again his right hand snaked into the pouch, groped around for a few more moments, then he pulled out two objects; he handed one of each to the Judge as well as Captain Taylor. The two men looked at the rolls of coins in their hands.

"You!" Captain Taylor erupted; "you're the one who's been handing out the golden dollars!? I should have known better; but I never guessed! And Mr. Forrester wouldn't even tell *me* where he was getting them from;" he declared indignantly. Gee looked up at Chief Taylor and just grinned; "One hand washes the other; I expect," he admitted.

Gee and Maria had lived in this place for nearly a month; as close as he could estimate it, and there were still considerable sections of it that he had never looked at; this, especially since it was still technically winter. He led his small group towards the west, or somewhat north of west, out towards where he got his kitty diggings from. He had never gone further than that because he never had reason to. The wall was made up of red brick, laid by someone who knew exactly what he, or they, were doing for the workmanship in the brickwork could not be faulted. "This," the Judge declared as they walked up to it, "is what I was talking about earlier. From this viewpoint, it looks to be just a very nice brick wall; lain by an expert. From the other side, it appears to be the same. Only from above can the truth be seen. This is actually two walls, carefully laid out on a very large, thick cement sub-base, some twelve or so inches apart and filled with concrete and rebar. That, no doubt, is the reason the bomblets didn't actually knock it down as I presumed. What I must have seen was just random junk tossed about by the explosions, and being as absent-minded as I sometimes am, I just forgot that little factoid."

They looked at what there was to see, and then continued on towards the north. The yard wasn't quite as big as Gee first supposed, but it wasn't small either. They waded through fairly tall, dead grass, for deep winter was not long since departed and the new grass was yet to actually start growing. They came to the north-most part of the wall, turned and headed east. They hadn't gotten far when the wall took a very sudden left turn to the north. On the west face of the resulting wall was a door; well-built and carefully locked shut. Gee walked up to the door, stared at it thoughtfully and carefully turned the knob: the four walked in.

There was a very nice, but smallish, living room facing them and further north was what appeared to be perhaps a bedroom. More to the east was unmistakably a kitchen while north of that looked to be a bathroom; all of the needs for a small, but self-contained place for, perhaps, a bachelor of sorts.

"Martin Kodak," Judge Clark said, nodding his head as to confirm his thoughts to himself. "He and Eddie met while they were in the Army. Eddie, as rich and powerful as he was, was drafted. Instead of using his money and power to duck out of the draft, he just went on in. He was highly intelligent and well educated and instead of going in as a private, he went in as a second lieutenant. Somewhere along the line the two men met; the exact reasons thereof I either never knew, or equally likely, have forgotten. But they were best pals . . . as well as sparing partners; no doubt: the two could most definitely have their disagreements and neither were the least bit bashful about giving the other both barrels of their opinions. Sometimes, just listening to them, you'd think they were about to cut each other's throats, but just the opposite; in spite of both of them being pig-headed about things at times; they were instead the best of friends. At each other's throats at times; but in a friendly way. You'd have had to see them together to actually understand."

The listeners all nodded their heads, then in an effort to learn yet more; began to search the place. There was a door off to one side that was locked; this, Gee took care of in stride as he usually did and they found yet another, smaller room, that almost predictably was filled with yet more items that included not only salt and sugar and other spices and flavorings but also a goodly amount of raw grains in the form of wheat, oats, corn, rice and others; all of which could be ground into meal – on a conveniently placed grinder for such - or equally obviously; planted to grow yet more grains for the future. So many people had done with so little for so long, that the raw product was often hard to find. This was a very good discovery indeed.

There was yet another door they had not opened; Gee went over to it and tried to turn the knob; to no avail. He stared into the knob, found the objects that needed to be moved and moved them. He turned the knob and the door opened. The group entered yet another room; but a room that was not an actual part of the whole. After a very few moments examination, they decided that this was a garage. It had all the earmarking's of such; there was a charging station setting in a logical place and the door leading out of the place was clearly intended to permit a vehicle of sorts to enter or exit at its need. Yet another standard door was set into the same wall. The four walked over to it, and since the locking mechanism was on their side, Gee just turned it and pulled the door open; the four walked outside.

They were now standing in a courtyard of sorts, between tall buildings, not all of which were demolished, nor were any of them entirely intact, and much of the residue left from the damaged buildings were strewn across what was clearly an entryway where a car could come and go at its need. As Gee stood and stared up at the surrounding buildings his own 'finder' inside his head began to buzz with an almost insistent whine. Yet more things he could search. Oh goody! The four walked out what was left of the entrance and onto a side street. This showed unmistakable evidence of heavy pounding by bomblets; the street that was thus bisected wasn't remotely accessible by anything less than a tank or other tracked vehicle; nor would it be in the foreseeable future. What a mess! Having seen everything worth looking at, the four turned around and retraced their steps back to the apartments that Gee was interested in.

They were now back where they began. The three males began to talk about the apartments in general and Gee's future with them; Maria, who had been involving herself in many things throughout the day, started drifting more off into her own private world; thinking her own thoughts; instead of being actively involved as she had been most of the time. Gee noticed the drift-factor; added two plus two and came up with an impression that seemed to fit. He turned to her. "Dearest;" he said softly, turning her around with his words; "you've been more than a love, putting up with this 'boy business' all this time. But I think that maybe for a while you'd like to be with others of your own sex. Perhaps back with Carol. She might be able to help you learn some of the things young girls need to know about keeping their hair so beautiful; for one thing. Another thought comes to mind; you might also find time to ask of herself; if she's dating; who she's seeing if - anyone, and not coincidently, what does she think of Judge Clark; both as a human and as an available male? And does she show any interest in that direction; you might casually mention that you were watching him - watching her - and that you think that he might be interested. Sometimes; a single word to the wise can move mountains. Or even a single hill; for that matter." In a blink; Maria erupted. She threw her arms around his neck and began showering his face and lips with passionate kisses; eight-year-old girl style.

He went along with it as males have done for endless ages and once she had it out of her system, at least for the present, the four formed a ring and clasping hands, blinked back inside the Captain's room. There was no Benny waiting inside this time though. Benny, upon finally awaking, could not recall being in the Captain's office; had no idea how he got there and not only was there a considerable apparent gap in his memory, his nose was broken and both upper front teeth were snapped off just above the gum-line and his entire outlook on life had undergone a monumental shift. He was, in many ways, a new person. He certainly didn't look the same anymore.

Several police women, who were presently not busy, took Maria by the hands and the three of them walked out the door and headed south; towards where Carol now was. This was a win-win situation for all for Maria was able to hang out with other females and learn yet more things a young girl needs to know in order to make her way in the world; and the males were now free to pursue things that were more of interest to the male mind.

Captain Taylor, Judge Clark and Gee got their heads together, and with a pre-explosion map to go on, began to plan on the best way to get things started. The one thing that was the most obvious of all was also the easiest to address. All of the junk; both in front and both sides, and eventually in the back, would have to be removed. At least some of it, in the way of unbroken bricks, could be salvaged and reused to build yet other walls or whatever was needed. At the present, there was only one company in the area that did such, and that was the company the Brandon boys now worked for. Judge Clark called the number and before the phone had rung the second time a person picked it up and answered: it was Walt Brandon. Gee, recognizing the voice as well as Walt identifying himself, grinned and nodded his head.

"Hello, Mr. Brandon; this is Judge Clark. I represent a client, someone you know quite well; he has a job for you, for the people you work for; rather. He has fronted up . . . and the Judge stared at Gee. He held up five fingers and mouthed the word 'thousand'. Judge Clark grinned and nodded. "He has fronted up five thousand dollars to do a job. This is likely just a start because the area he needs cleaning up is going to require quite a few men and is going to take weeks, rather than a few hours or days to clean up. Are you interested?"

"Hell ye . . . I mean, yessir; we definitely *are* interested. Um, we're talking cash money, right, not some down and the rest when you can?" Gee nodded his head, then turning slightly, stuck his hand into the pouch at his belly. A moment later he produced a thick wad of hundred dollar bills and laid them on the Captain's desk; "They's more where that came from," he said very softly.

"Definitely cash money;" Judge Clark assured Walt. "The party involved has more than enough money for this project. If you do it well, he also has a number of other projects that also need to be done. It is logical that if you do it right; he will stay with you. By the way, for what it's worth to you, your new boss is none other than Gee; the boy you used to chase. The best news is; Gee doesn't hold grudges. As long as you can do the job, and as long as you do it according to spec, he will be more than happy. The greatest news of all, as far as your end of it goes, once this first is cleaned up; I believe that he has a lot more that needs to be done. Enough so to keep at least some of your people busy well into next year; if not beyond."

"That *is* good news; Your Honor. And the next time you see Gee, tell him that Paul and I are sorry for all the things that we did; to him and to a lot of others. We honestly thought we were doing what Mom wanted; we should have figured it out long before. And he was right; Arvin was lying to us the same as he was to everyone else. Paul and I got to talking it over later that same night and we decided that Gee had the right of it. We faced Arvin and told him 'no more' and when he started throwing his weight around we both tied into him. Most of the time before, we were scared of him, because he was so much bigger than we; but by then we'd had all we wanted and we were both on him like stink on a skunk. By the time we were done; he had a lot more than a shot-off earlobe to think about it . . . and, Gee, if you're there and listening to this; 'thanks:' more than we can ever say."

Gee reached for the phone and Judge Clark handed it to him. "Hi; this is Gee, and I've been here all along, listening to what's been going on. I never did think you two were bad; you were just following a very bad example. And I'm more than glad that you quit what you were doing; because not only were you hurting a lot of young and innocent people, you were hurting yourselves even more. The worse of it was; you didn't actually see the truth of it; you just couldn't understand. What I'd like now, is tomorrow, fairly early; show up at the last place you three were looking for me; the one where you three had chased me into a blind alleyway and then couldn't find me. Meet me there about 8 AM or thereabouts and I'll show you what I want done and you can tell me what you can do and then we'll go from there; deal?"

"Done deal," Walt said and then both hung up.

Gee and Judge Clark looked into each other's eyes for a few moments; Gee nodded. "There was something else I was going to say, but in those few moments, I forgot what it was. Bottom lining it; I think that with a 'bit of luck and a tail wind', as my Da used to say, we've got a good start on things. Now; for the next bit of news . . . or whatever . . . I'm hungry! If I don't get something to eat pretty soon I'm going to start gnawing on the furniture!"

Not surprisingly; the Courthouse also had a small restaurant of sorts and the Judge, having yet more time on his hands, joined both Gee and Captain Taylor there. The room wasn't specifically large, but was bigger than he was used to. Best of all, from his viewpoint, being with two such well known and esteemed people, they were waited on almost before he could get seated. The menu was both a bother and a blessing; bother, because he still could not read all that well; blessing, for the exact same reason. He read through what he could; what he didn't quite understand, he asked one of the two adults. As he worked his way down the list, he came to something that was utterly foreign to him; something called 'hamburger and fries.' Not only had did he not know what this was; he had never knowingly eaten such. He immediately put his forefinger on the words and showed it to Captain Taylor. "What be this?" he asked innocently. Captain Taylor looked where Gee's finger lay, took the menu from out of his hands and underlining the words with his own index finger, showed it to the Judge. The two looked each other in the eyes; "a virgin" they said, speaking with a single voice.

A woman came over to take their orders; both the Judge and Chief made their choices and when that was done, both looked at Gee; "and our young friend here wants to try his first ever hamburger and fries. And tell the fry-guy that it better be done to perfection or I'm tossing him in jail for 'contempt of court;'" Judge Clark announced. "And I'll lock the cell door with my personal key;" Captain Taylor added. The waitress nodded her head, and giggling, headed for the order desk.

It didn't take as long as Gee expected; the waitress first served the Judge; which was only logical; then Captain Taylor, and then his burgers and fries. Gee looked at his plate and could feel the saliva in his mouth starting to flow; even before his nose got a whiff of what was before him. He picked the burger up, cautiously as it was still fairly hot, and took a careful bite. For a few moments the world seemed to drift away. For one; he really was very hungry. For the second, his taste buds came in contact with the burger and each and every bite thereafter was pure ambrosia as far as he was concerned. His Mom actually wasn't that good of a cook: like her conversations, her menus were quite limited. But this . . . this was to die for. Except . . . it needed salt. He glanced around; no one seemed to be paying him the least amount of attention. Plus, he had the advantage that there really weren't all that many people in the room at the time. Taking a chance, he glanced around to see if he was being watched; he didn't seem to be. He reached into his pouch and carefully grabbed the same small salt shaker he'd grabbed before; the one that had caused Mr. Coldbrick to come unglued; flicking the lid back he carefully shook a generous amount over fries and burger. He started to put the shaker back into his pouch, only to discover that both the Judge as well as the Chief was watching him . . . as was the waitress and several other diners. He just shrugged his shoulders and stuffing the burger up into his mouth, took another bite. Much better; perhaps they had a better class of clientele than in Forrester's diner, but other than watch for a few moments; no one had anything else further to say. Then again; now that salt was more available, maybe it didn't cause as great a stir. At least there were no brick walls falling on anyone.

Once the food was little more than a faint belch within, the Judge headed back to his courtroom; he has cases coming up that he needed to preside over; plus he now had all the information he needed to start researching Gee's needs and getting the property moved over into his name. The two of them headed back to the police station. They walked in; people turned to see who it was and what they might want, but the two people he was actually looking for were not there. He glanced at his watch. He still wasn't that good with it, but he was getting better and it actually wasn't all that long since he and Maria had parted. He decided that she was likely just having a good time with the girls. Waving goodbye to the Chief, he turned and headed out the door. He got as far as the corner; in the blink of an eye he vanished, only to appear in his own living room.

He no sooner got in his place when niggles began to eat at him. This was, perhaps, the same niggle he'd felt earlier; but with the Judge and Chief with him and all else that was going on; he'd not paid attention like he might have otherwise. He walked out what was actually his back door and headed down the steps. As he reached the ground, he looked ahead and slightly to his right, sort of north by northeast as it were. Two of his kittens were back in the same area they'd been when the three of them had come through; an hour or so earlier. The animals seemed concerned about something; maybe they had a bug or something similar cornered? He walked that way. Before; the two animals had scattered, running for nearby bushes, but at the time he was with people strange to them. This time; both were meowing piteously and there was that about them that did not seem right; he headed straight towards them.

They seemed to be gathered around a section of green plastic pipe that was sticking up out of the ground; it was a section of sewer pipe but instead of laid flat, it was on end, and one of the two kittens was on the edge of the pipe; looking in. He walked up and peered down;

two faint glowing eyes looked back up at him and in that instant he understood. Without hesitation, he focused his mind and a moment later a small, bedraggled and hungry kitten hung in the air; seemingly held aloft by the lack of gravity; if nothing else. He reached out and plucked the small animal up and promptly cuddled it up to his chest. The kitten repaid his kindness by sinking a small paw full of claws into him; he didn't mind. He turned and headed back up to his apartment; all the time shuffling his feet around to keep from stepping on one frantic little animal or the other.

It wasn't easy, but he managed to get back up to the apartment without tripping over one or more kittens. He went into the kitchen and carefully set the bedraggled animal on the countertop, A moment later he found a small bowl and filed it at least half-way full of water and put it just in front of the little animal's nose. It sniffed twice and then on very wobbly paws it moved over and sticking its face into the bowl; began to lap almost frantically. Next, he brought out some solid cat food as well as a can of the fish; the latter he was doling out more carefully as the greedy little wretches would eat nothing else; had they the choice; much like kids and a plateful of cookies; no doubt. He left a gracious plenty of both in front of the small animal, and then because the other two had caught the scent of fish and were meowing their little brains out, he got another dish and put perhaps half of what was left in that. This he put down where the other two could get at it. They promptly pounced on it and snarling and growling at each other in little kitten voices, gobbled up as much of it as they could before the other little pig ate it all up. He capped the can with the lid it came with and stuck it in the fridge for future use.

He glanced at the watch on his wrist. Since discovering it and learning how to use it, he wore it constantly. He made it a habit to wind it carefully twice a day; once in the morning, before brushing his teeth and then again just before going to bed; again, after brushing his teeth. Like most such, it seemed to drift a bit on time, but less than a minute a day. He took care of this by setting his watch every time he went over to the police station; or in that general area. He presumed, being the Courthouse and all, they would be most likely to make sure that all of their clocks were set to the correct time. Looking at his watch he decided that Maria had been gone for perhaps just over an hour. That might be enough time with the girls for her. It might also be more time than she liked being gone from him. He made sure that the northern door was fully shut to keep the small ones inside; at least until the one got over its latest experience. For a moment he thought of swinging by Foresters, but decided that once he'd gotten Maria; they both could swing by; this way she could personally choose whichever apples she wanted. He focused his mind briefly and in a blink he was standing right at the corner leading to the Courthouse. Placing one foot ahead of the other; he began to walk.

It didn't take long. As he walked, he glanced around, looking at other people and whatever there was to see; his wandering gaze glanced to the southeast. Once again a layer of dark clouds hovered near the horizon. The Brandon boys and whoever they would bring with them were supposed to show up at his place first thing in the morning. If a major storm moved in during the night; that was likely to turn into a no-show. If so; he'd just try again the next day, and the next; if the weather didn't cooperate. He walked up the appropriate steps, turned the proper corner and walked down the usual hallway. Opening the door; he was there.

"Gee!" a young female voice squealed. A moment later Maria attacked him, smothering his face with happy, excited kisses and hugging him without restraint. He returned pound for pound and was the happier for it. Maria was up to the top of her ears in happy talk. She told of everything that had happened while she was in the hair salon; but the part that took up most of her delighted chatter was the simple fact that; 1) Carol was not at the moment seeing anyone, and 2) she was both delighted and astonished that Judge Clark even knew she was alive; much less potentially interested, for she thought him a most handsome, suave and sophisticated male. Gee made a mental note to pass that on to Judge Clark; verbatim.

It turned out that she hadn't eaten since that morning. He had a very good sense of direction as well as an exceedingly good memory; upon learning the last, he took her gently with his arm around her shoulder and steered he in the direction of the diner. They walked in. There were more people in there than there had been earlier; he found an empty table and the two sat down; opposite each other.

"Who said you two guttersnipes could come in here?" a female voice sniffed off to his left.

"Judge Clark and Chief Taylor said they could; Mrs. Topperwien," a woman said as she walked up; it was the same woman who had waited on him earlier. He glanced at the woman who stared at him out of suspicious eyes; she had light auburn hair and a thought popped into Gee's mind.

"I likes your hair; ma'am," he said politely; "can't hardly tell by just lookin' it's a wig." He nodded; smiled, and turned back to the menu he'd just been handed. Mrs. Topperwien gasped, stood up and pivoting on her feet, stomped out. Gee's eyes seemed to shoot green fire at the woman's back as she flounced out of the diner; without paying for her meal and without finishing it either. Maria clapped both hands across her mouth; trying to stifle the giggles that were all but bubbling out of her ears; the woman who was waiting on them wasn't doing much better. Gee's emerald-green eyes followed the woman much like a carnivore watching a prey animal moving away; and for similar reasons; at that. "Not sure what a 'guttersnipe' be, but she got no cause to call us that;" he muttered softly to himself. The waitress stomped her right foot to the floor twice and erupted into squeals of giggles.

Gee ordered two hamburgers and fries for he had enjoyed the first round so much that he was more than ready for an encore; and if he liked it, he was positive that Maria would too. He took the small salt shaker out of his pouch and salted his own and then handed it to Maria that she could do so to hers. The two ate their meal in peace. The waitress got herself off with others that also worked there and repeated the entire sequence to those who had missed out on it. As it turned out; Mrs. Topperwien was not the most liked person in the Capitol; largely due to her opinionated attitude towards anyone she didn't approve of; which was, basically, everyone who wasn't her. The average listener who heard of the fiasco were more than pleased to pass the news on and like some sort of virulent disease the incident wove its way throughout the building in record time; gaining mass with every telling.

Gee and Maria, once done with their meal, swung by the Judge's quarters to speak a few bits of news into his ears. With that done, the headed out, first to Forester's where they stocked up on some more food as well as more apples for Maria as she was rapidly getting low. While doing these things he filled her in on what had happened while they were apart, starting with the three of them jumping to their place; on through him finding a small kitten down at the bottom of a green pipe. Between them, they tried to figure out the best way of making sure that never happened again. First; Gee thought of just digging it up, or perhaps trying to pull it up out of the ground, but neither of them could figure out why it would be there in the first place; would pulling it out cause further problems? Perhaps there had been a drainage problem there and the pipe was set up so water could run down to a lower and better aerated level. Ultimately; Gee decided that if anything could no longer get into the pipe, then nothing could fall down it. They now had a great abundance of busted brick laying everywhere. Gee thought that simply dropping pieces and chunks of brick down the pipe until it was clear full would guarantee that no kitten, nor any other small animal, would ever fall down there again and the loose chunks would allow water to flow out; if that was the original intent. Unless a better idea came up; this is what they intended to do. As it turned out, for at least one of the kittens, their efforts were totally wasted; for that specific animal, it had seen all the inside of that green pipe that it ever wanted to see, as far into the future as it could imagine. For a kitten; that actually wasn't all that long.

While Maria was getting her personal affairs in order, he popped outside his place and picking up one piece of broken brick after another he 'dropped' them down the pipe. Even with all of the pieces down inside the hole, if was it used as a water drainage system of sort, the water could freely flow between the bricks and down into the lower levels. If that was the reason for it to be there in the first place; if not that; then what?

Chapter 12

The next day dawned fairly clear with only scattered clouds where the potential had been for rain. The two were up well before the appointed time; ate their breakfast and fed the kittens; which, for various reasons, did not seem to be in any hurry to go outside; at least one of them had endured all the "outside" it wanted for the immediate future. Almost exactly 8AM a truck pulled up before his place, followed by a flatbed with a fairly large number of men wearing mostly boots, jeans or coveralls and gloves; all got out of the vehicles and began to look around. Gee popped down, mostly to their backs and walked up; the first two he looked at were Walt and Paul; both spotted him and both got guilty expressions on their faces. He understood their problem; with a broad smile pasted to his face; he reached out his hand to greet them.

"How-do;" he said with a welcoming grin. "Welcome to my place. I've been working with Judge Clark and have come up with his price and he is in the process of getting this switched over to my name. Once it's cleaned up, and fixed up, it's going to be very nice indeed. For now; my problems are obvious; the bombs that blew this neighborhood to shreds, tossed brick every which way with much of it being broken and yet other bricks basically still in useable condition. What I need is to have this all cleared up;" and he gestured to the front of his building; which was a monumental mess. And this was the good side. "I want all of the bricks that are still usable to be carefully stacked in one section over there;" and he gestured in the direction he wanted; "with the unusable pieces either carried off and dumped somewhere, or else

214

tossed over onto one of these otherwise vacant lots. I don't like the latter option as eventually they will most likely have to be moved yet again."

He led the two men over to his right, which was more easterly, and then stepping carefully he led them as far into the building's atria as he could; this was where the serious rubble began because not only was it left over from collapsed walls but also the entire section of what had once been the roof was laying both atop as well as adjoined with all the thousands of bricks and pieces thereof. The two men stared, whistled appreciatively, and nodded their heads. "And you have enough money to do all of this?" Paul Brandon demanded cautiously.

"I do; and then some;" he admitted. "As you both most obviously know, I'm a 'finder' by trade and inclination. That is, I go and look and snoop and pry and peek and search out various corners and I don't stop until either it's time to go home and eat or I find something that makes it all worthwhile. Many times I've come back empty-handed. Other times, I've done very well, but most of the time it's somewhere in between. In a way, I owe all three of you for finding this; it was when I was running and trying to get away from you that I found it."

"I hope you don't mind my asking you this;" Paul Brandon said with an apprehensive look on his face, "but back then, we all but tore this section apart; looking for you and we couldn't find you anywhere. And we all three saw you walk into this exact place. Where were you hiding?" His face showed confusion, frustration, concern and even anger.

Gee looked up into first Walt's face and then Paul's. He stared for a few moments, nodded to himself and then looked back up at the two boys who were considerably taller than he. "I guesses I can tells you." He took Paul by one arm and Walt by the other and led them to the exact site the three had stood, staring about in complete confusion. "You was standin' about here; he moved Paul a bit further, "and you was standin' about here. Arvin was standin' over about here." He moved a bit further, forming a loose triangle between the three of them. You all were gawking around, tryin' t'see; but the whole times I was squattin' down, awatchin' the three of you. Right out in plain sight. But you couldn't sees me. Does you knows why?" The two boys were staring at him with rapt attention; both shook their heads. He pointed to the rickety-looking railing sticking out of the side of the building; they looked in that direction. 'Cause the whole time I was squattin' up there; watchin' you. Did you looks up; you'da seed me starin' down atcha. But typical, folks don't looks up; they just looks around."

"You're lyin'" Walt snarled at him. In his face and eyes Gee could see the residuals of what he boy had once been . . . and the view was not nice.

"A'right;" he said softly, looking directly at Walt; "tells you what you do. You stand right here and watches me. You; stand right there, now," he said to Paul; "but 'sted o' watchin' me; looks direct at that railing. Got's it? Doesn't blinks now 'cause this don't take very long."

The two did as they were directed and in the next blink Gee was standing on the railing, looking down at the two. Walt gave a massive flinch, jerked his head left and right, and began to bellow; "Hey; where'd he . . . " then he looked up towards the railing where Gee now stood, waving at the pair of them. In the next moment he was gone and his voice sounded just behind them. "I'm baaack" he said softly. The two gasped in astonishment, swung about, and stared as if there was nothing else left to see.

"I guess that's about it for 'show and tell.' What that be called, is 'teleportation;' it be. . . is a way of moving from one spot to another, instantly, without moving a muscle because it's done with the mind and not the body. As an aside; the brain tells the body what to do and the muscles obey; and the brain also triggers teleportation; they are, in fact, two different facets of doing basically the same thing. This is only one of the things I now know I can do. It may be that I've always been able to do this; or maybe, in my fear as you three came looking for me, I somehow spontaneously developed it . . . hey! I'm startin' to sound like my Da! That's only too cool. And in a way; I partially owes it to you three boys. Or at least; you helped 'jump start' the process."

He led the two back to where people were already starting to go through the rubble; separating broken from whole and putting each in its respective place. The men had not been at it very long but already he could see a small section starting to look somewhat cleaner than the area immediately around it. He left Walt and Paul to direct their forces in the ways they wished and turning, headed back in the direction he had come from. As he moved out of line of sight of the group he triggered the response within and in the next instant he was standing right outside what he thought of as his 'back door.' He walked back in and found Maria; standing, staring at him with the biggest smile on her face he could imagine.

"I was watching you," she announced breathlessly, "I saw and heard everything you said to the Brandon boys!"

For just a moment the world seemed to go away. Was Maria starting to become like him? He wasn't sure exactly how he would take that! In part; he didn't want to be the only one on the planet to be able to do these things. Yet again; he wasn't sure that he wanted his Maria to be the next one to do so. He stared at her; scarcely breathing. "Come here; I'll show you," she said, beckoning to him: he followed her footsteps. She walked to their front door; the one that lead to the front part of the building. She opened the door and led him over to the emergency exit door; stood and then pointed out the window. "When you popped up here I was just behind you. If you'd turned around you'd have seen me." She beamed up at him happily.

Both relief and embarrassment flooded through him in equal proportions; he was glad that it wasn't what he thought and at the same time ashamed he had felt that way in the first place. He held out his arms and when she came rushing in he hugged and kissed her and told her again and again what a smart and beautiful young lady she was; and never once mentioned what he thought she meant.

By this time, Gee had kept to his original vow. Over the space of nearly a month now, he had been gradually removing the more ragged parts of his apparel, and replacing them with more presentable wear; this gave him a more attractive appearance. Since Maria had delved into the younger of the two girls clothing, she too, came up in appearance, although truth be told; she had never been as ragged as he was at one time. Over the same period of time, he kept going down into Eddy's place and over some days, he and Maria got all of the rugs in the place thoroughly shampooed . . . twice, with the second round consisting of very little soap, and intended more as a rinse. They had also wiped down the walls they could reach and with the only exception of the ceiling, had done a first-rate job of cleansing of the place and by now the scent of whatever it had been that smelled so foul, had basically gotten tired of them and had departed to other environs . . .and good riddance; was their thought. The lower section had multiple advantages over their first apartment; the most obvious was the fact that they didn't have to go up or down three flights of stairs each and every time they wanted to go out into the yard for kitty digging's and other reasons. Not to mention that the kittens also liked it for the exact same reason; although, being cats, they didn't have much to say about it.

One of the disadvantages of the ground floor lay directly south of them; the people who had been hired to do the work were steadily getting rid of much of the eastern part; that which they could reach, but further in where the piles lay more than man-high, the progress was far slower. One such day, Paul Brandon, sided by his brother; walked up to him as yet other men kept chipping away at the monumental pile of junk that still kept him from using his front door. "We just about of money," Paul announced, "when are you gonna get us some more?" The two boys glanced at each other and then looked back at him; interest clear in their eyes. Five thousand dollars in less than a month, and for the amount of work that was done, seemed more than excessive to him.

"You'll have to talk to Judge Clark about that," he quietly informed the pair. Both straightened up at those words.

"Judge Clark?" one of the two gasped; the other seemed to pale a bit around the ears.

"Yup;" he replied. "Y'see; I'm not all that good on the money end of things; just don't know when a price be right and when it be higher'n' the sky; so I lets him do the payin' and I just gives him what he tells me he needs. "Y'see; th' Judge; he gots a firm rep for bein' hones' 'bout things; someone a body can trust. You two, on the other hand, got a rep that be just the other way around. So I use him for a go-between; you needs more money, you talks to him: not to me; it saves me a lot of fuss and feathers, and in the long run, a lot of money toos. Y'see; you two boys don't have a name for being honest in everything and sometimes old habits are hard to break, so I let him decide which is what." The two glanced at each other, nodded their heads at him and without further words, turned around and walked off. Gee made a mental note to mention the event to the Judge . . . or at least Captain Taylor, who could easily pass the message along. He watched the two for a few moments, shook his head sadly, and muttered to himself: "sometimes old habits die hard." He turned and went back into his own apartment, taking the long way around for it would be some time yet before the men got enough of the detritus out of the way that he could remotely use the front door. Providing it even worked: that was something he'd never even thought of. "Maybe later today;" he muttered to himself. He turned and went back to what he'd been doing before the pair had walked up on him. What the Judge had to say to him about it later was something else.

Gee was squatted down on his heels before one of Eddy Case's safes; a number of letters, envelopes, and other papers spread out before him; just to his right. To his left was a fairly large pile of money: bills in fives and tens; some in twenties; yet others in fifties. But the biggest pile was in hundreds: this was many thousands of dollars; how much, he couldn't be sure because he basically ran out of numbers when he ran out of fingers and toes. Well; maybe not quite that bad; but it wasn't good. In any case, there was enough money before him to potentially pay for, not only the removal of all of the detritus from in front of his new home; but also to have much, if not all of it, rebuilt. And that didn't begin to take into account the money he'd seen in yet other safes. But the thing that was currently taking most of his time and attention was a folder with a cord wrapped around it. His reading skills were getting better; he could understand most of the words he read; providing they were words he recognized and used at least fairly often. What the file held; did not fit anywhere within in that category. The words that most caught his attention were written on the front, and was the reason he'd opened this specific folder in the first place; read: 'In The Case of My Death;' and it was stuffed almost to capacity with both sheets of papers as well as thick envelopes that many times were written in script; something he still did not know how to read; and neither did Maria. His only recourse lay in the form of Captain Taylor, and even more important, Judge Clark. He took the folder, replaced what few items he'd removed; retied the strap that held the whole together and set it off to one side where he would be sure to access it once he got before the Judge. Or at least Captain Taylor.

Tomorrow would be another day. He and Maria took separate showers and then each got into what they thought of as their "night clothes;" they gave each other a quick little kiss goodnight, and then with the three kittens jockeying about for their own sleeping space; the two nodded off into dreamland.

They awoke just as the sun was peeking over the eastern horizon, filling their bedroom with the first glimmering of reflected light. They got up, took care of what everyone takes care of first thing in the morning and once they got the kitten's bowls refilled with water and food and got the flushable out of the cat box; they found something for breakfast and consumed it with gusto for both were more than hungry and they had a full day planned ahead.

With the basics taken care of the two popped over to their favorite spot and began walking towards Forrester's Groceries. Neither had been there for several days now and their own supplies were dwindling down. They were almost there when three raggedy males stepped out from behind some trash piles where they'd been hiding and all walked up; bold and ready for trouble. "Give us all your money and we'll let you go," the larger of the three stated. "Oh yeah; y'gotta leave the little dolly too; that'll be our dessert." The other two males laughed sycophantly.

Gee stared at the three before him. As he stared, his eyes saw behind them; Patrolman Trent and his woman were coming up on the trio, moving as quickly as they could and at the same time, making as little noise as possible. "Nope" Gee replied. "The little 'dolly' you mentioned belongs to me; and as far as the money goes; nope on that also. And there's not much any of you can do about it. You see; in your greed and lust, you didn't look around very careful; and that especially goes for behind you."

"Bull sh . . ." before the male could finish his comment, Patrolman Trent reached out, grabbed him by his left shoulder and yanked him around; as his face tried to catch up with his torso, a duke came out nowhere and nailed him on the jaw; he dropped to the ground without so much as a twitch; he'd been switched off instantly by Trent's right fist. The other two started an aborted effort at running; but Molly Trent appeared only a very few steps from her husband; she had her revolver out and even as their eyes locked on the gun she held, she thumbed the hammer back to full cock. The two immediately put both hand in the air and stopped all other activity. There was a time when a perp would have chanced running for it, but here of late, cops had gotten into the nasty habit of just shooting them in the back instead of the front, and in either case; they were dead. And the two knew it.

Patrolman Trent walked up to the pair and removing his own cuffs off his belt, cuffed the first. Molly, still covering the second with a cocked revolver aimed directly at his chest, reached for her own belt with her left hand and handed her husband her cuffs; an eye-blink later and the second one was cuffed; both hands together as well as run between the first man's hands and back to back; this was a little touch that discouraged either of them from making a break for it. That left only the third, who was at that moment trying vainly to come back to consciousness. "Gee; what a pity we only have two cuffs;" Patrolman Trent said softly, hanging his head in apparent sorrow; "if we only just had yet one more pair." Molly looked at her husband and began to laugh softly. "Gee; where do you think we could get another pair?" she asked him concernedly. "Gee; I just don't know;" he moaned quietly in reply.

Gee looked at Maria, dropped his head and shook it sadly; while taking two short steps he reached inside his pouch; an instant later he produced yet a third set and handed them to Molly. She, laughing softly, took them from him and between her and her husband, got the semiconscious perp properly cuffed and awaiting transportation to carry them off to their new home for the next several days.

With the latest bit of excitement behind them Gee and Maria headed out towards the Courthouse; Forrester's was something they needed to go to sometime today, but for the moment, both were remembering the diner and the burger and fries. Gee had only eaten two and Maria just the one, but with some drugs, only a single hit can create a lifelong addiction; and food is no different. The two walked into the Courthouse, turned right and headed towards the precinct; they entered, took no more than two or three steps before they were spotted: "They're here, Captain Taylor," a voice rang out. A moment later his office door swung open and he popped into view; a broad smile on his face.

"What's this I hear about three perps trying to hold you up?" Captain Taylor demanded.

"Yup; said he was going to take all of my money and Maria too;" Gee admitted quietly.'

"I bet that didn't go over very well;" Captain Taylor opined.

"Nope;" Gee admitted; "thing was, none of them looked around before they made their advance; which was incredibly stupid on their part. Then the biggest dumb of them all said they wanted all my money and to leave Maria behind for their 'dessert;' that didn't go over at all well."

"They said what?" The words came from numerous people and in glorious surround sound. "I bet that went over like a turd in a punch bowl;" Captain Taylor added.

"Fact;" Gee admitted. "Truth be told; Patrolman Trent and Molly likely saved them all their lives. Had any of them laid a finger on Maria I'd of been on them like stink on a skunk; they wouldn't have liked that at all. Presuming they were still alive; that is." For just a moment his face showed implacable fury, and the glare in his green eyes was that of Death; being released upon the guilty. Captain Taylor gave a slight shudder. His experience with the youth had always been on the good side of things; but he was well aware that Gee had yet another facet to him; a side that was rarely seen by anyone for more than a very few moments. Thus far; immediately thereafter, death arrived, and that particular one was no more . . . for a least four cannibals; anyway.

Captain Taylor headed back toward his office, his right hand wind-milling in circles; beckoning the two on. They arrived in his office; he closed the door, leaving the narrowest of cracks in case someone had a legitimate need. He moved over to his desk, pulled his chair out, and sat down. He turned and looked at the pair. "So; what brings you two here on such a nice spring morning; not that either of you actually need a reason."

"Wull; it was you that introduced me to that burger and fries and my stomach hasn't been agreeable with anything I've stuck down on top of it ever since." With those words, Captain Trent burst into a roar of laughter. Gee stared at him in modest confusion; he couldn't think of anything humorous about food. The Captain, obviously aware that things might not be quite so obvious, roared out "Mrs. Topperwien." Again he dissolved into gales of laughter; enough so that within moments multiple heads peered in through his door, trying to see, first; exactly what he was laughing about, because second, they were always interested in a good belly laugh themselves and Gee was noted for supplying that very thing. The Captain, seeing all the faces peering in through his door, again exclaimed; "Mrs. Topperwien" and again dissolved into near-hysterical laughter. This time, most of the faces peering in also dissolved into gales of giggles. He turned and stared at Maria; confusion clear on his face.

Except for being male, Gee was in so many ways an ingénue, that the most obvious things could pass right before him and he would not remotely understand what was happening. Maria took him by his hand and gently led him off to one side; away from the frenzy that was threatening to overcome the people inside who were all but helpless in the grip of hysterical laughter. "It has to do with Mrs. Topperwien;" she began. "For the first, she evidently is hopelessly in love with herself; and no other. To put it bluntly; she doesn't think 'hers' stinks. She's always putting others down, making other people look and feel small: she's just mean spirited. When she started in on us, calling us "guttersnipes," that's what she was doing then. You responded with what sounds like a compliment; but because you revealed to all that she was in fact wearing a wig, which is apparently not cool, it makes her look . . . not necessarily bad, but . . . human; I guess. And from her viewpoint; that was a slap; which in truth, she richly deserved. And everyone is happy about it. Not her; obviously, but everyone else. And I'm proud of you for it." And she leaned over and kissed him affectionately on his lips. He smiled and returned like for like. As it turned out; bricks weren't the only thing he could hurl with impunity; he was also getting quite adept with words.

At least for the moment the people in the precinct were laughed out and everyone returned to their own desk to carry on whatever they were doing before Gee had arrived. Captain Taylor, still not fully recovered from his laughter, picked up his phone and dialed the Judge. He waited briefly, and then responded. "Hello; your Honor," he began; "I've got Gee and Maria here; both of them came in, intending to swing by our diner and get yet another burger and fries. Evidently, the one he bought the other day, has started an addiction in him . . . both of them for that matter; as Maria is also here with him: no surprise there." He listened quietly for a few moments, and then nodded; "I'll pass the word along," he said and then hung up. The Judge says to tell you that if you'll give him just a few more minutes, he will join us and have lunch with us; I guess he has a few questions to ask you about that property."

"Wull; I gots . . . I mean; well I have some things about that to pass on to him; things I think he's going to be very interested in. As a matter of fact, as long as you have a few minutes, I've a few things to pass on to you." Maria was out in the main office, talking with a number of other women and it was just the two of them in the Captain's office at the moment. Captain Taylor nodded his head. "It has to do with the Brandon boys." And he proceeded to give Captain Taylor all the details, from the time when the two boys had walked up to him until they slunk away with their figurative tails between their legs. The Captain listened; at first with open interest, then with a measure of hostility and finally with a certain degree of anger. "To finish it up, I don't entirely blame either of them. They were raised by an older brother who was morally bankrupt; just had absolutely no honor in him. At the same time, they've got some very bad habits that they need to outgrow. To put an edge on it; I don't specifically think the two ought to get their tails in a crack over it, just yet, but I do think that both you and Judge Clark need to be aware that the two are not yet exactly finished products either. And that they probably need at least a loose watch on them; maybe not every day, but often enough. Maybe in time they'll finally kick their past; maybe their past will in time kick them. It remains to be seen; but they both need guidance as well as maybe the fear of a beating: so to say."

At that moment Captain Taylor's phone rang; he picked it up and listened. "I got it, Your Honor; the three of us will meet you there in . . . Yes sir; three of us; Maria is also here. That's right then; ten minutes, fifteen tops. You've got it; see you then. Oh, before I forget; Gee tells me that he also has something to tell you . . . no sir; he didn't tell me what. I expect we'll just have to wait and find out; right; no more than fifteen minutes. Out here;" and he hung up.

Gee looked Captain Taylor in the eyes. "If we have ten or fifteen minutes, we best start right now. Knowing Maria as I do, either she'll be ready to leave immediately or need at least twenty minutes more just to say goodbye. Girls: you'll never understand them; but you'll never stop loving them either."

"Truer words were never spoken; young man; I think you are wise well beyond your tender years. Let's get a start on it immediately just in case." The two got up, gathered what they had and needed, and both headed for the door. Gee got to the door a half-step ahead of Captain Taylor; grasping the doorknob he twisted it open and then permitted the officer to precede him through the door and out into the room. As Captain Taylor passed him he spoke very softly: "M'da told me to always let the other fella go thru the door firstest; that way, does they be a bear or such on t'other side, the fella gets eat up first and you gets a chance to duck down low and runs fast away." He, in turn, broke out in laughter. "Smart man; your Dad. My Dad use to tell me that's the real reason gentlemen always let the lady go through the door first; in case of a bear or such." Both laughed softly and continued on into the room.

Gee and Captain Taylor walked up to where Maria and Carol Donovan were in a lively discussion about something that was interesting to the female mind; but tentatively not as much to the male. He nodded to Carol and reached out to pull Maria to him. As he touched her; a thought popped into his mind. Both the Judge and Carol had admitted to mutual attractions, but thus far, he hadn't seen any results. He turned to Carol and smiled up at her. "We're about to head over to the diner to get something to eat; have you eaten yet? If not; why don't you join us?" She looked at him, broke into a beautiful smile and nodded; "Yes; I would like that, I think."

Captain Taylor and Maria both stared at him and both gave him the evil eye. "Gee; exactly what do you think you are doing?" Captain Taylor hissed at him. Maria's eyes weren't exactly friendlier.

"Doin' the will of my Father," he said and pointed an index finger at the ceiling. The Captain did a double-take, his face seemed to pale slightly, and then admitted softly; "There are six person tables over there; many of which are rarely used."

"I know; I saw 'em the last I was there:" Gee admitted softly.

"You're a rat; you know that; right?" Maria hissed at him. "Squeak, squeak," he replied.

He took Carol by her left arm; she looked down at him and gave him a brilliant smile; "Such a gentleman;" she said. She reached over with her right hand and gave his hand a gentle pat; the four of them headed out in the proper direction. Carol was in a very good mood and was chatting happily; talking about her job over at the salon as well as other things at the police station. Either she hadn't noticed how quiet the rest were or was just ignoring it. Maria was staring holes in him; she would give him an earful just as soon as she got a chance; Gee knew that without being told. The four of them went down hallways and turned corners and almost before anyone was ready; they rounded a corner and the diner was before them. Judge Clark turned his head, spotted them and then locked upon exactly who was with them and his smile slowly slipped away. Carol wasn't much better. "Damn you Gee;" she hissed at him.

"Yessum;" he said softly. "Tell me; did Molly Trent ever tell you about the time she first met me; down in that bombed-out house and how she had to crawl between fallen timbers and walk around broken glass, just so she could pick me up and rescue me? I was only about 18 months old at the time, but I still remember some of it. Did she ever tell you?" Carol stared at him and gave her head the tiniest nod she could. "Fourteen hours; she said. Fourteen hours I was in Gabriel's arms, sheltered from falling glass and brick and roofing; all that junk around me, but I was not only unharmed, but clean; there wasn't a speck of dust on me, my diapers weren't even soiled. And that was fourteen hours later. Did she ever tell you this?" Again; she gave the tiniest nod of her head.

They were now less than a full step away from Judge Clark; and not only could he hear Gee clearly, Gee now had his absolute, undivided attention. "I can do things I can't explain; I know things I don't understand; but know that they are true and that there's a reason for them; even though I don't understand. Do you believe this?" She was staring at him as if her very life depended upon that exact fact; she again nodded her head. "Then know this: I am human in every respect, even though I can do things I cannot explain; know things I cannot define. Also; believe things, things that I cannot prove, but believe to be so in any case; and I absolutely believe that there's a reason why we five people are here right now; doing this exact thing. And I believe that you should reach out your left hand and take Judge Clark's right hand and let him seat you. And then I believe we should all sit down, order what we want to eat and do our best to forget this conversation ever took place, because I also believe there are things we are not meant to know; not because it's a deep-dark secret; but because it's not healthy for our minds and souls to know or try to understand. Do you understand this much? Again; she nodded her head. He turned to Judge Clark and gently extended her hand towards him; he, with barely a moment's hesitation, took it and as the gentleman that he was; properly seated her.

As Gee looked around the room, he noticed that many people seemed paused, as if in deep thought or distracted by yet something else. In that moment, he realized that only they five were aware of what had just happened and the rest were unaware that anything at all had just taken place. He seated Maria, who had gone from staring daggers at him to watching him with wide-eyed interest. She; and Captain Taylor. The rest of the people seemed to be staring off into space; as if fascinated by some bug or other object on the wall. Slowly, and then with greater speed, every thing went back to the way it was and people once again went about their business and continued eating and talking as if nothing extraordinary had just taken place. For them; it hadn't.

The waitress came up and handed out menus to everyone there; a moment later another person brought out a tray with glasses on them while yet another held a large pitcher filled almost to the brim with clear water. The two did what they'd come for and then politely nodded at them and departed. The waitress handed out the menus; he glanced at his and gave his head a single shake. This was the same one who had waited on him the last time; she recalled his reaction to the burger and fries and immediately broke out into a sunny smile: "Burger and fries for you; I suppose;" she chirped. He gave her his best smile and nodded. It was the same for Maria. The other three looked over the menus, made their choices and the waitress, quickly writing everything down, smiled, nodded and left.

Gee looked around. There were four pair of eyes looking steadfastly at him; eyes that held questions he wasn't sure he was able to answer; right then or even later. He got around that quick enough by changing the subject even before it came up. "I specially wanted to see you; Your Honor," he said, starting things off in the direction he actually want to go in. "As you no doubt already know, I've been going through some of Mr. Case's properties; trying to make sense out of things I often know little about. Some of these directly affect you, and maybe even yet others. Earlier today, I had my nose in one of Eddy's safes, going through some of his papers as well as money he had laying around. There's a thing I don't know the name of; maybe some of you can help. It's kind of a bag, made out of paper and the end parts have folds in them, so it can get smaller and bigger. This specific thing, whatever it's called, is full of papers and envelopes; some of which is got what is called 'script;' I think it's called. Whatever it is, neither Maria nor I can read it. But the part I think might interest you, Your Honor, is the words printed on the outside of it. It says "In The Case of My Death;" in pretty big letters."

Judge Clark had been watching Gee carefully the entire time; but with the last few words his facial expression changed from polite interest to almost rabid need. "You said 'In Case of My Death" and it belonged to Eddy; is that what you're telling me?"

"Yes, Your Honor, that's exactly what I'm saying. As you already know, my reading skills leave much to be desired, but I am getting better. And the container, whatever it's called, is clear full to the top with all kinds of paper; some with writing on it; some of what you say is 'type-written'; some maybe with printing; which I'm getting better at reading: that sort of stuff. I've only looked through part of it, but most of what I've looked at, I don't actual understand."

"As far as I can guess, the item you're talking about is called a 'folder;'" Judge Clark said; "among other things. Largely because of the way it folds flat when it's not in use; it is commonly used to hold valuable papers; among else; and would be the logical place to put any 'last will and testament' that Eddy might have. While there's no way you could conceivably know this, Eddy owned the electric company, along with a great many other things in this city. While the power plant itself wasn't hit, very obviously a great many other things were, and many people either died outright or just showed missing. That's the way Eddy was for most of eight years; right up until you explained about finding his skeleton." With this comment, Carol gave Gee a quick glance because she knew nothing about the skeleton and there is within human nature, be the human male or female, that which is curious about such things.

"Which opens yet an entirely new pail of worms;" Judge Clark continued. "There is a man here locally named Thomas Price. He was a custodian of sorts for our main power company. With so very many people turning up either dead or missing, he has stepped in and in his own authority has claimed ownership of the power plant. He doesn't actually have anything to prove that he has this right, and up until now, I've never been able to prove that he doesn't. I won't know until I've reviewed all the papers involved, but I suspect that Mr. Price is soon going to be out of a job and position that I'm not convinced he had a right to in the first place; which may also mean that he now owes somebody, probably meaning you, a great deal of money that he's usurped. He is not going to be remotely happy to learn that. If I may; can I be the one to tell him?"

"Well; let's wait until you've reviewed all the papers and make sure that's the way of it. If it be; you have my permission;" Gee admitted.

There are times when even the mind, no matter how lofty the thoughts might be, must succumb to the stomach. As the first few platters were brought in, along with all of the enchanting odors that accompanied such, trivial matters of thoughts had to postpone in order that the stomach could rule; however short that reign might be. Everything tasted as good as he expected, and that included his own anticipations: it was delicious. Except for needing some salt; of course. That, he took care of in his own manner, first his own; and then handed the shaker off to Maria. She, without asking, offered it next to Carol. She looked at Gee; he glanced back and nodded his head. The shaker made the rounds and everyone made use of it; in time it came back to him and he placed it back into his belly pouch and thence, on the shelf where he usually kept it. A number of people watched him, but no one approached, or made mention of it. In time, everyone was done; they got up, Gee picked up the tab; glanced at the total and reached into his pouch and pulled out a twenty dollar bill; that was more than enough to cover the costs. In a very short while he got his change; that, he stuck back into his pouch and thence onto the shelf next to someone's parents; it was just the way he did business.

Each picked up what they came in with and started to head out. For a few brief moments, neither Judge Clark nor Carol seemed to know what to do with themselves. Gee waited for just a few heartbeats and then moved slightly between them and behind. He guided the Judge to lift his left arm slightly away from his body; in the same moment, he guided Carol's right hand under and over the Judge's arm. "As my Da once tol' me; gentlemen and ladies use to walk like this. The man's arm gave her something to hold onto in case she should stumble or trip over anything; and because the people of the time used swords and such, it gave the man use of his right hand in case he needed to draw his sword in defense of the lady. And it gave the lady use of her left hand to slap him into a different time zone did he use that right hand for anything else." He looked up at the two; first Carol and then

Judge Clark and gave them both the wickedest grin he was capable of. The two burst into laughter and stepped slightly apart. He smiled up at them. "Don't be so concerned 'bout what others might think; be concern 'bout what each of you thinks of the other. While you both likely have lots of time left before you run out; that don't mean you should waste it." He bowed respectfully to each of them, first to Carol and then to the Judge, and then backed away and towards where Maria was watching him with wide eyed interest. He held out his left arm and she, without hesitation, curled her right hand over his forearm; exactly as Carol was now holding Judge Clark's arm. Both turned as of a single mind and headed out of the room, closely followed by Chief Taylor; who was both shaking his head and stifling laughter.

The three headed towards the Captain's office; he walked up to it, inserted a key, unlocked it and first he and then the pair walked into his office. Since the event with the mysterious safe had taken place, Captain Taylor made a space open in one corner of his office. It wasn't a large room but there was enough room for such, and since the subsequent event of Benny being caught inside his office, he now made room within the safe for anything that would fit inside as well as everything he wanted to keep out of reach of nosy Parkers. Ever since the 'Benny' affair, nosy Parkers seemed to be somewhat limited in number . . . or at minimum; far more discrete about their activities. In a few moments Chief Taylor divested himself of both his snub-nosed revolver and badge; both were unneeded in his office and both tended to chafe and poke him when he moved about. His routine completed, he turned and stared at Gee.

Before he could form his next thought, much less vocalize it, his phone rang. He gave it one more ring and then picked it up; "Captain Taylor speaking; what is your need?" He listened carefully and then nodded his head; he stared at Gee and spoke softly; "It's the Judge; he wants to know how soon you can get Eddy's folder up here so he can examine it." Gee looked back at the Captain and then reached out where nothing was; in the next instant he pulled his hand back and he was holding a folder; on the front, in large printed letters were the words: "In The Case of My Death," were printed. He set the folder, which was obviously full to the top with papers, on the Chief's desk; he stopped what he was doing and looked the Chief in the eyes.

"He once again pulled a 'Gee' on me, Your Honor; he pulled it out of thin air and just this moment placed it on my desk. What is your pleasure?" Chief Taylor listened attentively and then nodded his head. "About five minutes? I'm sure we can manage that." He looked at Gee and Maria; "His Honor wants to look into this matter as soon as he can get over here; is that well with you?" Gee nodded his head. Chief Taylor turned his attention back to the phone in his hand. "Will when you get here be soon enough; Your Honor?" he asked politely.

don't know how you do these things, young man, but I must admit; you don't waste much time doing them," he confessed.

"I'm not sure how I manage to do these things either, Captain Taylor, but I concede that it do . . . I mean 'does' make things easier at times. I've got to tell the truth about it; sometimes it scares the 'willies' out of me; on one hand it seems as natural to me as breathing; on another level, it doesn't seem I should be able to do it when no one else can; it just doesn't seem fair in some ways. Yet again . . . I gotta admit I'll be the saddest boy in town if it ever goes away from me; that's only one of the reasons I'm so careful how I use it, and also who knows about it: I'd hate to be proud of something that's a gift and not anything I could have ever earned. And to be blunt; even though I sometimes like being the only one who can do this, did I ever have the right or ability, I'd pass it on to others. Not just anyone, of course: Benny comes to mind."

What would have happened or said next was lost to history for at that exact moment Judge Clark rapped on the door twice with his knuckles and promptly walked in. He stopped for a moment, glanced around and in the next instant his eyes fell upon the folder that sat upright between Gee and Captain Taylor. He beamed joyously and promptly headed directly for it. "So this is it?" he asked in anticipation. He took a single, long look at it, reached out and carefully lifted it up slightly off the desk where it sat and gave a single, low whistle of appreciation. "So this is it? My word; it's heavy; there must be an enormous amount of papers inside to make it weigh this much. If you trust me enough, young man, I'll take this back to my office for a more thorough investigation, but at this moment, I'm most anxious to at least give it a quick over-view. Does this meet with your needs and interests?" Gee promptly nodded his head and agreed. The Judge untied the knot that kept the folder closed up and reasonably in one piece and one by one, began to lift out papers and envelopes, scanning them sometimes briefly, sometimes in depth. "Oh yes; this is to do with some of his other properties; this is something to do with one of the Fire Stations; sad, that, one of the bomblets hit that square on; a total loss. Only good thing about it; being Christmas night as it was, no one was inside; not even the dog."

A moment later he pulled yet another envelope out, removed the paper from within and scanned it briefly. He stared at in and read it again, more carefully and a smile began to slowly crawl across his face: he turned to Gee. "God is truly with you, son, he began. "It's almost like Eddy knew the future, that he wouldn't be here, and that he wanted someone to take over his holdings. What I have here is a writ that names the undersigned to be sole owner and protector of his assets. He even went so far as to have it notarized and has signed it. The only thing he didn't do is put in the name of whom would take over his assets; he's left that . . . to you." And he stared Gee directly in his eyes.

"Me?" Gee exclaimed; "how could he do that?"

"It's not that hard; not for one who actually trusts in God. Simply put; he left that part blank. All anyone has to do is to carefully print his name in this space right here, and then sign on the dotted line just below. Do you know how to print your name? I know that your reading is getting better; do you know how to print; how to sign?" Gee shook his head 'no.' "Come over here, Son, and I'll show you; what is your full name? I'm afraid that it's going to have to be more than just 'Gee." It took some careful assist, but along with learning to read, Gee was also trying to learn to write; often just copying things out of one book or another to the best of his ability. One thing he had been practicing was printing his name. He carefully, to the best of his ability, printed: 'George Elandier Evansen'. Judge Clark carefully wrote the three words in script, then provided Gee with a piece of scrap paper and had him practice.

At first; he took a ballpoint pen; with the cartridge retracted, and carefully traced what the Judge had just done. He was a very intelligent boy and he understood quickly. After a few attempts, he tried it out on a blank piece of paper. His efforts were almost an unintelligible scrawl but he rapidly caught on, and after only a very few tries, he could write his name legibly enough that it could be fairly easily read. With this in his favor; he signed on the dotted line; managing to do a respectable job of it; all things considered. Judge Clark co-signed on the line indicating first witness; Captain Taylor signed the next line as second witness. And he discovered that he now owned the power station that supplied the city with electricity; and having been witnessed and attested by both the Judge and Chief of Police, there wasn't much Thomas Price would be able to do about it. Except perhaps throw a fit, fall down on the ground, roll around and whine. Other than that; his options were few.

Gee never learned whether or not Mr. Price threw a fit and rolled around on the ground or not; that he was deeply displeased, however, was made abundantly clear when he learned from both the Judge as well as Police Chief that he not only was no longer in control of the power station; either to direct it the way he desired, nor benefit from the monies that it still managed to generate: this latter was far more important to him than the former. For one; the place he lived in was above his ability to pay for; once the revenue from the power company was removed from his grasp. Typically; he tried to hire an attorney to represent him, but once the agent understood all the details, that one would simply present him with a bill for services rendered and promptly back off. It was not a good time to be Mr. Price; no, not even a bit. It all came to a point several days later when Gee, accompanied by Maria, stopped by the Police Station to 1) visit the Chief, and not at all coincidently, 2) swing by the café that was still up and running inside the building and get their fix of burger and fries.

The pair walked inside the Police Department, as they often did and only started to turn towards the Captain's office when Molly Trent hissed at both of them and quickly shook her head. "You shouldn't even be here," she whispered to the pair; "Mr. Price is in the Captain's office and he's having kittens!"

"Alright; now we won't be the onlyst in town with kitties;" Gee exclaimed.

"No, Gee, that's just an expression;" Molly quickly explained.
"It means that Mr. Price is exceedingly angry and is looking for a fight with just about anyone. And if he knew that you are Mr. Evansen; he would most likely try and tear your head off. Not that he would succeed; knowing you as I do."

"Cool; that!" Gee replied, and leaving Molly Trent behind, promptly headed for the Captain's office; closely tailed by Maria. The two walked in as they usually did. There wasn't anything dainty about Mr. Price. He wasn't remotely Lendl Holms big; but he wasn't small. Captain Taylor, spotting Gee, immediately tried waving him off; saying that he was busy and to come back some other time. Gee ignored the Captain. "What you be bellerin' about?" he demanded of the man. He, in turn, swung about and began to yell at him; ordering him to leave. Gee stared up at the brute standing before him.

"Wull; makes up you mind;" he demanded. "Seconds ago you was bellerin' my name; now I'm here you wants me t'leave. For what it's worth . . . I'm George Evansen." He stared the bully directly in the eyes and didn't blink.

The brute roared. He pulled back his fist and started to strike; Maria, trying to protect him, darted between them. In the next instant she flew on in the same direction she started in, flew through the air, and well out of the range of festivities, she came to land gently on the wooden floor; much like a dandelion seed wafting softly to the ground. A moment later; Price's fist swooped through the air she had just recently occupied. In the next instant, Gee doubled up his right fist, and much as he had when he had stopped the woman in the boutique from attacking Maria; he punched from his shoulder and chest; but this time, he didn't pull his punch. He thought 'brick' and in the next instant it was, for all intents, a brick that struck Price on the point of his chin. He stumbled backwards two steps and crashed to the floor. He hit, and did not twitch, because he was out cold before he even started to fall. That; and a number of teeth that had previously been inside his mouth had now taken residence; scattered across the floor. Chief Taylor stared, his mouth agape, his body in the exact position it had been in before the festivities began. He looked a moment longer, slowly closed his mouth, and feeling behind him for his chair; he found it and carefully sat down. "Son," he said softly, "should you ever get mad at me; I beg of you, please; just call me on the phone. Or better yet; write me a letter: you're getting better at that and I think I'd live a lot longer if I just read about it and not end up on the floor like him." And he nodded at the brute that lay wadded up on the floor; much like a used and discarded tissue.

People brought in a stretcher as it was obvious to them all that Mr. Price was not going to wake up in the immediate future. Four grown men packed him down to medical; he was given an exam and mouth x-ray, revealing not only missing teeth but also a lower jaw that showed fracture lines along the lower part where much of the impact had been directed. This, the man did not complain about, because he was still unconscious. It wasn't until after the medics released him and he was yet again packed down to the jail room and put into one of the smaller, private cells that he finally woke up . . . and had no idea where he was; nor why he was in a cell; much less why his mouth hurt so. In fact; either he was lying about everything, or he couldn't recall being in the Captain's office nor of his ill-fated attack on a ten-year-old boy who had basically mopped the floor with him. He was a far more humble and meek man; once he finally stopped hurting so much. And, much to his dismay, he was also a man without a job or money.

Thomas Price was merely the tip of the iceberg. There were a number of people who had, knowingly or not, followed in his footsteps and sequestered different business and positions that actually did not belong to them. These, almost inevitably, were the possessions of Eddy Case. And in the majority of cases, were people who saw a chance at taking something they did not own; and pretend that they did. As Tom Price hit the floor in Captain Taylor's office, the reverberations began to spread outward, and more than one individual found reason to grab up as much cash and other valuables as they could and just leave town. Even though it remained a little-known reason exactly why Gee held such sway within the judicial system of their city; it was documented that he did. Also documented was the mere fact that thus far; everyone who had gone up against him did not remotely come out on top. And that factoid did not even include what he'd done to the cannibals within the city limits. Not long after he'd taken the four out with a few bricks; and then put Cops into yet another building that was directly next to one of the cannibal hot-spots; the rest, feeling unloved and unwanted, began to leave the city in droves and within a very short time, cannibalism was no longer practiced within at least this city's limits. This was most pleasing to those who lived there and only wanted to try their best to get their lives back to what they were before the bomblets fell.

Spring delayed it arrival beyond what was reasonable, then in a burst of enthusiasm, blossoms and new leaves burst forth in joyous exultation. Gee's home was rapidly getting cleaned up. Once the Brandon's understood both the factoids that Gee's position within the courthouse was unshakable, and that the quickest way they could return to their former ways was to try and cheat him on just about anything, quit messing about. Focusing their forces in a more professional manner, they quickly had the front of his place cleaned up, and approaching what it had been before the bomblets had fallen. That was the outside part. The inner; that which was over their heads in debris was yet another thing. They asked around and found a few men who actually knew how to lay brick; one of whom wasn't exactly the man who had done the job in the first place, but was instead, his oldest son. The boy, now a man, looked the site over; recalled how his Father had worked for many months at this exact site. After talking it over with both Gee and others, began to get the main, inner mess taken care of. This was not something that would be done in a matter of days; but rather months; if not several years.

One good thing was discovered at this time; Gee tried his front door, the one opening to the South, and found out that it worked just fine. The main part of the mass had dropped straight down and out away from the lower part of the building, not only leaving the door as access to the outside, but also clear of the steps that led up to the second and third level. That, obviously, caught a great many people's attention and virtually overnight he was besieged with those who were looking for a better place to live. This wasn't remotely possible just yet; while the front had been reasonably cleaned, the atria was more than half-full of debris that hadn't been hauled off and the surrounding areas were rapidly starting to fill in with broken bricks and other effluvia that had been out in front.

One day, while out in what was his back yard, trying to whack down a growing mass of grass, Gee once again began thinking of the buzzing in his head that he'd felt the time all of them were on the north side of his property; out where the multitude of damaged buildings were. He had gotten a tingle then but had not as yet gone to investigate. Maria was, at the moment, off with Molly Taylor; doing something 'female' he presumed. The remains of shirt that still had some part of a pocket left, was rapidly turning into rags; even at his worst, he didn't like wearing it any more. And thus far; he had not found anything that could remotely replace it. But it seemed to him that almost every time he thought of the pocket; he thought of those buildings; especially those on the eastern side. He laid the small scythe that he held down, and turning in the direction he wanted, he began to walk.

He headed directly for the place where Martin Kodak had once lived. There were many ways of getting to where he actually wanted to go, but by taking the longer, slower route, he was able to look for and potentially find yet other useful things that might be needed; either immediately or potentially in the near or more distant future.

He unlocked the door with his mind and entered in. The place was exactly as it was when he was last there; which was logical. But this time he was alone; he moved more slowly, more carefully, and examined all the walls and corners, but he found nothing that was new to him. He made his slow way through the small apartment and then exited out the back, into the brick strewn lot that had once held multiple cars; parked by people who once lived within the apartments that surrounded the open area. He paused and stared about; looking with his mind as well as his eyes Slowly at first and then with increasing speed, his 'meller began to function, and as it did, he began to get 'niggles' about where he wanted to go next.

He 'felt' for anything that might pull him and found several little niggles that nudged him first one way and then the next. He felt for the one that seemed the strongest, then instead of just 'popping' in as he usually did, he tried out his levitation. At first slowly and then with increasing speed, he floated upward and forward, headed in the general direction his strongest niggle pulled him. A few moments later he gently landed on a small sundeck that was attached to one of the apartments. He looked at the base of the sliding door; there was the familiar locking mechanism; he nudged it with his mind and it moved obediently out of the way; he pushed the door sideways and started in. He got no more than two or three steps when his lungs drew air in; he immediately coughed and in a blink was once more standing out in the vacant area between the buildings. He glanced around; startled. How had he managed to do this; he wondered.

He breathed in and out, in and out, and everything seemed to work as it should. It was, seemingly, only the air inside that was offensive. 'What if,' he wondered to himself, 'I could be inside, looking, but breathing outside; might that make it better?' He focused himself, unsure that this was remotely possible, and then popped back to where he had been just a few moments before. He cautiously inhaled and then exhaled and the air seemed just fine to him. He started looking about.

He was inside a smallish-sized living room. There was a TV over in one corner; along a different wall was a bookshelf with numerous books of one type or another. He cautiously eased himself down a hallway. There was a door to his right; he opened it. The first thing he saw was some human remains; from the size and position it was of a fairly young child; whether male or female he couldn't tell. He moved yet further down the hall. Another door beckoned; he opened it. It was a repeat of the first room, but in this room the remains still lay in bed, covered with blankets very much as if death had taken its victim while slumbering peacefully. He started to continue on but his 'meller began to twitch vigorously in protest: "go, look in the closet," the 'meller seemed to be prompting him. He moved that way and slid the closet door aside. The victim evidently was a young boy, perhaps near his own age, and to his utter astonishment, hanging from coat hangers were a number of pants and shirts and best of all, two sweat shirts with the pockets in front; exactly as he'd been looking for. He reached in, took the two – hangers and all - as well as yet other clothes that interested him, and headed for the door. He was still breathing normally and still wasn't having problems with the foul odor; but he didn't want to take any chance. He moved about in the apartment, opening every door and window that he could find, and once that was done, he popped back into his own apartment; his left arm crowded with the clothing he had found.

He popped in, not in the lower apartment where he and Maria now spent most of their time; but into the upper place they had called their home for nearly two months. He still had quite a bit of his things up there, including much of his clothes. He took the new clothing as well as everything he was still wearing and tossed them all into the washing machine. He put in the proper amount of detergent, turned the water on and while the machine did its thing, he took a shower to rinse the last of the residue off of him.

Gee stood in the bathroom, towel in hand, drying off. As he toweled himself vigorously, he glanced into the mirror in the bathroom that was just in front of him. When he first moved into this place, now over two months ago, he could see the light switch on the wall in the reflection of the mirror. Then, the base of the switch was comfortably above the top of his head; perhaps even a tiny wisp of wall just below the plate was visible. Now, as he looked, the top of his head came well up into the plate, perhaps even with the toggle itself. In the short time he had lived there, he had grown that much. He believed that it was, no doubt, a combination of his normal growth patterns as well as the mere fact that not only was he eating much better than he had before, he had also discovered Eddy's pharmaceuticals; including a gracious plenty of vitamins, minerals and other things needed by a growing body, and his own body was making good use of these very things. He also noticed that Maria seemed to be squirting up; though he had no idea how far she came up next to the light switch; because when she climbed into the shower, nude, she didn't want him in the same apartment as she; much less in the same room. Girls! Go figure!

He dug his clothes out of the dryer and put them on. The shirt with the pocket in front fit him a bit loosely, but he knew that well before he had the shirt worn out he would have outgrown it anyway. He put other clothes on and his shoes. He now had shoes that were actual leather and not the tennis he had worn for so long. He now looked to be exactly what he was; a young male who had at least some money and who knew what he liked and what he didn't. He gave himself a last look over, then deciding that he was as done as he was going to get, turned around and grabbing what he needed most, popped out of the room and into his favorite spot and began walking towards the Police Station, where he presumed Maria and Carol were now were.

He spotted several groups of young toughs who were eyeing him with evil intent, but the word had gotten out among them that anything more than eyeing him; got them quick trips to a jail cell and then a few moments before a judge who had very little patience with people like them. They watched him, muttered among themselves, and quietly eased further away. Which please him immensely; he didn't approve of the way they conducted their business but neither did he wish them any evil; at least he didn't as long as they didn't try causing him any trouble.

In time, he walked up the steps of the building, made the usual right turn and in the process of time, walked into the police station. At his entrance, heads turned, first just to see who had entered and then to comment among them-selves when they saw who it was. It was Gee, but not the one they were more used to. Now, dressed as he was, he was both familiar and not; somehow it was him and wasn't. It was, of course, the mere fact that the badly decayed shirt he'd been wearing for the last year or more was missing and it its place was another; looking, if not brand new, then at least hardly worn. People gazed, commented among themselves and pondered where he'd gotten the new clothing from. This, of course, did not include Maria. She marched herself up to him; eyed him from shoulder to beltline and back again.

"Where did you get this from?" she demanded; poking him first in the chest with her forefinger and then in the belly.

"I'm a finder;" he admitted quietly; "I might have mentioned that a time or three. I presume that you remember that open area right behind where Martin Kodak used to live; out in back behind where he presumably parked his car." He looked her in the eyes and she nodded her head.

Talking quietly; he continued; "You'll remember the open area that was covered with bricks and other junk?" She again nodded her head. "Some of those buildings still stand, but they're not that easy to get into. Earlier today, I got a 'niggle' that prompted me to go up into one of the places that are still partly standing. I found at least two human remains as well as other belongings; and with them, I found this shirt. Since I like the front pocket so much and since my other one has long since outlived its useful life; I've replaced it with this one. I also have one more; but all of them are pretty much the same."

Maria stared up into his eyes, a soft, introspective expression on her face. "Gee; I don't know if you're aware of it or not, but people and stores have just about completely run out of clothing; any kind of clothing, for male or female; young or old. If you, or anyone else, can come across such, we really need to get at least some of it out to where people can buy it to replace what they've already got. And that's especially true of people with young kids; kids who not only are growing, but being kids, wear their clothes out faster than adults because kids are so much more active."

"Yeah; and I suppose you'll decide you want to get paid for those clothes, too," a pugnacious voice declared from one side. He turned and faced the speaker; one of the men who worked there; but what the man did, besides stand around and sneer, Gee didn't know. He looked at the man and stared back.

"Why not?" he asked the man; "you come here and do whatever it is you do. Besides stand around and sneer; that is. And you want to be paid for it. If you think that 'finding' is such an easy job I suggest that you quit this one and go out and try it for yourself. A few things you might consider before you do. I've scared myself spitless more times than I can count. One time I was gone for almost two days before I managed to get myself out of the crack I fell into and back home. And it was several weeks before I went out again; not because it had scared me so bad, but because it took me that long just to heal up. And, yes, I have the scars on my body to prove it. And it's not just a matter of going out, looking around for a few minutes, picking out what I like best and coming back home. There for a long time, I'd go out day after day and not come back with anything. Like anything else; you have to learn the ropes; have to learn what works and what doesn't. And last but not least, I know of other boys who started out doing the same and at least two of them went out and were never seen again." He stared at the man with the mouth and his eyes were like glowing green coals within his head. The man promptly backed down and muttering some sort of excuse; eased away.

Gee watched the man slip himself from the room, then quietly shook his head. "It seems to me that my Da once told me; "they's three kind of people in the world. Them that go out and make things happen; them that stand around and watch; and them that stand around and scratch; unaware anything is happening anywhere." Which of the three we are is completely up to us; and our rewards are allotted according to what we do with what we're given." He stared in the direction the man had gone, shook his head once more in disbelief, and then turned and moved away.

The next few days passed peacefully into history. The front of his place was rapidly becoming more like it once was, but one could only take a very few steps into what was left of the front lobby before that feeling evaporated right before one's eyes. The inside of the atria was still entirely too full of junk for anyone to remotely be able to access the stairs and doors that loomed above them just barely tucked back into the shadows enough to give at least some of them an eerie, dismal look that boded no good to anyone. Some people, those who only days before were clamoring for access to the places; to go into and snoop and steal if nothing else, abruptly forgot their previous preoccupations: it really didn't look all that safe, if one didn't notice the thick cement supports that held everything up. In fact, it was the strength of these supports that were responsible for the building not being a gigantic pile of rubble; instead of apartments that were actually much better than many of the observers supposed.

By now, most of the front was cleared off, and with a bit of scratching around in the Police mainframe, the location of a reasonable amount of cement was found. The young man whose father had actually laid much of the original brickwork was himself a skilled mason. He had come just a few days before, and after clearing off the cement base to the brick walls, was now recreating the walls that had been demolished. There was one problem though. Only a small percentage of the original bricks were still intact; the rest were broken, sometimes in large pieces and chunks with other times shattered almost beyond recognition. And there were no brick yards in the general area where one could go and simply buy more. The most logical source, then, were the buildings that were only partially destroyed; but destroyed enough that they were not in and of themselves repairable. This wasn't quite as serious as it might have otherwise been because one of the most obvious and glaring source lay not all that far away; it was the remains of the brick wall that had fallen on the unfortunate Mr. Coldbrick when he made his ill-timed advance upon that specific spot.

This, in itself, was unfortunate as the dead have a habit of decaying, and it isn't long before that fact is wafted through the air by whichever vagrant breeze that might be floating through. Oddly enough; the odors lingering nearby didn't suggest that this was going to be that serious of a problem. People came in, and directed by those who actually understood such, began to carefully chip the grout between the bricks away, but not all of the grout and not between every brick. The bricks could also be removed in sections; provided the sections were not squared off, but were instead asymmetrical in size and shape. Properly done, the bricks could be laid into the developing wall almost as if it were a very large oversized brick; instead of many bricks stuck together. Days slipped into weeks and weeks into a month.

It was during one of days when several of the workmen who had been toiling in what was actually towards the center of what was once a very large wall; stopped what they were doing and came over to where he was standing, talking to Patrolman Trent. "Excuse me, Mr. Evansen," the worker began, "but I think you might want to come and see this; especially after what you've told us about Mr. Coldbrick."

Gee nodded his head and both he and Patrolman Trent followed after the man. Much of the wall was in the process of being reduced back into both individual bricks as well as small sections that could be manually picked up and moved to the new site. They walked up to where several men were in the process of digging out yet more bricks, rubbing them against each other to wear off the dried cement and then into yet another pile where they would in time be loaded up and moved to their new location. As they walked up, several men who were watching them come, moved to one side, reveling what appeared to be smashed human bones. Gee watched as several men moved yet other sections of brick away from where they had laid for some months now, revealing yet other pieces of what had once been a human being. In a short period of time they had the remains of Tom Coldbrick out where they could be easily seen.

"There doesn't seem to be anything except bones;" one of the men said thoughtfully.

Gee nodded his head. "I suspect that because it's fairly early yet; both in time of day as well as time of year, the ants haven't completely come out. And I also suspect that the reason there's so little left of Tom Coldbrick is because of ants. That also means that once this area has warmed up a bit; you'll be up to your ears in ants. You might want to consider moving your operations more to the east and start working this way. One thing though; from the way the bones are lying, my thought is that Mr. Coldbrick was trying to do something with this safe; maybe trying to open it up and find out what was inside. My best guess is that he had his back to the main wall and was unaware it was even falling. He even might have been killed by the falling brick before he knew he was in danger. In a very real way, that's the ideal way to exit life, to die before you even know you're in trouble."

"What do you think might be in that safe?" one of the men watching asked him.

"No way of telling; short of drilling and nitro, considering the damage done to the safe's door;" Gee admitted. "And that last part I base on what people say at times like this. But my best bet; would be nothing. From what I understand and remember; this building was empty well before the bomblets fell: not from personal observation, but from what I've heard people say. And people don't usually leave anything inside a safe if they're moving out. They might leave it unlocked with a slip of paper inside with the numbers needed to unlock it; this, for the next people who move in. Who will most likely call in an expert in such and have the numbers changed anyway. The fact of the matter is; a safe isn't always all that safe."

"Not when you're around it isn't;" officer Trent murmured softly; giving Gee a sly glance out of the corners of his eyes. Gee stared at him for just a moment, then sticking his tongue slightly out between his lips; blew the officer a raspberry. He, in turn, shook his head sadly and laughing softly and giving him a dismissive wave over his shoulder, moved off in the direction where he was actually supposed to be. His wife, Molly, stood watching the two. They were far away enough that she couldn't actually hear what they were saying, but the expressions on their faces and Gee's tongue explained it all; she clapped her hand over her mouth and vainly fought a battle with her giggles.

Time moved on as time has a habit of doing. The front part of Gee's new residence was starting to look very much as it had before the bombing; and even the inside; the atria, was looking more open. Soon; those skilled is such things would come and with materials scavenged from one place or another, would once again create the broad arches that once had covered the interior, creating a sort of indoors place where people could meet when the weather outside was being unreasonable about such.

All over the city and the land; people were trying their best to copy him. Ever so slowly, and then with increasing speed, dilapidated and otherwise destroyed buildings were more gently brought to the ground; that the brick work and other supplies represented within the walls could be reused to build yet new buildings. In the process thereof, a great many things were found in the way of clothing and other needs that others were able to buy, that which was unobtainable only a few days or weeks earlier. Other cities, both near and far, were both copying his progress and in and of themselves doing the same; for it is within Man's mind to rebuild what he had destroyed; through the passions of anger and hatred as well as brute ignorance. Ever so slowly did the race of man begin to bring itself back from the very brink of destruction where its own foolish pride and lust had led it.

The setting sun sunk slowly in the west; as it has been doing since the dawn of time. But it is a truism that one man's sunset is yet another's sunrise. And so, on the opposite side of the planet and in the southern half of the globe, the same sun was just now gradually rising; shedding his light upon the land. There before it lay the ruins of what once was the world's oldest, and among the most beautiful, city; once thought the most beautiful city in the world. But it had been prophesied that before the end, Damascus would be so totally destroyed, that not even a goat would be able to make a living in it.

The End

D L Davies